Florence in Ecstasy

The Unnamed Press
P.O. Box 411272
Los Angeles, CA 90041

Published in North America by The Unnamed Press.

1 3 5 7 9 10 8 6 4 2

Copyright © 2017 by Jessie Chaffee

ISBN: 978-1944700171

Library of Congress Control Number: 2017937451

This book is distributed by Publishers Group West

Cover design & typeset by Jaya Nicely

Florence in Ecstasy

a novel

Jessie Chaffee

For my parents, Heide and John, and my brother, Joshua.
And for my husband, Brendan.

And then at once she was filled with love and inestimable satiety, which, although it satiated, generated at the same time inestimable hunger.

— *The Book of the Blessed Angela of Foligno*

You imagine the carefully-pruned, shaped thing that is presented to you is truth. That is just what it isn't. The truth is improbable, the truth is fantastic; it's in what you think is a distorting mirror that you see the truth.

— Jean Rhys, *Good Morning, Midnight*

Prologue

This morning is every morning. I've been here almost a month, and still I wake too frequently, too early, to the buzz of mosquitoes, gray light, and the window shutters swinging open and closed. I wake from violent dreams filled with strong winds and slamming doors. Bodies thrown against windows loose in their frames, frames loose in their sleeves. I wake in Florence, afraid. The shutters swing open and each time I catch just a glimpse of the Palazzo Vecchio's tower against violet sky before they swing closed again. The image is familiar now. This empty apartment is mine. Still, this is not quite life. On this morning, I relight the citronella coil and walk to the window. In the alley, a man puts on a magenta helmet, climbs onto a moped, and pulls out onto Via Malenchini, the last to leave the bar below. Once he's gone there are only the birds that shoot past my window like darts thrown screaming from an unseen hand. It is feeding time.

I wait, as I do every morning, for the sun to come into view. When it does, it shines at such an angle that the hidden city emerges. I no longer see edges and perimeters. Instead, the roof tiles, drainpipes, plaster walls, cobblestones, and glass panes become a single canvas for the pattern drawn by this glow. All I see is the pattern, etched in light and shadow. I am in a new place, unmarked and alive. This moment is an answer, a stopping point. This morning is every morning. This is when I do not feel alone, when I feel held by this city. Until the sun is fully up and the pattern fades like exposed film, the rooftops, drainpipes, stones, and windows regaining their edges and returning to the foreground. Another long day stretches ahead. But something is shifting.

I walk to the bathroom, pull my T-shirt up over my head, let my pants drop to the floor, and drag the orange scale away from the wall. It rattles across the blue tiles, catching in each valley. I adjust the needle to zero. Not cheating—never cheating—I watch the numbers spin like a slot machine until they stop, predictably. "It's good," I say aloud, running my hand along my face, my arm, my stomach. "It's good," I repeat, overly decisive and sober, trying to coax my reflection into agreement. *Today,* I think as I dress, tie back my hair, and climb the three stone steps to the kitchen, *will be different.*

I open the long slatted doors and step out onto the small balcony, which is so steeply pitched it feels like it may topple into the courtyard below. It is one of the reasons I took this apartment, even when the landlady quoted the rent and I felt my stomach drop. She felt it, too, saw the fear in my face, and showed me another place, smaller and darker, said, *Much better price,* in her raspy voice, but I couldn't, I couldn't. I needed the light. *The other one,* I said, *the bright one,* as she eyed me skeptically and repeated, *Caro, caro, caro. It's not a problem,* I lied, *I need the light, the light, the light.* When I pass her on the stairs now, she always gives me that same look.

It is the end of August. For weeks the other windows have been quiet and dark, except for the apartment across the way and one floor down, where an old woman sits all day, her arm spreading on the sill. She is sometimes staring out, sometimes cooking sauce I can smell as steam climbs out and over the terra-cotta roofs. But even her window is vacant this morning. The Italians have fled the cities for the coast, and all over Florence there are handwritten signs taped to shop doors. CHIUSO PER FERIE FINO AL 1 SETTEMBRE. The type of scrawl that normally says "back in five"—only, in this case, it's "back next month." The signs do not deter the tourists who fill the piazza around the Duomo, who line up at dawn to be the first into the Uffizi Gallery, who haggle and hassle at the Mercato Centrale, who shout at the buses that lumber down the narrow streets and heed no one, who walk the bridges with gelato dripping down their hands in the evenings and watch Italian bands playing the Beatles. A manic, frenzied movement repeated day after day, night after night. They are looking up, always up. Up at the frescoed ceilings of churches; at the parade of Madonnas in museums; at the oversized head, hands, and feet of the *David*; at the performers dressed as mummies who move only at the sound of money in their jars; at the buildings edged in angels that circle and circle.

I am no different. I still cannot cross Piazza della Signoria at night without looking up to the golden lion at the top of the Palazzo Vecchio, to the harsh glare of Neptune who rules the fountain outside, to the writhing sculptures in the loggia at the piazza's corner—lit from below, the Sabine woman twists and twists out of the grasp of her attacker, all that stone tapering from the massive base to the single point of her finger reaching toward the sky. *There is something more*, it says.

Chapter One

"Signorina."

Signora Rosa. Such a delicate name. She must be someone's grand-mother, stout and soft with a halo of white hair; this had tricked me into thinking that she would be soft with me. But she is all hard edges. No sooner have I closed the door than she is there on the stairs with that same side-eyed look. Why? It is almost September. Almost a new month. *Only cash,* she'd said when she agreed to rent me this bright apartment, even though it was *caro, caro, caro.* Only cash. Up front.

"Signorina," she rasps. A term meant for someone much younger than me, a little girl, and I'd like to upend her assumptions, tell her I had every intention of paying her, but I can't form the words. Instead I mumble, *"Sì, sì, mi scusi, momento,"* and scurry around the corner to the bank to face my dwindling funds. I have enough to get through September, and that will be it. Every last cent. But as soon as I hand her the bills in that old stone lobby, I feel free.

And then I walk. Every morning I walk, circling the bones of Florence, treading a well-worn path through the bodies of tran-sients to whom I am invisible. Today I walk until my skin is on fire and my legs are slick and shaking. Until I'm ill with the smell of sewage that the heat pulls from every crevice. Until I grow dizzy and my mind grows numb and I arrive at the place where I always end these walks: by the wall of the Arno River at the city's center. I lean into it, feel the heat coming off the stone, feel the bodies press-ing against me, tourists burrowing in to snap photos of the Ponte Vecchio, their cameras storing the same image again and again.

The rowing club sits below on a narrow embankment in the bridge's shadow. It is a launching point for the boats that, even in this heat, cut lines up and down the lazy Arno. For days I've watched from this perch the young Italian men carrying sculls down to the river. There is something calming in their movements, in the quiet way that they shoulder those boats, like pallbearers, and lay them down on the water's surface.

But today is different. Because for the first time, a woman emerg-es on the embankment, a boat balanced on her shoulder, oars bal-anced on her hip. She is alone. She is at ease. I watch as she lowers the body into the water, slides one oar into the metal U-ring, then the other. She pauses, glancing up and down the Arno—there is no one else out yet, it is hers alone—then steps carefully into the shell. She nudges the dock with one hand, and the river offers no resis-tance as she pushes off gracefully, adjusts the oars, and begins her course, making her way toward the next bridge with purposeful movements. It is a separate existence, one far from this city with its crush of bodies and sounds and smells. I watch until she disap-pears from sight, a single body at peace.

Tucked into the busy street behind me is a green door that I have also watched on these mornings and, beside it, a small plaque—SOCIETÀ CANOTTIERI FIRENZE, it reads, "Florence Rowing Club" —half hidden by a vendor's cart heavy with belts hanging thick and dark like vines. To the right is the long courtyard framed by the arms of the Uffizi Gallery; to the left is this green door.

Today will be different. I inhale sharply and push against bodies, launching myself across the street. But before I reach it, the door swings open with a rush of cool air, and a group of teenagers clam-bers out, jostling by me with a chorus of *permesso, scusi, permesso.* Another figure is behind them. A man, tall, with dark hair brushed back.

"*Attenzione, ragazzi,*" he calls as they disappear down the street in an explosion of sound. "*Scusi, eh?*" he says to me, his hand propping the door. The skin gathers around his eyes in bursts as his cheek-bones stretch to accommodate an expansive smile. I feel surrounded by it.

"*Dove va?*" *Where are you going?*

I look past him into the darkness, my face still hot from my walk, my dress sticking.

"*Mi dica,*" he says then.

Tell him what? "*Questa è la Canottieri Firenze?*" The words catch strange in my mouth, half swallowed.

"*Sì, sì.*" He gestures for me to enter. "*Che cosa vuole, signora?*"

"*Vorrei...*" I put my arms out to the surroundings, foolish, and I can smell my sweat now. It smells sour to me, acrid, like an infection—it has for months, and I don't know if it is my sense or the odor that has changed. "To join," I say finally, hugging my arms back to my sides.

"*Va bene,*" the man says, and chuckles. He pushes the door open wider. "*Allora,* you must speak with Stefano."

"*Grazie,*" I mumble, scooting past him into the dark foyer.

"*Certo. Arrivaderla, signora, arrivaderla.*" I hear him still laughing until the door abruptly shuts, taking with it the heat, the light, and this laughing man.

I walk down a flight of steps, blind until my eyes adjust—an office glowing fluorescent, another door. There is no one here. I should leave. But I think about the woman on the water, and then I hear distant punctuations of sound that must be human. *Stefano.* I cling to the name and keep going, through the door and down more stairs. I am tunneling into a cave, a warren, down and down until I reach a low stone doorway I have to bend under to clear, and when I do, I'm accosted by the smell of coffee and sweat. A little bar filled with tables, and daylight beyond. An old man in a unisuit looks up from his paper, squinting like an angry gnome. I wait for him to ask me a riddle, but he shakes the paper and lowers his eyes.

Behind the counter a man with a white mustache fills a glass with bright pink juice. He's watching me. "*Buongiorno,*" he says. "*Americana?*" He places a spoon in the glass, then points to himself. "Manuele."

"Hannah." I relax. No riddles, no tricks. "Is Stefano here?"

"Anna," he says, losing the *h*. "Anna *di*..." He raises his eyebrows.
"*Di* Boston."

"Anna di Boston—*ecco* Nico." He nods at the old man, who sighs
and shuffles to the counter.

"'*Sera*," he mumbles, before taking a sip of his juice.

Manuele winks, then calls, "Stefano!" and a third man appears in
the sunlit doorway. He's tall and deeply tanned, his mouth a sharp
line. Manuele speaks to him too quickly for me to follow until I
hear "Anna di Boston."

"Hannah," I say. "I'd like to join. The man upstairs told me—"

"*Sì, certo*." Stefano's smile is still tight, his brow now furrowed.
"You row?"

"No."

"Never?"

I hesitate. I know how I must look to him—it is written across
me in spaces and hollows. But I've come this far, and so I continue.
"No. I'd like to learn, though."

Stefano says nothing, then, "*Va bene*. You'll learn. *Andiamo*," and
gestures for me to follow him out into the sunlight. Above us, the
Ponte Vecchio sprawls, a triple-bellied beast, reflections catching in
its arches and water pouring between its supports like a churning
shadow. Tourists lean over the river's wall where I stood moments
before, but that world is distant now. It feels like the city itself has
opened up, as though I'm peering out at it from the inside.

"Oh," I exhale softly.

"*Bello, no?*"

I look around for the woman I'd seen, but the river is empty, and
there is no one on the stretch of grass or the long brick steps that
lead to the Arno's edge.

"Today it is quiet," Stefano says, "because of vacation. But tomorrow people will return." Then, in a mixture of English and
Italian, he explains that this was originally a stable for the Medici
horses. As he speaks, his smile loses its tension. He is the club's
manager and his father was before him.

"Hey, Stefano," a young man says brightly as he passes us on his
way down to the dock.

"He's American, too," Stefano explains. "A student." He leads me back inside and shows me the locker rooms, the weight rooms, then walks me down a dark, boat-lined corridor—at the end, an old man is tending to one of the sculls, laid out like a body before him. He gently polishes its bowed wooden sides.

"Ciao, Correggio," Stefano calls, before leading me into a room crowded with rowing machines. Against one wall is a raised pool of water, four sliding seats balanced along its lip. "For practice in the bad weather," he says. "This is a special room. You know why?" I look at the quiet ergometers, the placid water, our reflections in the mirrored wall, until Stefano points to the ceiling, smiling wryly: "Uffizi," he says, letting me in on the secret. "*C'è state?*"

"Of course." I smile, really smile, for the first time in days, maybe weeks. We're right below the museum. I imagine the crowds wandering the galleries above, and that could be me, had been me, and yet in a month, a day, a single afternoon, you can become something new, can become undone but also transformed.

And so when Stefano tells me the cost of membership and says, "It's okay?" I nod, though I barely have enough to get through the month, but still I nod.

"It's perfect," I say.

"Okay. Tomorrow my assistant is back—you register with her. Then you begin here, in this room—to practice, to learn, okay? One week, two weeks. And then the river!"

"So quickly?"

"*Sì. Certo.* And why not?"

"And why not," I echo, taking the warm hand he offers me.

Before I leave, I walk up and down the hallway lined with wooden boats. They are overturned on shelves, spines raised, bodies stretched, stacked floor to ceiling in rows running from the largest eight-man boats to the small one-man sculls at the far end. I have the sensation of the past hovering just below the present, as I so often do here, my own past leaping out, fast and fierce, and suddenly I remember. I walk slowly, examining the names stenciled in white block letters along their sides—FORTUNATO, BOREA, PERSEFONE. I search for inconsistencies in the repeated symbol of the red-and-white rowing flag that ripples across each boat, trying to find a place where the human hand had wavered.

Boston. The museum was dark. It was a Monday in July and after hours—it had been planned this way, so that I could come and go barely seen, and now I was going, or was supposed to be. I ducked into the bathroom, eyed my face in the mirror, hollowed. I threw up.

Then I walked through the vacant galleries, clutching the envelope—a severance, handed to me with lowered eyes because I had brought myself to this place, to the bottom—until I reached the painting. A sea-filled nocturne. Blue and silver, but up close, mostly gray, a fog heavy with shadows, the only break in the haze a few orange gestures, the brightest near the center—a fire on a distant shore?—but so faint and far off you knew you'd never reach it. That was how I had felt. For years, maybe. As though everyone around me had figured something out that I couldn't quite grasp. And so I remained in this fog.

I was exhausted, in fact I could barely stand, but still I stopped in front of this painting to stare at that bit of orange near the center, that place beyond this place where I found myself, inexplicably. I put my hand out to touch it—and why not? what could they do to me now?—to touch, only lightly, that vanishing point where everything disappeared and came together. It was a shallow valley, rough under my finger. I felt the events of the previous months slipping away. I felt a door opening, the crack widening into something I could slip through.

"Hannah?" A voice came from the end of the corridor and I hurried out into the gray summer evening without looking back.

I choose my evening meals in Florence carefully. Early on I made the mistake of going to a traditional spot, candlelit, with couples who eyed me suspiciously. I had not anticipated such stares. Disapproving and reproachful, they presented a uniform front, said,

This place is ours, as I took too long reading the menu, inevitably falling on the *contorni*—the *side dishes*—and then ordered quickly, avoiding the waiter's skeptical gaze: *È tutto?* Yes, that's all. When my small plates arrived, the stares returned, the pairs glancing up from their own dishes piled high with meat or pasta—glistening, those items stared at me, too. I took in their stares and ate quickly.

So I choose carefully. There is Fuori Porta, or "Outside the Gate," a wine bar just beyond one of the city's large doors, the last lit building in a trendy quarter before the road winds up into the dark hills. Between six and nine each night, appetizers line the counter. I dine on pickles and carrots. I drink three glasses of wine. I listen to the hum. When the young bartender asks if I would like a fourth glass, I smile and say no. *I'm meeting a friend for dinner,* I think, *for all he knows.* I always leave Fuori Porta feeling better. Something in the walk home through the silent streets, past the dusty buildings, and across the Ponte alle Grazie—bridge of thanks—leaves me lighter.

And then there is Shiso, a sushi place where I go when I feel alert enough to face conversation with the owner, Dario. Tonight I turn the corner to find him arguing with one of the drunkards who fill the square outside—their hair is stringy with grease, their eyes drained of color. Sometimes I feel their hot breath as I pass and a phrase is thrown my way, but they go no further. I am no threat to them. And there is something of them in me, too.

"*Dai! Dai!*" Dario shouts at one of these shades, a cigarette hanging from his hand. When he catches sight of me, he drops his voice low and presses something into the man's palm. Then he throws his shoulders back and inhales deeply, looking off into the distance as the man disappears down the alley. He's pretending he hasn't seen me.

"Ciao," he says, overly familiar once I'm upon him. "*Come stai?*"

"*Bene.* How are you?"

"Busy, always busy," he says with a sigh. This is his mantra, though there are never more than a handful of people in the restaurant. I am, I believe, his only repeat customer.

He puts out his cigarette and opens the door, placing a hand on my elbow to guide me in. The interior is steel and red, about a decade too late to be modern. This place is his passion, opened after his travels in Japan. He explained it all to me one evening. *Very good*, I lied, picking at the small strips of overpriced fish. Because it's good, sometimes, to be known. I let him walk me home one night, let him kiss me outside my door. But not tonight. Tonight will be different.

There is only one table occupied—a young American couple—and the waitress, unsmiling, doesn't move from her post by the kitchen. Dario wipes down the counter and pours me a generous glass of wine.

"A good day?" he asks.

"Very good," I say, meaning it for the first time.

"You are lucky to be on such a vacation. For me it is always work, always busy. What is your work—in Boston?"

It catches me off guard. "I do fund-raising," I say, as though it were still true. "For a museum."

"*Cosa?*"

"I work with art."

"Ah. An artist."

I don't correct him. What would be the point of explaining that my job had nothing to do with art—though that was why I'd taken it—and everything to do with money. I was good at it at first. Pretending that I gave a shit, I mean. Pretending that it mattered.

"Then you understand what it is," he continues, "to be always busy."

I nod. His confidence is aggressive and catching, and I, too, act as though I don't see the empty tables, the waitress's frown as she takes my order, the sweat that beads on Dario's forehead and scalp where his hair is thinning. I accept a second glass of wine and eat slowly once my food arrives, thinking back on the day. Dario crosses his thick arms and commences a fresh monologue.

"I have this place for three years, you know. *Tre anni*, almost."

As he speaks, I begin my necessary ritual—the list. I construct it carefully in my mind.

"I think, sometimes..."

The coffee this morning—no milk, no sugar.

"...*è brutto*, Hannah. *Davvero.*"

On top of it I place the toast—two slices, choked down.

"*Sicilia. Penso di...*"

The salad, after my walk, is more challenging.

"...*è sempre la stessa cosa.*"

I nod. Dario pauses, refills my glass.

"*Allora* I go on vacation..."

I start over: break the list up into compartments, slide the toast to one side, put the wine in its own square—a larger square, it's true. Alcohol counts, isn't air, I know this. But it gets me through, so I account for it. Leave room.

"...*è diverso...*"

I return to the salad. Take it apart. Compress the pieces.

"...*che cazzo...*"

A roll of green. Slivered tomatoes. A sheet of cheese, almost translucent.

"...*non voglio ma...*"

There is no place for the almonds, a handful this evening before going out.

"...*è un casino.*"

Finally the salmon. Five pieces. Slimy. I feel them already swimming in my stomach.

"She says to me, 'Dario...'"

Then I stack the items, one on top of the next. They become a tower, tall and spindly.

"*Che posso fare?*"

But it does not feel spindly, this tower. I feel the weight of it.

"*Così è la vita...*"

The almonds sit to the side, disturbing. I cannot place them on top.

"...*però in futuro...*"

I dare not.

"...*credere—*" Dario's phone rings. "*Cazzo,*" he bellows, picking it up and walking quickly to the corner of the bar.

I look again at the tower. Close my eyes. Try to figure it out. Start over.

Giggling behind me. I open my eyes. In the mirror I can see the American couple—they are looking this way, the woman with her hand over her mouth. Why? I look at my reflection. What does she see? A woman, almost thirty, older than her, I must be older than her, my face drawn and serious. My hair is limp. I blew it dry before going out, in spite of the heat, and it should frame my features, dark. But it didn't work and it's gone limp, sits flat, hangs to my shoulders in strings. Like the men outside. Like dribble. Strings of dribble.

There is something I've forgotten to do. Somehow during the day, over the course of this evening, I lost it. I try to focus, to grasp it, but it's gone, out of reach, disappeared. Why can't I hold on to anything? Always it slips and slips and slips.

A voice shouting. Is it mine? No. Outside. A man is shouting at someone or something in the street.

"*Magari.*" Dario sighs loudly. "*Hai visto?* What I have to do. Always busy." He disappears outside, and I open my purse and leave money on the counter. Too much I think, but I'll go. Before Dario comes back and I let him walk me out, I'll go. I glance quickly for the waitress, but she's disappeared as well. There's only the smug couple now.

Outside it is dark, but still the air sticks. I hear raised voices behind me and they chase me on. The stones catch my heels, echoing loud each time. There is something I've forgotten to do. My street is empty and the music from the club beats loud. The door of the building feels heavy, the air in the lobby is heavy, too. I hit the switch of the timed light and, with a click, the stairwell illuminates but goes dark by the time I reach the third floor. I put my hand on the wall and find my way up, my steps loud and clumsy, and somewhere below a door opens.

"*Signorina?*" The landlady—what else does she want from me?— and I speed up, catch my thigh on the edge of the banister rounding the corner. It feels hot, spreads, will bruise. I hear the phone ringing, shrill, as I get to my landing.

Yes, that's it. I've forgotten again. Four, five, six rings. I find my door, put the key in the lock. Turn one, two, three times. The ringing continues. Seven, eight, nine. The door swings in and the sound pierces. Ten, eleven, twelve.

"Hannah?" My sister's voice hits like cold water, pulls me in. Even this far away, I feel pulled. Weighted. I breathe in, breathe out.

"Honey, are you okay?"

I nod. I will not cry.

"Hannah?"

"I'm fine. I just hurt my leg."

"What? What do you mean?" Kate is suspicious. She is always suspicious.

"Nothing. I don't know. I just got home."

"The list, Hannah. It's been five days. You didn't—"

The list. My inventory. The tower swims in front of me now in the dark. Laughter bubbles up from downstairs. "*Bastardo!*" a man shouts. More laughter.

"You can't do this, Hannah." I see her seated on a stool by her counter, dialing and redialing, intent on mending. She is a mender.

"I'm fine." I see the words and then say them. "I've just been busy."

"With what? What do you do all day?" She stops. "I'm sorry. How are things?"

"I went out to dinner," I say. "And I was going to write you, but I forgot."

"Hannah, you can't forget. That's the deal."

That is our agreement. Every three days: the list. That and no scales—but Kate doesn't know about the orange scale, purchased on my first day here. And I do send the list. Today was different, though, and my words begin tumbling now, spilling out of me as I explain—the meal, the wine, the men, the shouting, the wad of money left on the bar. "Too much, but I needed to leave before Dario came back. And then I forgot to write you. Because of everything that was happening."

I've fucked it up. I know it before she speaks.

"What are you talking about? Who's Dario?"

I think through it. The mirror, the almonds, the shouting. There's an answer in it I can't find. It slips and slips and slips. I give up—it won't make sense to her. Kate breathes in sharply, and I can see her looking out her window as though she can see me all these miles away.

"We'll talk about it next week," she says. "When you're back."

And now I'll have to tell her. "I'm not leaving."

"What? Are you—"

"I'm staying. A little while longer. I already changed it—my ticket. It's done."

"Are you sure? Don't you think it's time to come home? To start looking for work? Have you started looking? Or don't worry about that. You can stay with us."

"No," I say quietly.

"Hannah—" Her voice catches. "You can't just disappear."

That's what she's afraid of, my total erasure. *I am disappearing.* But not anymore. Not anymore.

"This was supposed to be a break," she pleads. "A break. That's what you said. But it's been a month. What are you going to do for money? How are you going to live?"

"I'm fine," I say, focusing on the words.

"I don't understand this. I don't know what to do."

It is the same voice I heard months ago, when I had gone as deep and as low as I would go. The voice that reflected back to me the rock bottomness of my existence.

"Won't you come home?"

My anger surges up, cuts through the fog, and I'm surprised at the growl in my voice when I say, again, "*No.*" It doesn't sound anything like me. *It's mine,* I want to say. I don't know what it is, but it's mine.

Kate is crying now. I need something—something to convince her. And then an image emerges from the fog of the day. The woman on the water, her body at peace.

"I've been rowing," I say. "I joined a rowing club. It's helping. It's beautiful on the river. Quiet." And it's not really a lie—not if I make it true, which I will. If I can just get past this call, get to sleep, get to the next morning with its clean slate.

"That sounds nice," Kate says softly. Then, "Call tomorrow. Call tomorrow when you're feeling better."

I hang up the phone and take off my skirt, my body racing. I lie down on my bed. Dinner seems far away now. The club seems far away. Home, farther still. I am propped up here without a backdrop. I am stiff, straight. Not soft like my sister, as I should be. She is a question mark, I think, before I fall asleep. Miles away, curled in the dark, she is a question mark and I am an exclamation point. And it seems to make everything come clear that all I need is to become a question mark again.

Tomorrow, I will begin to bend. I will begin tomorrow.

Chapter Two

A gymnasium. Three girls lined up, standing at attention—why? The boy, smirking. I dreaded this boy who went down the line pointing his finger, labeling our breasts. *Flat as a board. Mosquito bites. Melons.* He was no taller, no stronger, and still we took in his smirk and watched him take in our blank faces, our failure to respond. His smile grew, became something I couldn't find my way around. He walked away then, satisfied. We did not look at one another. We did not speak of it.

But that's not right. That was a story people told me. *This is where it begins,* they said, pointing at screens and billboards and smirking boys with sharp fingers who would become men who lose the smirk and do not point and yet both are felt. But that is not where it began. Not for me. Still, years later when I saw school groups at the museum, I waited for this boy to emerge with that same small smirk. I watched as he circled girls like me, wanted to silence him before he could speak, wanted to follow him into the cluster and make them all scatter like birds. Would that have helped? Children do this, after all. Children do this and they don't end up like me.

The next morning I find the city transformed. The Italians have returned, reclaiming Florence at this early hour, and the city moves, not yet weighed down by the slow stroll of tourist traffic, amoebic and unpredictable. Instead the old stones rumble with cars and rattle with bikes; buses pull up and just as quickly away as suited men and women hop on and off; the mopeds that have lined the curbs in double layers all night zip out one by one and join the buzz over bridges; and delivery trucks sit stubbornly outside grocery stores, bringing whole streets to a roaring standstill. I feel high on the new energy as I cut through the center. This is Florence in September.

I use a self-service photo booth near the train station, blinking hard each time it flashes. The four photos are identical. My eyes look surprised, my nose large, my smile too wide. *Look at you.* Is this me?

But no one hassles me as I make my way to the club. No one sees me, it seems. Not the men in crisp shirts and loafers. Not the women in heels and sleek skirts who dismount their scooters with ease. All weaving in and out of the din of cramped coffee bars—each one a humming polis this morning—before disappearing through doors that must lead to offices and schools, vanishing from the scene before it fills with the second wave, and I'm relieved to be able to join them in my own way as I duck into the club, determined to make true my words to Kate.

"Per la carta," I explain to a woman in the office, handing her the photo after she charges my credit card.

She looks at the photo, doesn't say, *Look at you,* only *"Sì"* with a smile. She slides it into a membership card and hands it to me. *"Eccola."* I am official.

Tracing yesterday's path, I tunnel down to the locker rooms. Voices echo loud from the men's room, but the women's room is empty, tiled in cool white and hushed. I change quickly.

"Ciao, Anna of Boston," Manuele says when I enter the coffee bar, full today. Like the city above, the locals have returned, only here they are all men and I'm no longer invisible as eyes dart up. I hurry out into the sunlight. More eyes. Old men—Nico in his unisuit among them—are parked in chairs on the grass. They peer up over their newspapers and the murmuring begins. It fills me with rage, their whispering. And it makes me want to hide.

"*Attenta,* Hannah!"

I turn and almost collide with a large boat that rests heavy on the shoulders of Stefano and two other men.

"*Buongiorno,*" one of them says as they pass, their uneven steps pounding the length of the metal dock. They transfer the boat from their shoulders to their palms, the movements automatic, then rotate the wooden body, gripping its edges before lowering it into the water. Stefano stands up, wiping his hands on his thighs.

"*Aspetta,*" he says to his companions. He gestures to me to come down and takes my hands in his, kissing each of my cheeks, and this quiets the grumbling of the old men.

"*Ti presento* Sergio." Stefano grasps the forearm of his teammate, a compact man with uncharacteristic red hair and large teeth who smiles at me broadly.

"*E* Giovanni."

The third man—tall with a small beard and sparkling eyes—takes my hands: "*Per gli amici,* 'Gianni.'"

I haven't had this much physical contact in weeks. Not since Kate gripped me tight at the airport, my body stiff in her arms, rejecting the embrace. *Take care of yourself,* she kept saying. Then, *I love you,* but it felt like a chokehold.

These hands aren't prying or controlling, though—only warm—and I feel elated. As if sensing this, Gianni releases me, spreads his arms wide, and throws his head back. "*Che bello giornata, no?* Sunshiiiiiine!" he shouts, a tall elegant bird greeting the day in neon stretch pants.

"Our first day of training since the vacation," Stefano explains.

"*Ragazzi, che giornata!*" A fourth figure emerges from the darkness, four oars gathered on his shoulder.

"*Ecco* Luca," Stefano says.

Luca smiles, surprised, and I recognize him then as the laughing man I'd met at the club's entrance the day before.

"Hannah," I say, my face hot again.

"*Buongiorno,* Hannah. Welcome back," he says with that same laugh. He doesn't say more, though, doesn't give me away. He slaps Stefano on the shoulder and passes the oars to Gianni and Sergio, who slide them into the rings at the boat's edge. Then he steps into the shell, one hand on the dock, and lowers himself onto the second seat.

"We train together for years," Stefano says. "Since..." He puts his hand at waist level. "*Questi ragazzi sono i miei*—how do you say?—old friends."

"Best friends," Gianni shouts, taking his place in the boat, followed by Sergio.

"*Sì. I miei grandi amici,*" Stefano says expansively.

They all nod except for Luca, who looks up at me, unsmiling. "My great friends? *Io, no,*" he says, "I don't like these guys," provoking a chorus of moans.

"*Allora*, Hannah. You practice today?" Stefano asks.

"Inside on the machines."

"*Ci vediamo presto*, okay?" Stefano gives my arm a squeeze before taking his place in the first seat.

"Alessandro, *vieni qua!*" Gianni shouts, and an adolescent boy dashes past me and climbs into the front of the boat, facing Stefano, his legs folded beneath him. He grasps a rope that connects him like reins to the rudder behind him. The coxswain. They push away from the dock and pause.

"*Pronti!*" Stefano's voice cuts a straight line, and the boy adjusts the rope, pulls it taut, as each man lifts his oar in preparation. "*Via!*" Stefano calls, and they dip their oars in unison and begin to row with small strokes, using only their arms. They move slowly up the Arno toward the Ponte alle Grazie, where they carve a diagonal and then bring the boat around so that their backs are to the club. They come to a full stop, a single breath in and out, before I hear Stefano's voice again—"*Pronti... Via!*"—and with a deep *whoosh*, they are off with unbelievable speed, using their legs now, too, as Stefano calls, "*Tutti insieme! Uno! Due!*" When they pass the club, I can see that they move as one, their bodies folding and stretching, folding and stretching, their muscles flexing and releasing in time.

"*Uno! Due! Uno! Due!*" Stefano's voice echoes across the water as they approach the Ponte Vecchio. Within seconds, they are in the bridge's shadow and then lost to the sunlight on the other side.

Four months ago. I stood in front of an annunciation surrounded by people, all potential donors. It was a special tour I was chosen to lead because I'd studied these things and because one of the prospects spoke Italian, and I'd studied that, too, though as soon as he began speaking, my blank stare stopped him.

It was bright in the gallery, hard to make out the features on the faces around me, except for the well-heeled woman in the center, the one who'd asked, *Aren't you warm, honey?* at the beginning of the tour, nodding at my cardigan. It was May, but I was always chilled then.

I was talking about perspective when the ground grew unstable and the faces blurred, as though someone were erasing them, one by one. And then I must have fallen, hard. Darkness. Nothing. Then a voice, light, a face that I knew. One of the guards helping me stand. He liked me. He wouldn't tell, didn't tell. But someone did. Someone had.

Because the next day, Claudia invited me to lunch. She was so unlike me, but we had history. She'd helped to hire me five years before, became my mentor and then my friend. I trusted her.

We went to a café by the museum. The sun was merciless, the traffic screaming around us, but Claudia was composed as always— seated cool and tall, her lips a decisive line as she looked over the menu. I hesitated. Ordered fruit and yogurt, a splurge.

"You haven't been yourself, Hannah," she pressed as soon as we were alone. Her eyes—sharp and blue, blue, blue—didn't leave room for questions or doubts. "You've been making mistakes."

I nodded. I'd always been good at my job. Not good like Claudia, who handled the major gifts. But I could smile and smile. I was competent and, most of the time, invisible. Unless I made a mistake. Which I had, more than once.

"These aren't small errors."

There were gaps in my days. The details consumed by the next meal, the exercise to negate it, whether I'd need to throw up and how and where. And then that voice, always that voice. *If only you were.* Each day I felt closer to it.

"They cost money."

I'd grow dizzy scanning the screen, pull the wrong file, approve the wrong payment—

"That e-mail was a bomb."

—forward the wrong message. And suddenly I wasn't invisible at all.

"And there was a complaint about the event. One of the guests said you collapsed."

I nodded dumbly. If we could just keep the conversation to work, to my many mistakes.

"I told them you were sick," Claudia said. "Robert doesn't know about it." The director.

Our food arrived and I watched her eat. I didn't defend myself. I thought it would end there. But she had arrived with knives.

"I think you have a problem," she said, her eyes catching mine again. They looked right through me.

My yogurt sat cold in front of me. I couldn't lift my spoon.

"Hannah?"

I took a breath, tried to assure her that I was all right. She didn't realize, perhaps. But I couldn't look her in the eye.

"I don't think you understand," Claudia said. "You have a real problem."

Something stopped in me. The scene began to unravel. I was not a reliable source, I knew, and still.

"I'm fine," I said quietly.

"You're not fine, though. You're starving. Look at you. Your eyelashes are falling out."

This image would stay with me, maybe forever. It wasn't true, but it stuck. This was the end of our friendship. I lost other friends, too, though not in quite the same way.

I meet Francesca at the end of my first week at the club.

I've been here every day, working out on an ergometer in the room below the Uffizi, and the movements of this new routine are slowly growing familiar: I position myself on the rowing machine's small sliding seat and grasp the wooden handle. When I push with my legs, the seat slides back along the metal bar. I draw the handle all the way into my chest, the pressure of the cord it is attached to mimicking the resistance of water. Then I allow it to pull me back toward my feet, the seat sliding in, my body curling forward, my knees folding up to my chin. The spinning wheel exhales a breeze that cools me before I spring back again. I've lost so much muscle this past year, and the first few pulls are difficult—my arms and legs shaking and the seat shuddering beneath me—until I get into a rhythm. Curling forward, springing back. Slow and then faster. The movement is a relief; the expended energy counterbalances the ever-expanding list, my inventory. Still, I don't look at myself in the wall of mirrors. I keep my eyes on the handle, on the wheel, on my feet.

Finding me battling the machine in these first days, Stefano has helped. I've spoken with only him and Manuele, not with any of the others, all men, no matter what time of day. In the morning, the old men's banter echoes through the corridors with the *clang, clang, clang* of the weight machines. Midday the working men arrive to train while the city has its siesta. After school, it's the boys—they flail about on the river as Stefano calls instructions from a speed-boat, his reassuring smiles interspersed with grimaces as they tee-ter and totter and cut too close to the rubbish-filled banks of the Arno. The old men are still on the embankment at that hour, round-ing out the day with criticisms as the silhouetted teens slide past in small wooden sculls.

All men and boys. And then I enter the locker room on Saturday and find Francesca bent over the sink naked, examining her eyes in the mirror. They are red-rimmed.

"How are you?" she tosses my way in flawless English. "I'm Francesca. You're the American."

"Hannah." My voice sounds strange.

"Hannah. You a student?"

She must be flattering me. "No. Not studying. Just visiting."

"How long are you here for?" She spreads cream under and then over her eyes, massaging it in.

"I'm not sure."

"Huh. Well, watch out—time is different here." She rubs her fingers together. "Slippery. It feels like it's moving slower, but it's a trick. You see my face?" She eyes me in the mirror as she pulls her skin taut. "You can always tell how I'm feeling. I can't be too sad. You see it right away. It sticks, you know."

"You mean—"

"Wrinkles. Age. Anyway, you're too young to know. How old are you?"

"Twenty-nine."

"Huh." She returns to her reflection. "I thought you were younger."

Her comment would irritate me, except that I'm more concerned with how I'm going to change. Normally I wouldn't undress out in the open, would avoid the glances that might become questions. Even after I began eating again, the flesh kept falling away, and still my bones protrude. And then there are the bruises. They appear some mornings, without cause, blooming across my body like evidence. But there are no private spaces here, and so I change carefully, trading one piece of clothing for another. I look at Francesca. I'm not frail compared with her. I am an Amazon—much taller, with large hands, large feet. Some echo of the women of my past. Francesca is of different stock. Petite and lithe. She must be in her forties, but except for the lines around her eyes, she seems ageless.

Laughter from the men's locker room bursts through the vent.

"They're crazy." Francesca rolls her eyes toward the sound and strolls back to her locker. "Those men, crazy. There was an Australian girl here—she got burned three times! *Three times!*" She pulls on her own small leggings and glances up at me soberly. "She was thirty-three. You think she would've known better. Acted like she was about thirteen. Bad news, these guys. That boy from Chicago seems nice, though. Have you met him?"

I nod. Peter. The student. He's a serious rower. He walks around the club with his toned arms held slightly out from his body as though they've just been inflated. He's young, even for me.

"American boys are nice. Simple. I spent some time in America. I should have stayed—ha! The guys here, you just can't tell. Three times she got burned."

"What do you mean... burned?"

Francesca purses her lips and makes a motion with her hand. "She was humiliated. Everyone knew. And two of the guys were married."

"Didn't anyone tell her?"

"Tell her what?"

"That they were married."

"I thought she knew! You think she would have been smarter about it. Thirty-three years old! It got so she couldn't show up here. What can you do?" Francesca returns to the mirror, twisting her hair up into a coil, silent now, and I hear another eruption of laughter from the adjoining room. Our area feels like a vault, a mausoleum. We are rarities, like the red tiles scattered across the stark white walls. Chance blocks of color.

"Not a lot of women at this club, huh?" I ask.

"A few." Francesca shrugs. "It's mostly men. Doesn't bother me as long as my husband isn't one of them. If he was a member here, I wouldn't be. That's for sure."

I don't say anything, but she locks eyes with me and continues. "I don't see him all day. Just a half an hour at night. Then I go walking with the dogs so I don't have to see him." She pulls on her little ankle socks and the cloud passes over us, forgotten. She's practiced at transitioning, but I'm curious now.

"Are you from Florence?"

"Me? God, no. I'm from a real city. Milano. I've been here twenty years." She sighs at the burden. "Like I said—you lose time."

"Did you meet your husband in Florence?"

Another sigh, a flick of the hand. "Yes. I was twenty-one. How old are you again?"

"Twenty-nine," I repeat.

"*Ah, sì.* Twenty-nine. So you understand. I was only twenty-one. Too young to know better. *He's* one of those real loud types, you know? Real neurotic. I see it in my daughter sometimes. She's at that awkward stage—all pimply, short hair." She pauses. "Peter's single, isn't he?"

"I don't know. I mean, he's a student." What is she thinking?

"Yeah, he's single. All men are at that age." She closes her locker decisively. "You going to the game Monday?"

"I don't think so." Stefano has distributed invitations for the event—a soccer match, one of the first of the season. He bought tickets for the members at a discount, and though I accepted one and said that, yes, I'd see him there, I'm not sure I will. It's one thing to come to the club, to exchange a few words with him over a smooth shot of espresso. It's another thing entirely to see people out in the world.

"You should come," Francesca says. "I could use another woman there, you know? And the game's wild. Well, take care. Ask me about any of these guys." She pauses to glance back at herself in the mirror. "I appreciate it, you know. The bad thing."

I'm not sure anymore whom or what she's talking about.

"It's taught me. But it's a shame to learn like that," she says, then strolls to the door. "Ciao."

"Ciao," I say, but she doesn't appear to hear me as she smiles and joins the voices on the other side.

Later in the afternoon, I'm again struggling with the ergometer, intent on getting it right. I look down at my arms, which seem thicker, and look away. My face in the mirror is red, growing with the heat. I can feel it growing. *Look at you.* I close my eyes, slide the seat forward, roll my body in, push back with my legs, and pull with my arms. I hear footsteps and Stefano enters followed by Luca, who has a bag slung across one shoulder. I watch their reflections.

"*Eccola,*" Stefano says. "*Troppo veloce.*"

"Too fast?" I ask.

"You must wait."

"Wait for what?"

"*Spingi e poi—*"

"Stefano!" A voice from down the hall.

"*Scusi,*" he says, and disappears.

Luca watches me in the mirror and I stop moving. He smiles but says nothing. He's a person at ease with himself and the world. It makes me nervous.

"You must wait," he says finally, crossing the room. "Push with the legs *e poi* pull with the hands. Try."

I lean forward, curl in, and then spring backward, pulling the handle with me.

"Too fast," Luca says. "*Di nuovo.* Slow."

I lean forward, curl in, and begin to pull, but a pressure on my back stops me. I glance at him in the mirror. He's leaning down, his hand supporting me. I look for a loaded smile, wait for a line.

"*Aspetta*" is all he says. Then, "Push with the legs."

He keeps his hand steady, releasing the pressure gradually as I slide back. When my legs are almost straight he says, "*Adesso,*" and I draw the handle all the way into my chest.

"*Così,*" he says. "You understand?"

I nod.

"*Di nuovo.*"

I repeat the motion, alone this time.

"*Brava.*" He stands up, smiling, and skin gathers around his eyes. Like Francesca, he must be older than he looks, but he does not carry the weight of age or the gravity of too much experience.

"*Grazie.*"

"*Di niente.*" He turns to leave.

"Are you here tomorrow?" My voice echoes loud and he turns around, surprised.

"*Domani? No.*" He looks confused. I've done something wrong, misread his casual kindness for something else. "Tomorrow is Sunday," he explains. "The *canottieri* is closed."

"Oh." Of course. Sunday.

"*Allora,* until soon. Maybe Monday, yes? At the game?" He tilts his head, smiles, and is gone, leaving a lightness in his wake that I try to hold on to as I curl forward and push back, waiting to pull with my arms. I stop then and let the wheel spin slowly to a rest.

Chapter Three

Sunday. The club is closed and the city is closed, too. It isn't the soft closed of American cities—the change in hours or the farther walk for groceries—but an imperative *rest* that shutters all the shops. I should begin looking for jobs back home. Instead, I hurry to the train station, buy a second-class ticket to Siena, and leave Florence for the first time since my arrival.

As the train pulls out of the station the car doors inhale and then exhale a small man in wire-rimmed glasses. He grips a cigarette, looking down the aisle for the smoking car. Across from me are two young women: one with large eyes and tiny doll lips reads aloud self-assuredly from a novel to her companion, whose feet rest on the large backpack on the floor between us. I try not to stare as she reenacts the story with great hand and facial movements, her eyes growing wider in one moment, narrowing in the next, her free hand rising up and then dropping back to her knee each time she turns a page. With every gesture, she is a new painting. In a few minutes, we're in the suburbs of Florence. We're in the hills by the time she pauses for a breath and stretches her arm comfortably across the seat behind her friend, glancing at me wisely out of the corner of her eye as if she knows I am searching for a crack or a defect. Finding none, I close my eyes, glad to know these girls exist.

The sun is not quite up and the hills are swallowing us now, one side green and the other black like a shadow puppet theater. We are going south. Nothing sounds better and it feels good to know, as the train stops and starts at each city along the way and the sun emerges hazy behind the clouds, that I'm going somewhere new on this gray day. With each curve, we burrow deeper, the surroundings growing more remote, until the homes disappear and there is only land for long stretches broken by blocked letters on train platforms. MONTELUPO. EMPOLI. CASTELFIORENTINO. How many of these first impressions will come undone?

Across the way the listening girl slides out from under her friend's arm and extracts from her bag an enormous cucumber and a pocketknife. She passes it to the first girl, who flips open the blade and begins to peel away the skin in strips without looking at it, still reading from the book somehow, no energy lost or wasted, and again she is a painting. She knows where she is going just as she knows how to peel that fruit, tracing easily the skin and losing none of the meat. Something in the gesture reminds me of my own history. Somewhere I had the confidence of that girl.

In Boston, I would look over the rooftops, leaning out my window with my stomach resting against the radiator. I knew that landscape, its edges and extensions and how they all connected. Knew the pinpoints within it—the people and places of my past and my present, the constellation of my existence. I held that periphery always in my mind. I did not realize then, but now I know how much I held. I did not think then, but now I know that every time I spoke the name of a street, a neighborhood, a friend, I was saying, too, *This is mine, this is mine, this is mine.* Now I am a single point and the distance of my gaze: that field to the left, that edge of trees to the right, these girls before me.

The listener reaches back into her bag and finds a little package of dried soup mix and a tin of crackers. The girl who is a painting finally abandons the novel and slices the cucumber thin onto a napkin on the seat between them. Then I watch them both, concentrated and silent, place the cucumber on the crackers and sprinkle the secret mix on top. It is a meal they have stolen from their mothers. Their task complete, they glance up at me and I turn back to the window, embarrassed. *I am known somewhere,* I want to shout.

Late June. It is impossible that it was less than three months ago. I stood at my sister's window, looking out. The world below was a toy set: the tops of trees, bodies stretched out on a square of green, a playground, and, beyond it all, half hidden, the Charles River. It was manageable, reasonable, ordered. I wished I were a child looking at those pockets of life. I wished I were a child reveling in spring, anticipating the summer, the days growing longer. I didn't know what to attach my unhappiness to—loss, work, stress. Julian was the easy one. *Leave me alone*, I'd said. Until he did.

Kate's apartment was a clean slate, untouched by wars and recession. You could stand in her living room—with its white couch, white walls, nothing to compete with the view over that toy world—and believe that none of it had happened. But it had happened. It was real. And what had happened to me was real, too.

"You can see the river in the winter," my sister said, coming to stand beside me.

"I lost my job."

"I know," she said quietly.

"I embarrassed them in front of the board. That's the only reason. They wouldn't have cared otherwise." There's more, but Kate didn't need to know about the rest. She wouldn't understand.

"It doesn't matter now. You need to take care of yourself," she said. She was a mender, the mender since our parents split, our father disappearing into a new family, our mother disappearing into work, unshaken and unshakable. She was not a mender, my mother. She was a *pull yourself together*. Kate was both. A survivor and a mender.

"You can stay here. Give up your apartment."

"I'm subletting." I wished I'd beat her to it. "I have a plan."

"What plan?"

"I'm going to leave Boston. Get away for a while."

"For god's sakes, Hannah. I'm sorry, but this is serious. You need help, not a vacation." She said nothing for a moment, then softly, "When did this start?"

I stopped breathing. She was thinking, I knew, of my near tears over dinner, when I'd admitted to her what she'd already figured out. I was a child, a child.

"It wasn't Julian, was it? He seemed so nice. I still don't understand why—"

"Stop trying to blame something." Julian was nice, had been nice
for months, and then concerned, and then suspicious, like Kate. And
now he was gone and the ache remained. It had been there long before him, and it always returned, like an old injury before rain.

"I'm alone and I'm fine," I said, turning to face her, turning on
her. "What else do you want?"

"I just want you to be—to be yourself." Kate said this in the same
voice she had used on the phone that morning. That voice that had
found me in my bed where I'd been for three days, unmoving. It
was a voice that could break my heart if I let it.

"I am myself," I said louder. "Quit trying to help." I should have
stopped there, but I was angry. I was so angry. "Maybe you're the
problem. You think I don't notice you watching me? You watch me
all the time. I'm not an experiment."

She dropped her head.

"I know what you're doing," I said, "and it's not helping. I wish
you'd leave me alone. *You're not helping.*"

She put her hand to her face, but I continued throwing words
at her, hard, until she whispered, "When did you slip through the
net?" and began to sob. Still I kept going until she went into her
bedroom, locked the door, and I could hear her on the phone. I
stayed by the window. It was getting dark and people were leaving
the park, filtering out through different gates with languid steps.

She doesn't know what I can be, I thought then, looking out over
that ordered world. There were these things that I could be. I just
needed to get away from the eyes, from the watching.

Following signs that lead me through the original walls, I walk into
the old center of Siena. It's early afternoon, the church services are
over, and the shop windows are dark. Only the occasional coffee
bar is open, the interior a cool rectangle broken by no more than
one or two bodies gripping espresso and glancing up at a small
television. Soccer.

The streets are tighter than Florence's and the buildings on either side too close to me, slicing the sky into narrow strips. Siena is an older generation, cloistered and closed, and I feel trapped with nowhere to look but up at the church towers or down at my feet. *Medieval*. So this is what it means. Tunneling between buildings, I find my way to the only open space, the Piazza del Campo, a cobbled Tilt-A-Whirl of a square edged in cafés. I visit the unfinished duomo, then drift to the edge of town, to a church balanced high on one of Siena's hills. It is massive but plain, and a worn wooden door on its side is almost unnoticeable. The door is open a crack, and I enter to find a similarly sparse interior, cool and hushed. I like the simplicity of this space—the walls are light stone, the ceiling wooden beams. I would like to stay here to read and write and think. I would like to stay here to wait for answers. I breathe out and then in and catch the scent of incense. Halfway up the nave a woman kneels by a side chapel, but otherwise the basilica is empty. As soon as I take a few steps, however, a priest appears. He is small and old with tufts of white hair around his ears. He squints at me, smiling, his lips folding into his face, and offers me a tour.

"*Grazie*," I say, and then realize my error. He begins speaking rapidly in Italian but with such excitement that I don't stop him. He takes the edge of my sleeve and leads me to the back of the church, to a small fresco.

"*Conosce* Santa Caterina?" he asks.

I nod. Catherine of Siena. I studied her in college—or paintings of her, anyway, and this one is familiar. She wears a black-and-white habit and holds a stalk of lilies. It is pre-Renaissance—her features are flat, her almond eyes lowered without expression, the proportions slightly off, and she has a greenish glow. Eerie. On each of her hands sits a drop of blood, the stigmata. What else? She had visions and ecstasies like St. Teresa, I think. And she claimed that she had married Jesus in a dream.

We stand for a moment longer, the priest gazing up at the portrait and shaking his head. He looks close to tears. Then he takes the edge of my sleeve again and we are off—he speaking and I not understanding, his feet shuffling along the marble floor with a *shhh, shhh, shhh,* and I try to step more lightly. He walks me up the left side of the church, stops at several paintings along the way, gestures to the ceilings and I catch a series of dates. When we get to the front of the cathedral, he points to each of the stained-glass windows, naming them. Then he leads me to a chapel that is frescoed on three sides. At its center is a small ornate shrine, a mini-cathedral.

"*Questa è la sua testa,*" he says gravely.

"Her head?" I ask.

"*Sì*, her head," he confirms.

Indeed, within the shrine is St. Catherine's mummified head shrinking into a crisp white habit. The cheeks are sunken, the nose almost gone, the upper teeth visible, the eyes closed but the eyebrows seemingly raised. I look around to see if there are any children who might be traumatized by this medieval mummy, but it's only me and the priest and St. Catherine now.

"*E anche il suo dito.*" He gestures to a glass case off to the side where a single finger, crooked, points heavenward.

"Her finger?"

He nods happily and points upward, too. He keeps smiling—this must be the end of the tour. He shakes his head when I offer him money but gestures with great enthusiasm to the frescoed walls of the chapel and bows slightly before disappearing.

I leave the dismembered saint to herself and look at the frescoes, which piece together Catherine's life. These images are more relatable. They must have been painted a century or more after she died. They have perspective and expression, and instead of a blank background, Catherine is out in the city, architecture and landscape behind her. In one image she is collapsed, receiving the stigmata. She looks upward in ecstasy, her body not her own. On another wall, she prays for a man's soul as he is executed. His head, like hers, has been torn from its body.

The third fresco stops me short. St. Catherine, right hand raised, stands over a young woman possessed by demons. A crowd has formed, but the people peer at her from behind pillars or hide their faces, shrinking back from the scene. Cowards. Only St. Catherine is calm, her eyes down, her raised hand unmoving. The possessed woman writhes on the ground beneath her, her arms straining up at unnatural angles, her head thrown back.

Which of these women am I? The one straining madly toward something unseen, or the calm one looking on? I have been both. In this past year, I have been both. I have been the madwoman screaming, straining, digging ditches around the bone. Sculpting.

When did this start?—my sister's voice, a flat note as she watched me disappear. And still I could not stop digging, could not stop sculpting. I *would* be well sculpted. But I was not mad. I was calm. She couldn't see. She couldn't see that I was not only taking away. I was reaching for something. I was creating.

I stand for what must be a long time in the little chapel in front of this fresco. Catherine's face belies nothing as she gazes at the possessed woman, but even the saint, I decide, was more than her patient reserve. I look at the first painting of Catherine in ecstasy and then back to the image of this writhing woman. They seem the same, and I wonder if, in looking at this madwoman, St. Catherine recognized herself, frozen in one of her ecstasies, envisioning. Of course, she had been told that the woman was inhabited by an evil being, not God. Still, it seems to me that Catherine is looking in a mirror, and I wonder if she realized this and if it struck her as odd that she had been asked to heal her own reflection.

I stop in a gift shop, the only place open, and find a book on the saint's life. But as the train pulls out of the city at dusk, I can't focus on the words. I put the book on the seat beside me and close my eyes.

I see myself already back in Florence. For a moment I am in two places at once. It is always this way when you travel. You exist in two places at once, as two people at once. There is the place you are now and the imagined place you are going, where you are already wandering streets, having dinner, strolling back to your hotel. There is the you that is here and the future you already there, smiling and confident. And that future place is not a busy intersection in Florence at night, or a darkened alley where words chase me. It is not the place I feel I am perched, always precariously perched, these days. The future place is better and in it is a better me. Not the me riding lonely on a train, running from everything I knew and everything I was, but the me that is knowing, flirtatious, unfettered, savvy, healed. The thought is reassuring, but then it turns and is terrifying. That future woman is not me and I know how she will look at me, the past her. I know how she will pity, patronize, want to expunge, destroy. She will say, *I remember what I was, before I learned.* She will want to erase what is mine. But this is me and this is mine. This lonely train ride is mine, too.

Out the window is a parade of shadows and I am a single point in the dark, one lit window passing by. *This is the first day,* I think, looking out at the darkness and seeing suddenly my own face. *This is the first day of the rest of your. The rest of your. The rest. This is the first day. This is the first. The rest. Your life.* Then: *The rest of your life. What if this is the rest of your life?*

But this is the place where I am: on a train in the dark. And, in truth, the place that I'm going doesn't exist. She does not yet exist.

Chapter Four

At the stadium the next night, the crowd is roaring before the game has even started. The rain has kept no one away. As I take out my ticket by the entrance, I hear my name and I see someone running toward me, his umbrella flying behind him.

"Hey!" He grins once he's upon me. The American student. His cheeks are red, his nose dripping. "I'm Peter. From the club."

"Hannah." I put out my hand, but he swings an arm around me, gives me a wink, and exclaims, "I know!"

We enter together and I scan the bleachers for familiar faces as we make our way closer to the field where the serious fans cram together, all purple and red, the colors of the Fiorentina.

"Isn't this amazing?" Peter shouts as we pull out our tickets for another official and walk down a level. "First game of the season. I bought a scarf at the market, even though it's too warm for it. Damn, this is great. Ever been to a game?"

"No, I haven't!" I try to match his enthusiasm, an impossible task, especially as I'm beginning to feel uneasy. High Plexiglas walls on either end of our section separate the home fans from the visitors. I look across and down, across and down, and finally see a row of red windbreakers that identify the club members, Stefano and Luca somewhere among them, but before we reach them I feel a hand on my arm—Francesca.

"Ciao!" Her eyes are wide, encircled with dark makeup. "Come here, you two. Sit by me."

I want to join the rest of the group, but I don't want to go down there alone, so I squeeze past Francesca and take a seat next to the clear wall. She and Peter immediately begin speaking in Italian, and I look away and find an old woman staring at me through the divider. Beyond her is a sea of bodies, all in yellow. The Parma fans. I turn my gaze to the field, where the players are warming up. Aligned behind the goals are police officers with guard dogs and guns. Francesca and Peter are still completely caught up in each other and I try not to listen in, try not to judge this woman, who had cautioned me with such alarm but who clearly has her own plans for this much younger man. This boy, really. Can't she see that he's a boy?

There's a gust of wind and I cross my arms tight, wishing I'd brought a jacket. I spent the afternoon with St. Catherine, reading in a park near the river. She was born to cloth-dyers and her parents had hopes of a good marriage, but she had a vision of God at age six—saw him quite clearly hovering above her, blessing her with the sign of the cross, as she walked one of Siena's narrow streets—and from then on she thought of nothing else. When she turned twelve, her mother tried to take her out to be seen, to attract a husband. Instead, she shaved her head and wrapped it in a scarf. She refused visitors, slept on a board, and wore a thin cross-covered chain with small hooks around her waist, pulling it tight so that it drew blood when she moved. *Take that* is what those hooks said to her parents, to her would-be suitors, to the people who didn't believe her visions. *Believe this*. That was as far as I got when it began to rain, the skies opening up and drenching me.

The whistle begins the game, and instantly I can see nothing as all the spectators have risen. A flare gun goes off somewhere in the stands, and the guard dogs shift uneasily as smoke descends over the stadium, obliterating the figures in purple and yellow. There is history here tonight, centuries of competition on the faces of the people shouting around me. These regional rivalries run deep. To-night it is Parma, but it could be any team.

"Great, huh?" Francesca roars beside me.

Mariotti, the great hope of the Florentine team, has the ball. He flies down the field, his long hair trailing behind. He has a casual ruggedness that has secured him a spot on the cover of every gossip magazine. He misses a goal and the Parma fans begin to chant, "*Vaffanculo! Vaffanculo!*" *Fuck you! Fuck you!*

As if in response, Francesca weaves her arm through Peter's.

"Are you coming out after?" she asks twenty minutes into the match. There is a postgame party at a dance club owned by one of the rowing club's members. "Mariotti is supposed to be there. But who knows if he'll show his face now, huh? Anyway, you must come. It'll be fun."

There's another surge from the crowd before I can answer—the Fiorentina have scored—and a large man pushes between us, fist raised. I try to speak around his protruding middle, but as the big belly falls back, Francesca's face—her eyes wide, her mouth open and laughing—turns away from me and into Peter, her thin fingers grasping his cheeks. Then they are lost to the crowd as people jump up on their seats and I feel pressure against the backs of my knees. My right side is pressed into the divider, and there is no room now to even step back onto my own seat. The shouts around me rise and meld until a song grows out of the chaos, the tune familiar. Francesca's voice climbs in sharp staccato, breaking off only when I squeeze her arm: "I'll see you at the party."

I slide by her and then Peter, who continues belting out the song, his eyes luminous. When they reach the chorus I realize that it's a version of "Yellow Submarine"—"Fuck your yellow submarine," maybe. I push through bodies and fight my way up toward the exit. I'm almost there when I feel a vibration against my shoulder and turn to see a young boy—his hair slicked back and his yellow Parma jersey pressed against the wall—glaring at me and pounding on the glass. He begins shouting, "*Vaffanculo! Vaffanculo!*" And how could he know that his curse is wasted on an outsider? I continue to watch his busy lips until they are obliterated by a great wad of spit that makes me jump back even as it is caught, squashed, on the divider between us.

The dance club pulses in the middle of a dark park near the river. When I step up to the door hours later, the tattooed bouncer barely looks at me before waving me in. The first room is enormous, every inch filled, and the bass beat of music engulfs me. The crowd radiates out from a central circular bar that glows like a small city. The ceiling stretches up several stories, and high above, people lean over balcony rails, humming red. On the perimeter of the room is a series of dark doors that lead to other rooms, one of which the *canottieri* has rented out. I had two drinks with my meal at a café near the stadium, but I'm already anxious for another one.

I am underdressed—jeans, sandals, and a button-down seemed right for a game and then a bar, but I look juvenile compared with the women in this club, all wearing spiked heels and fabric that clings to their bodies. More than the clothes, it's the gesture that I'm missing. All around me they are talking, laughing, placing hands on arms, heads pitched back, backs arched, hips swaying right or left, all of these small movements melding to form a single S. A fluid motion in and away, a curling S with a strong spine. Leaning in, leaning out, but still bound to that core. It invites whatever the night might bring; it attracts and intimidates. I don't have this gesture, don't have any gesture. I just *am*. I feel a tug at my hair and turn, but there are no eyes on me. I run my hand across my head and keep moving.

At the third doorway, partially obscured by a thick velvet curtain, is a handwritten sign: FLORENCE ROWING. I descend into a room where everything is lower—low ceiling, low lighting, low tables with candles lining the back wall where people are seated in low clusters. The center, a small dance floor, is empty. I scan the room for Francesca, for anyone—I thought I'd be late, but I'm early, and I recognize no one in those little circles: not the men and not the women, who in this room have mastered an easy movement as well. I order a vodka and soda from the young bartender. He must be used to American students because he doesn't blink when I drink it fast and order a second.

I look up when the curtain moves, hoping for a familiar face, then glance at my reflection between the bottles on the back of the bar and try to appear natural. I roll up one sleeve of my shirt, push it back down. I lean to one side, then the other, resting my elbow lightly on the bar's edge. *Look at you.* I put my hand to my face, feeling for more flesh, then drop it quickly and look away. When I order my third drink, I try on the gesture, moving toward the bartender a bit and smiling, but his face remains blank as he scoops ice into a new glass.

I am decided on leaving when there is an eruption by the door.

"Oh, Fiorentina..."

Stefano enters and pauses at the top step with his arms raised, a handful of men behind him. The air swells with sound as everyone around me begins singing.

"Oh, Fiorentina..."

Stefano takes the steps two at a time, leading the charge, and I spot Luca and Gianni among his companions. The song surges up and down and even the bartender joins in.

"Ricorda che del calcio è tua la storia. La la la la la..."

I try to catch Stefano's eye, but he doesn't see me as the group passes and then divides, the men splitting off to greet people. The song slowly dies but the room is buzzing now.

"Ne prende un altro?"

An older man with thinning hair. He's shorter than me and his shirt hangs too far open.

"No, grazie." I shake my nearly full glass at him.

He puts out his hand. *"Sono* Bernardo."

"Hannah," I say, taking just his fingers.

"Piacere, Anna." He stretches out the vowels, the grin not leaving. "You are at the *canottieri?"*

"I am."

"Why haven't I seen you before?"

I'm trying to think of a response that will end the conversation, but his frozen smile seems immovable.

"Basta, Bernardo. *Ciao, bella."* Stefano squeezes my hand and gives Bernardo a look—his smile drops and he shrugs, muttering something under his breath before turning away.

"Grazie," I say.

Stefano nods and calls for drinks. "A great game, yes? *Forza Fioren-tina!*"

"A great game," I echo, though I'd missed most of it.

With three glasses balanced between his hands, Stefano points to the back where a few other men sit hunched around a candle like a band of witches. When we get to the table, the conversation halts and Luca rises with a smile. "*'Sera,*" he says, his hands absorbing mine easily. Gianni and Sergio are sitting with him, along with a man I don't know, broader than the others and in a sharply pressed suit.

"Hannah di Boston," Stefano explains.

"Carlo," the man says, taking my hand and gripping it a bit too tightly. Then the conversation resumes and I am forgotten, except by Luca, who asks what I've been doing in Italy. I think for a moment and then tell him about my trip to Siena, which seems the safest answer.

"Siena," he says, and nods. "Beautiful city. *Ma Firenze è più bella, no?*"

I confirm that, yes, Florence is more beautiful, and he pats my knee approvingly, letting it linger a moment before reaching for his drink. I feel comfortable with him, trust his smile in this candle-light. I tell him about the chapel of St. Catherine.

"*Ah, Santa Caterina,*" he hums. "An interesting woman."

There is a church in Florence I should visit, he says. San Frediano in Cestello. *San Frediano in Cestello,* I repeat to myself. I finish my drink and go to order another. I walk with ease, glide through the crowd, and smile at the bartender, who now smiles back. People have begun dancing to a song that is vaguely familiar.

Francesca. I catch the name when I return as the table erupts in laughter.

"Francesca?" I repeat, and Luca turns, surprised, as the other men continue bantering.

"*Sì,* Francesca. It is really funny, *no?*" He grins and then takes in my blank look. "*Non hai capito?*"

"No, you speak too quickly."

"Hmm," he considers. "Only English, then. I practice, *va bene?*"

"All right."

"*Allora.*" Luca takes a deep breath and begins with effort. "You know Francesca, yes? She always goes out in the wide boats, *perché* she is afraid."

The larger wooden sculls. They sit firm in the water, don't tremble with each stroke like the sleek aluminum ones.

"So today," he continues, "we told her to try a little one. But she says, 'No! No! No!'" Here Luca does his best Francesca impression, pursing his lips and crossing his arms as he shakes his head tersely from side to side. "But we laugh at her *e poi* she says *va bene. Allora,* Correggio puts her in the boat and she goes. She has on little... sunglasses, yes? And she waves like we are stupid."

Luca is already starting to chuckle between words as he recounts the scene. I can feel the warmth coming off him.

"She has a few strokes *e poi* she screams. Just at the boat is, ah, *una nutria.*"

"A what?"

Luca pinches up his face and raises his hands in small fists. Carlo laughs roughly across the table.

"Oh." I grimace. "You mean the rats." I've seen them waddling along the riverbanks and paddling in open water with only their heads showing.

"*No!*" Luca says earnestly, putting his hand on my forearm. "Not a rat. *No. Una nutria.* Cute, yes?"

"No," I say definitively. "There is nothing cute about a massive river rodent."

Stefano returns with more drinks and Luca pauses to take one.

"*Allora,*" he continues. "They do not bother us. No problem. But Francesca waves her arms *e allora* the boat is shaking and we shout, '*Tranquilla!*' but she moves too much *e poi* she is in the water. *E la povera nutria*—"

"Poor Francesca." I laugh easily and the sound surprises me.

"Poor Francesca?" Carlo says loud. "*Macché povera Francesca.*"

Luca ignores him. "He tries to swim but Francesca, she moves *e poi* she hits *la nutria! Allora, la nutria* screams and tries to go away *però* he is stuck *nella... nella...*"

"In the current?" I suggest.

"*Sì*. In the current. Exactly. Crazy. Ah, Francesca," he says, and sighs.

Luca is about to say something more, but Carlo interrupts him again, his voice sloppy, and I catch the word *puttana*. *Slut*. All the men fall silent.

"Really?" I throw into the silence, feeling bolder with the alcohol coursing through me, and then all the eyes are on me, surprised.

But Carlo's gaze remains hard. "Why, you know her?"

"*Ma dai*," Luca says. "*Lascia perdere*, Carlo. You're drunk."

"He only acts like this to impress you," Carlo says with a smile that makes my skin crawl. "*Stai attenta*, eh? He's just like any man."

Luca pushes back his chair, but Stefano cuts in. "*Basta, ragazzi*. Carlo—it's enough."

"*Sì, basta*," Gianni echoes.

Carlo looks at Luca, still standing, and then shrugs. "And Mariotti? Where is that chicken shit?"

Luca shoots him a glance but sits back down. "Sorry," he says to me as the men's conversation picks up again.

"It's all right."

"If you can guess, it is not the first time Carlo speaks like this. But a crazy story, *no*?" And then he's drawn back into the group as though nothing had occurred.

I walk to the bar and get another drink, a little unsteady, but I make it back to the table. I sit down slowly and try to look interested. Then I begin with the morning. The coffee, the toast, choked down. The salad at lunch—strings of tuna, tomatoes rolled to the side. The evening—the bar after the game, and I remember the brusque waiter, the wooden table, the plastic menu with its grease stains, but what had I eaten? I can't remember. Not enough. Not enough for these drinks, and I feel something in my stomach now: dread.

I look to the men, try to follow their conversation, but something has changed and I can no longer understand it. I watch their lips move and try to stay calm as their voices spin, peppered with exclamations and laughter. *Prendere in giro*, a term I've come to know. *Take for a ride*. The Italians use it when they're teasing someone and, with these words spinning around me, I begin to suspect that I'm the reason for their laughter.

I anchor my gaze to Luca's profile to keep the evening from dissolving. For a while this works.

Things kept falling around me.

"What happened?" Julian asked, running his fingers along the inside of my forearm, the concern on his face growing. It was April. We were in the South End, back at the bar where we'd met eight months before, an anniversary of sorts.

Earlier that evening I had knocked everything off the glass shelves in my bathroom. Reaching for one item, I'd upended them all. They'd fallen everywhere, the lipstick cradled in the sink, the mascara rolling across the floor. My hands had darted out to stop the avalanche and my arm caught the edge of the mirror. Chipped for years, waiting to catch me, it had drawn a deep red line in my flesh. I'd tried to hide that bloody line, but he had found it. His thumb grazed over the wound.

"What happened?" he asked again.

"It was an accident."

"Another one?" His concern was tilting into suspicion and it made me bristle.

"I'm fine," I said. I still had my job. Everything was in balance. He could only disrupt it.

"Hannah, why won't you talk to me? This isn't normal."

I pulled my arm away, mean. "What's not normal? Maybe you're not normal."

He was right, though. It wasn't normal. Things were coming loose. The proof was on my body and in this wound that he read with his fingers.

We kept drinking until the edges of the night blurred, until I said, "Leave me alone," and began flirting with a stranger, faceless now, who wouldn't prod or pry. I asked the stranger to dance. And still Julian wouldn't go, not that night. But eventually, when I'd said it enough times and with enough venom—*Leave me alone*—he did.

"*E* Mariotti?" Carlo booms now.

"*Boh,*" Stefano says.

"He is too afraid," Luca whispers to me. I don't know what he's referring to, and still I nod and nod and sit up straighter, try to mirror the women around us, but the room is moving, coming apart in ribbons. I watch the men and hear their voices, but I can't make out the words. Until Gianni rises and announces, "*Su, balliamo.*"

Luca turns to me: "We dance?"

I don't want to dance, cannot imagine even standing now, but it is easier to follow than to explain, and so I follow him to the center of the room. And then we're dancing. And isn't this how it always happens? Things are fine and then they aren't, and I'm in a place I didn't mean to be, watching it all deteriorate. *Hold on to yourself,* I think, *hold on to yourself this time,* but everything is moving quickly. I'm coming loose. Luca smiles, his features large as he sways side to side, the smell of his cologne surrounding me. I try to mimic his movements but the floor is shifting. I remember the S of the Italian women, the easy movement of it. I lean in, lean out. But it's useless. I don't have the spine for it. I am pitching too far one way or the other. It is all I can do. All I can do to remain standing. The crowd becomes a single creature, tilting and stretching, closing in. I lean in. Lean out. Lean in. Lean out.

Darkness.

Then hands on my arms propping me up. Voices circling.

"*Andiamo.*" Luca's voice, his arm around me. "I take you home, *va bene?*"

The voices continue. I nod. I want to hear, want to know what they are saying about me. But it's impossible, even, placing one foot in front of the other now. Why? Why did I drink so much? What did I eat? I begin with the morning. The coffee. The toast.

The air outside hits cold, wakes me.

"Sorry," I muster as we walk slowly. "I mean, *mi dispiace.*"

"*Di niente,*" he says. "It is late for me also."

Luca's car is small and he drives quickly, the lights outside a blur as we race out of the park and into the old streets. It rattles and rattles and rattles. We take a sharp curve as we approach Piazza del

Duomo and my stomach jumps. I grip the door handle and shut my eyes, hoping he won't see. But he has seen.

"*Stai bene?*" he asks. "*Stai bene?*"

I can't speak. I concentrate on the hum of the engine, mute. In a second Luca veers to the curb outside a small bar. He ducks out and I watch him, bent, almost jogging into the bar. I want to hide, want to leave, but that would only make things worse. I look at the comically large Duomo, striped green and white, and its angles swim. I can never get a feel for the whole. It must be late, very late, but even now a juggler stands on the steps surrounded by a cluster of students. The juggler says something I can't make out and they laugh. The car door opens and Luca slides in with a bag and hands me a bottle of water, uncapped.

"*Grazie,*" I mumble, taking a large gulp, and try a smile. "*Mi dispiace.* Too much to drink. I must be confirming all your stereotypes. About Americans, I mean."

Luca doesn't smile back. He opens the satchel, producing a roll. "*Mangia.* You'll feel better."

I think, *What are you doing?* and in the same breath, *How did you know?* But there's no hiding now, so I take a piece, put it in my mouth, and chew slowly, trying not to think about it. I swallow and focus instead on the juggler, and then on two men who appear from around the corner of the cathedral holding forties. One of them pauses, hands his beer to his friend, and turns into one of the crevices to piss, the dark stream gleaming on the marble.

"*Che schifo,*" Luca says, watching them, too.

I don't know how long we sit in the car. Luca puts on the radio, hands me a few more hunks of bread. I accept them and listen to the music, chewing slowly until all of it is gone. The students disperse and the juggler sits on the steps of the Duomo counting his money.

"*Allora,*" Luca says finally. "We walk?"

I nod. He helps me out of his car, locking it behind me.

"I follow you," he says.

I know this much at least, my route home. We walk away from the Duomo, then down through Piazza della Signoria, empty now.

Possibilities seem to open up with the space, and if things were different, if I were different, this might be romantic. But the statues that I love are eerie in the moonlight, and I am a child who cannot keep a straight course, Luca's hand intermittently on my elbow to prevent me from drifting too close or too far. I remember my first boyfriend, years ago. We sat on a curb in the middle of a cold November and he took off one of my inadequate canvas shoes to warm my foot with his hands, and I knew that things were coming and I only had to wait. But now I'm not waiting, only walking. And Luca is tired and quiet. Finally we reach the river, where the reflections of streetlamps spread across the water in long pews of light.

"Which way?" Luca asks.

I gesture left and soon we're by my door and I can feel, already, the regret tomorrow will bring.

Luca takes my hands and kisses me quickly on each cheek. "*Buonanotte.*"

"'*Notte,*" I say, turning and putting my hand on the door for support as I search for my keys. I find them and choose, impossibly, the right one. I try to fit it into the lock.

"*Aspetta*"—Luca takes the key and easily opens the door—"I accompany you to your apartment?"

"*No,*" I respond quickly. I'm angry, swimming in it. Carlo was right about him. "I don't even know you."

He starts laughing, the sound of his voice gentle in the dark. "I will walk you to your door only, *sai?*"

I feel my face grow warm. "*Grazie,* I'm fine." I mean to right things, but he looks puzzled as I step into the lobby and shut the door.

The apartment is dark. I shuffle to the bedroom and unlatch the tall shutters. Luca walks slowly up the street and disappears around the corner. I'm shaking, and my body relaxes only when I lean on the sill smoking a cigarette, a habit reserved for nights like these. It is raining again and the air bites at my hands as I watch the ash drop. I begin with the morning. I close my eyes, see the familiar tower grow. Such a long day. So much to remember. The coffee. The salad. I make it to the club, but the drinks I'm forced to estimate. Then I remember the small bits of roll, broken gently and passed like Communion in the car. I try to forget, to see only the hand, the gesture, the kindness in it. But the hand is lost, the gesture lost. *Don't. Don't.* My head begins to buzz. I drop the cigarette, run to the bathroom, and it all comes up.

Chapter Five

I wake the next morning to rain that doesn't let up. At the club, everyone will be indoors—all bodies crowding in, all sounds echoing loud, all the older men clustered in the bar instead of on the embankment, all eyes and voices. I avoid it. I should open my laptop, look for work, but I avoid that, too.

I visit San Frediano in Cestello on the other side of the river, the Oltrarno. Luca was right—the church is beautiful. A small plaque on the wall outside announces that the mystic, Santa Maria Maddalena de' Pazzi, lived and died in the adjacent convent. Inside, there is a chapel dedicated to her with a painting of the saint in ecstasy, and in the chapel's belled ceiling she welcomes souls into Heaven with sweeping arms. This is why he sent me here. There is nothing more, though—not in the little brochure I was handed and not in my guidebook—and the gates leading to the convent beside the church are locked.

I find a small café not far from the church, glowing warm on this gray day. I stop for a coffee, but the place seeps in, holds me there, and I stay from early afternoon into evening, alternately reading and watching people battle the rain through the wide window. I return the next day and the day after that. The waitstaff has no qualms about my making the transition from a coffee and salad to a glass of wine when the café empties and they have their staff dinner, scraping at plates and laughing, while I watch the gray light stretch across the tables in shifting bands and catch in my glass.

I'm still reading about St. Catherine. As a teenager, she pleaded to join the Mantellate, a group of older widows cloistered in the Basilica of San Domenico, but her parents refused—she was not old and was not a widow. She would be married. Until she grew ill, so ill that even when her father took her to the thermals baths, the boiling waters had no effect. Her illness was a sign from God, she said, and so her parents acquiesced, allowing her to join the widows in prayer, and Catherine was healed.

Her career began with a movement inward, with visions and ecstasies. When in a trance, she did not wince at the needles that disbelievers jabbed into her feet. This and her vision of a mystical marriage to Christ secured her celebrity. As she grew older, she looked outward beyond San Domenico. She cured the lame, drew poison, and drank pus from the sores of the sick. She learned to read and became politically active, composing letters of criticism to the pope.

And she made herself empty for prayer. By age eight, she was slipping meat onto her brother's plate. By sixteen, she ate only fruits and vegetables, then used instruments—a stalk of fennel, a quill—to throw them back up.

As another steaming dish arrives nearby, the thick, smoky smell drifting my way, my stomach turns over—with desire, then revulsion—and in this, I understand the saint's denial. I remember well when my days became punctuated by sharp sensations:

Chills.

Sunlight too bright.

Sounds attacking.

Counting. And with the counting came praise and with the praise came questions. *How do you do it?* Claudia asked, one of a chorus when I began losing flesh, December into January into February. There was admiration in their voices, and I knew what they were asking: *How do you cut so close to the bone?* By the time Catherine joined the Mantellate, she had stopped eating almost entirely. *This body of mine remains without any food, without even a drop of water: in such sweet physical tortures as I never at any time endured.* She was empty, open. I'd like to think that she belonged to no one but herself, that the sweetness of the pain was hers alone. But she writes, *My body is Yours.*

Love. Her letters are filled with the word. *The soul cannot live without loving... The soul always unites itself with that which it loves, and is transformed by it.* I envy her ecstasies, emptied of everything. Is that love? All that emptiness and the trance that follows? Love is a tunneling, I think. An envisioning and then a tunneling of vision, the edges disappearing until all that remains is the beloved. I had hoped that I would feel that with Julian, that with him I might escape the mornings when I woke tamped down and pressed myself back into dreams that did not soothe. But he was no match for the other solace I found. He fell away with all the rest.

By the second day of my residency at the café I'm almost all the way through Catherine's life. *The soul is always sorrowful,* she writes, *and cannot endure itself.* Outside, people are hurrying through the rain to the evening service. The bells begin to clang furiously, ricocheting off one another as one of the staff appears.

"*Un altro bicchiere?*" he asks, lifting my glass.

"*Sì,*" I say, wanting him to leave me to listen to the bells. They are playing a hymn. It is familiar to me and I feel a rush of happiness, uninterrupted. Even in this gray light it grows, and I'm afraid of the moment when I'll slip over the peak and feel it dissipate. I close my eyes and the bells continue. They are asking a question: *Are you searching for? Are you searching for?*

On the third day, the sun returns and still I do not go to the club but to my café, book in hand. I've promised myself that when I've finished reading it, I will look for work. Three weeks left here. Three weeks.

I take a table outside now. The street is different in the sun, and the corner where this café sits is suddenly a stopping point for many. First a young woman leans against the building, high heels shining.

She pitches her head back, laughing at her companion's joke. She's replaced by an older man who stands with his eyes closed.

I'm afraid that with the good weather I'll see someone from the club, and, sure enough, just as afternoon is becoming evening, Francesca rounds that busy corner with her daughter in tow. She's almost as tall as Francesca, but she must be only eleven or twelve—she still has the face of a child. She is holding a balloon, a smiling sun that hangs from a piece of bamboo. She looks up at it as Francesca hurries her on, speaking emphatically, and a moment later I hear, "Hannah! *Come stai?*" and they are standing over me.

"*Bene.*" I hope my voice doesn't sound off. Her daughter looks at me and then looks back up at what I now realize is not a balloon but a paper lantern. She twists it slightly so that it swings side to side, the metallic paint catching the light.

"You really dropped out of sight," Francesca says. "Where have you been?"

I shrug, not trusting my voice to say more. I take a sip of water.

"Have you met Adriana?" She pinches her daughter's arm lightly and the girl puts out her hand.

"*Buonasera,*" she says, looking me straight in the eye. She flashes a smile but it disappears when her mother's voice cuts in.

"What are you reading?"

I show her the cover of my book.

"Santa Caterina? Interesting. You know they have her head in Siena?"

"I do. I've seen it."

"*Allora* we're on our way to Piazza della Santissima Annunziata for the Festa della Rificolona. You know it? It's a lantern festival—for the children. Little children, really." She drops her voice. "But this one wanted to go."

Adriana glances at me again.

"You should come. It's all kids and tourists, but you might like it. We can talk."

I feel light-headed and take another sip of water. But I can't think of an excuse not to go.

"Okay," I say, and stand carefully, leaving a few bills on the table.

We walk to the river, where the light off the water is blinding. People are crowded outside the *gelateria* at the end of the Ponte Vecchio and the jewelry shops lining the bridge are still open. The club is visible through the break in the shops—with the sun, the old men have returned to their posts outside, and Stefano stands at the edge of the dock, shading his eyes and shouting directions to the teens. I scan for Luca but I know he won't be there.

"I was wondering when I didn't see you at the *canottieri,*" Francesca says, as though reading my thoughts. "You avoiding someone?" She raises her eyebrows expectantly.

"No."

"Well, it happens."

"I've been busy," I say, but Francesca doesn't seem to hear me.

"Anyway, it's pointless. Florence is a tiny village. I don't care what people tell you. There's no avoiding anyone."

"Boston's the same. I guess most cities are like that once you get to know them."

"Not like Florence," she says, and shakes her head. As we approach the piazza, the crowd grows dense, and more children appear with lanterns. Francesca pushes Adriana along ahead of her and raises her voice to be heard over the chatter. "I came here from a city and I thought I was moving to a city. That's what *he* said. Center of culture, history. All that. Instead I've got this tiny village. Don't let anyone fool you. There's no hiding here," she says, and then, as though to prove her point, "So I heard you left the party with Luca."

My face flushes, giving me away, and still I say, "He just walked me out. That's all."

"Sure. You don't have to be embarrassed. You're an adult. Luca"— she nods—"he used to date a lot of women. And then one really messed him up—broke his heart. That changes a person, you know?"

"I don't," I say. "Nothing happened. I'm not looking for anything here."

"*Va bene.*" She shrugs. "Just thought you should know. These men —you can never tell."

Adriana looks back at us as we're funneled into the square.

"Do you study English?" I ask her, and she nods.

"Yeah, she speaks it perfectly," Francesca says loudly. Then to me, "When she talks, that is. Honestly, sometimes I feel like I'm living in a church."

I look at Adriana, but she's aleady broken away and her lantern becomes one of many as she disappears into the crowd, the orb swinging side to side.

Francesca pulls me to the stairs of the old foundling hospital that frames one edge of the piazza. Along its portico, in the spaces where the columns burst into arches, is a line of medallions stamped with swaddled children, white against powder blue. I look up at their bodies, tiny from here, and wonder when I will bleed, if I will bleed, my insides parched and brittle. At the end of the building, a large wooden wheel is set into the wall. I've read that centuries ago people could abandon their unwanted offspring there: place the child on the wheel and rotate the little foundling into the orphanage anonymously.

Tonight the piazza is filled with children, though, from the youngest sitting on their parents' shoulders to those Adriana's age, who anxiously search the crowd for other teens. Each child clutches a paper lantern.

"It's part of the Feast of the Madonna," Francesca explains as we look out over the square. "I swear, there are more feasts and festivals in this city... Don't get me wrong, I was raised Catholic. My parents put me through the ringer. You?"

"No. Not even close. My mother believes in yoga—that and work."

"Ha. What about your father?"

"I think he goes to church now because of his second wife. Anyway, finding God didn't change how he felt about us. He was still just not around."

"*Ho capito*. Sorry. Anyway, tomorrow's the big day," Francesca says. "Birth of the Madonna. Back to church."

The last bit of sun is lost behind the buildings and the air becomes sulfurous as each lantern is lit. Adriana reappears with another girl at her side, who greets Francesca quickly and then drops her voice to an excited whisper as Adriana leans her lantern toward us. Francesca pulls out a lighter to spark the candle from below and the sun's face ripples with light and shadow. Across the piazza, other lanterns glow to life, their patterns appearing. There are animal heads, starbursts, a Medici family seal. Adriana's friend has a broadly grinning cat. The images blur as the crowd begins to move and Francesca takes my arm. We walk out of the piazza behind the two girls and join the stream of lights that flows, sparkling, between the old buildings.

"The parade goes up the river," Francesca explains.

Suddenly there's a shout from the crowd and one of the lanterns explodes. Its owner, a very young girl, begins to cry as bits of paper fall to the ground. Adriana and her friend look around, their eyes wild with anticipation.

"What was that?" I ask.

"Don't worry," Francesca says. "It's normal. Some of the kids carry—what do you call it?" She purses her lips, then says, "Peashooters. Mostly boys." Her phone rings. "*Aspetta*," she says, glancing at it and smiling before picking it up. "*Pronto? Sì...* Yeah, I'm here with Hannah. You know Hannah... *Sì, certo.* Ponte alle Grazie. *Va bene. A dopo.*" She snaps it shut. "Look—there's one."

A boy darts through the crowds ahead of us. He raises the little peashooter to his lips and takes aim at a glowing lion. He blows and, in a moment, the lantern is deflated.

Francesca shakes her head. "Just like men, you know?"

He takes aim at another lantern but misses this time. Night has fallen, and above us, people are leaning out their windows to watch the lanterns pass. We take one turn and then another before we reach the river, where bodies pour in from the other streets to join the unbroken line of light. On the Arno, small glowing boats are carried fast by the current until they are caught in a mass at the base of the Ponte alle Grazie.

"Peter!" Francesca shouts, and I see him leaning against the wall by the bridge. She grabs his hand as we pass and kisses him on the cheeks.

"Ciao, Hannah," he says, flushed. Adriana looks back with a blank expression before she and her friend link arms and move ahead without speaking. He glances at Francesca.

"*Non ti preoccupare*," she says. "It's not a problem."

"So you started in the piazza?" Peter asks, his voice bright. "It's a great event. It only happens in Florence, you know." He pauses. "We've missed you at the *canottieri*."

"Thanks," I say, though after Francesca's gossip, I wonder who the "we" is. I try to remember the end of the night at the dance club—who saw me fall?—but the faces are gone, disappeared. More lost time.

"Have you been out on the water yet?" Peter asks.

"No, I don't think I'm ready."

"You should try. I can help you if you'd like. Francesca could, too. She's not half bad." Francesca hits his arm and Peter grins.

Around us the children begin to sing, the words become clearer as they repeat: "*Ona, ona, ona. Ma che bella rificolona. La mia l'è co' fiocchi e la tua l'è co' pidocchi.*"

What a beautiful lantern, mine is tied with bows. But the last phrase is confusing.

"*Pidocchi?*" I ask.

"Lice," Francesca says.

"Why lice?"

She shrugs. "Who knows?"

"Because of the history," Peter says, excited.

Francesca loops her arm through his. "The little professor. I told Hannah it was a Catholic thing. You going to show me up?"

"I'm not showing you up." He laughs, pulling her closer and then turning to me. "It *is* a Catholic thing. But the holiday was also one of the biggest market days of the year. Farmers came in from the countryside to sell their goods, but there wasn't enough space in the piazza—Santissima Annunziata—so they left the night before to get a spot."

"Ah," Francesca says, pleased. "So they came with lanterns."

"Exactly," Peter says.

"*Ona, ona, ona,*" the song continues, louder now. Up ahead at the next bridge the light is spreading horizontally as people disperse.

"And the lice?" I ask.

"Well, the farmers wore their best clothing. Coming to Florence was a big deal, you know. But the Florentines still saw them as lice-ridden peasants. And the children who lived in the city would shoot at their lanterns."

"*Sì.*" Francesca laughs. "The Florentines are a bit arrogant, *no*? Hundreds of years, and nothing changes." She sighs and leans her head on Peter's arm.

"I should go," I say as we approach the bridge. The parade is morphing into a party. The adults are gathering in groups, and the lanterns that have survived the snipers are falling forgotten to the street or becoming weapons themselves as children chase one another.

"I'm glad you came," Francesca says warmly, embracing me.

Peter kisses me on both cheeks. "Until tomorrow," he says insistently. "I'll see you out on the water, okay?"

I'm about to say no when Adriana runs up, clutching her lantern, which is hanging limp, pierced. She isn't crying but is instead elated.

"*È scoppiata!*" she says to Francesca, clutching it like a prize—the lost lantern means someone was aiming for her.

"*Brava, brava.*" Francesca smiles at her for the first time all evening.

"Okay," I say to Peter. "I'll see you on the water."

That night, before attempting sleep, I read the final chapter on the saint's life. Like all the greats, it seems, it was short. Catherine died at age thirty-three of a stroke, at which point she was eating almost nothing, subsisting on only water and the Eucharist.

Chapter Six

"*È la prima volta?*" Correggio asks. *First time?*

"*Sì.*" I try to sound confident.

We're in the hallway at the club choosing a scull. Correggio maintains the boats and helps the solo rowers, like me, carry them to the river. He is older and has a kind smile, but he speaks almost no English.

"*Allora.*" He looks at me, looks at the boats. "*Persefone,*" he says after a moment. It's not the widest scull but it still looks like a row-boat. Difficult to capsize. "*Sì. Persefone.*"

He grabs the nose of one end, sliding it slowly off the support and resting it on my shoulder. He skirts around me, lifts the other end onto his own shoulder, and I can feel the full weight of it then. It is heavy, digs into the bone, and I have to reach up with both hands to keep it from toppling off.

"*Andiamo,*" he instructs, and we walk the boat down the hall— "Ciao, Hannah of Boston," Manuele says as we pass—out into the sun, down the brick steps, and onto the metal dock. It is a brilliant day. It doesn't feel like a weekday in September. The sound of jazz from the Uffizi courtyard, the people leaning contentedly over the river's walls, and the flashing of cameras on the old bridge all suggest that this is still summer, that life is still free and open.

Correggio lifts the boat on his end and I mirror his movements. We spin the body, lower the spine down into the water. Then he grips the edge with one hand and offers me his other. I place one foot in—the boat shifts, the dock shakes—then the other, and crouch onto the small wooden seat, sick at the loss of solid ground. The river is empty today and I'm grateful for this. Correggio places my hand on the dock and squeezes it. "*Un momento.*" He disappears back into the dark tunnel and reemerges with two oars on his shoulder. He slides them into the metal casings, then holds the scull steady as I take the handles. *Don't let go,* I think.

But Correggio smiles encouragingly and, with an "*a dopo,*" pushes me off without a word of instruction. The momentum carries me away from the dock and the boat shifts side to side. He waves one last time before turning his back. I feel exposed, paralyzed, with nothing to anchor me. I look over my shoulder at the Ponte alle Grazie. I hadn't even thought about the fact that I'd be facing away from the direction I'd be rowing. I will have to navigate without seeing where I'm going. The boat begins to spin of its own volition, shaking me to action. I need to start moving. I need to find a rhythm. I imagine myself from above then. *This boat is a fish.* No—this boat is a bird with long wooden wings. Or a person with arms outstretched and curved palms striped red and white reaching down into the river.

Keeping my legs locked and using only my upper body to start, as I'd watched others do, I dip each oar. As I pull back against the water's resistance, I imagine those wooden arms are mine, those striped palms mine, my hands skimming just below the surface. But I dig too deep. One oar catches and the boat pitches left as the end surfaces with a splash. I breathe in, breathe out, realign the oars in a T, then lean my body forward and push the oars behind me, a diver preparing to launch. I close my eyes, dip them again, not too deep. I pull—my muscles shaking—and watch the wooden arms fold forward, taking with them a gulp of river. The ends emerge in unison this time, and I shift the handles so they are parallel to the water's surface, palms facing the sky, like St. Catherine in ecstasy, arms open, ready to receive.

I look over my shoulder—I'm close to the bridge now and I'll need to turn. I dip one oar into the water and use the other to pull myself around, the boat rocking one way and then the other, until I'm facing the Ponte alle Grazie. As I make my way back toward the Ponte Vecchio, I add my legs, sliding the seat forward, pushing against the footrests, then pulling with my arms. There's something wrong, though. The line of water in my wake is not straight but jagged. My right oar hits a rock with a loud clunk and the rattle reverberates through me. I stop, my body pulsing—I'm too close to the wall. I look at the club, directly across the river from me now, but there is no one on the embankment to witness this. I push off the rock, then use one oar to pull the boat back to center as I approach the Ponte Vecchio. I don't look up at the bodies leaning over the wall or at the sky bright above them. I keep my gaze fixed on a point behind me as I pass into the shadow of the middle arch. The underbelly of the bridge is brushed with soft reflections, and I can hear the water licking lightly at the supports. I pause, happy to be hidden here, and bring the oars into the boat. Their palms curl around my feet, dripping. The boat begins to spin on its own again, and I take one last breath of this cooler air before lifting the wooden arms and righting it.

I take one stroke and then another. With each one, I feel more centered. When had I last felt so centered? *How do you cut so close to the bone?* Back then, yes, even when the comments changed direction, praise replaced by suspicion and carefully framed questions. *They were envious,* I thought. The nerves in my face went numb, and still I felt centered. I stopped sleeping, I stopped bleeding, and still I felt sure.

May. I was seated in the museum's courtyard, where I went when I needed to mute the world. Students were scattered around the garden and up and down the arcaded walkways, separated into small groups. They were drawing and occasionally speaking, their voices absorbed into the vacant air above. They had each chosen a different model: Persephone, her hip cocked to one side; mosaicked Medusa screaming; a maenad reaching out to a figure unseen.

I sat cross-legged at a distance, watching. In the museum's café the cash register chimed and the sound hung in the air like a tuning fork struck. The world was foggy but I was clear. Centered. I could feel each of my vertebrae, buttons against the stone column, shallow ditches dug around the bone. My ring was loose, my pants were loose, my joints were loose, unbound. I was changing form.

The galleries upstairs held endless cycles of love and pain. I understood this movement. I heard Julian's voice grasping for me even as I said, *Leave me alone*. And now he was gone. He had disappeared, too. Or had been replaced, as though in reaching for one thing, I'd found something else entirely.

It was raining, drops tap-tapping on the glass ceiling above, and the light in the courtyard went blue and then gray. One of the students cried out, her voice cutting through the fog—when had the world grown so loud? She shrieked again.

Then loud heels on marble and there was Claudia, looking down at me.

"Hannah, here you are," she said in a tone that suggested that I was no different from the students, in need of a chaperone.

I struggled to get up, ticked through excuses in my mind, then said nothing because what did it matter? Claudia gave a small smile, put a hand on my arm, but it was false. *Look at you* is what her eyes said. She was wrong. She could not see who I was becoming. There were these things that I could be.

"Robert wants to see you."

"All right," I said.

The cash register chimed and I followed her out slowly. I was well sculpted. Close to something.

I don't know how much time has passed when another figure appears on the river. I've made a single loop, under the three bridges and back, and am approaching the Ponte Vecchio again when I see a flash of silver catching up to me. It's Peter. I stop rowing as he passes.

"Ciao, Hannah," he says, not slowing his pace but smiling broadly as he glides by, leaving a clean line framed by a perfect series of rings behind him. I look over my shoulder and watch as he and the boat become a single form again and pass under the next bridge.

He is a bird, he and that silver scull, a bird. Would I ever have that grace?

There are these things that I could be, I had thought in the gray light of the museum. But what did I know then? In the months that were a haze, were a dream—the world coming into and out of focus, the contrast sharper than the movement from the dark hum under the bridge to the sunlight on the other side—in those months, a voice arrived and kept returning. *If only you were...* It did not arrive as I had expected. Its grip was soft at first, and I welcomed it. *This is mine,* I said, wrapping it around me. I gave it words. I gave it language. I heard it, I embraced it, and I replied. Digging ditches around the bone, I replied. *If only I were...*

But now, pulling long these wooden arms, I know that there are things that I will never be. Never the bird that is Peter in that boat, never my sister's ordered apartment, never the S of the Italian women. The thought catches and catches and catches. It comforts me, terrifies me, breaks my heart. *If only you were... You will never be.* Pitching one way, then the other.

There must be a balance between the things that I can be and the things that I will never be. There must be a time when the spine of this boat will hold the body steady along a straight course. There must be words for that moment.

Chapter Seven

The descent into the club, Manuele's greeting, Correggio's smile, the weight of the boat on my shoulder, the explosion of sun on my face, the trembling of the metal dock under my feet, the settling into the seat, the footrests gripping my heels, the oars sliding into place, the first pull of water. This all becomes habit, this all becomes familiar.

You are here, each stroke says. *You. Are. Here.*

I go every morning. The river is quiet early in the day and I like the solitude. For the first time since my arrival in Florence, I don't feel lonely—it is only natural that I do this alone. My muscles ache in the mornings not from tossing and turning all night, but from this movement: sliding forward, pulling back, tracing a long ellipse. After a few days, the ache dulls and I begin doing five laps instead of four, up under three bridges and back.

In the afternoons I have lunch at my café—a salad, but with more to it now, and sometimes even a cup of soup. Except for the students, the city is less crowded with tourists—all returned to school and work in other countries—and I visit the city's churches. I take in the simple facade of Santo Spirito, the tombs of Michelangelo and Galileo in Santa Croce, the languishing figures of Dawn and Dusk in the Medici Chapels, all the things I've never seen but learned about years ago, and that past hovers close like a half-remembered dream. I take these things in and I do not think about my weight, do not look in the mirror, do not step onto the scale. I'm doing this on faith—not looking and not measuring. *When did this start?* It doesn't matter anymore. I need to move forward.

I no longer go out to dinner and I stay clear of Dario's restaurant. Instead, I walk to the supermarket in the evenings, weigh out tomatoes, zucchini, and eggplant on the scale and press their accompanying pictures to print the price. I have the young woman behind the deli counter measure *due etti* of cheese. She knows me well enough now that I no longer have to ask. I add rustic bread or a bag of potatoes. I prepare my meals at home and have just a single glass of wine. I'm falling in love with the details of my daily life here; I'm falling in love with this city.

I avoid Signora Rosa. The one time I do see her, I assure her that, yes, I will be out by the end of the month. I write Kate every three days with my list, call her once, and in this way, I keep that world silent. And when I receive an e-mail from Claudia with the subject "checking in," I don't open it. There will be nothing to upset this equilibrium.

Two weeks pass, and suddenly my departure looms close. I should be making plans, looking for jobs. But I don't. I need this time. I need this time like I need the light.

Monday morning as I'm leaving the club, my body glowing from being on the water, I find Luca seated in the little coffee bar reading a newspaper. His face opens up, deep lines appearing around his eyes, and with this, the past—my near collapse, our odd stroll back to my apartment—seems to vanish.

"*Come stai?*" He stands and takes my hands. "Where did you go? You left Firenze?"

"No, *qui*. I've been here." My words are broken, hovering between languages. "I've been here every day."

I'd seen him several times from the water, bent until he arrived at the large glass doors, where he straightened, a lightness emerging in his step.

"You've been in the *palestra*?"

"No. In a boat—on the water."

He raises his eyebrows. *"Brava,"* he says. "You like this?"

"It's beautiful." I pause, trying to convey the depth of it. *"Molto calmo. Molto tranquillo. E anche...* comforting."

"Sì. It is like a friend."

"Exactly."

Luca considers me for a moment, as though trying to figure something out. Then the thought is broken and he smiles again. "And now? You go to meet other friends?"

"No. I don't know many people. I mean, I've been busy. Visiting churches, seeing the city. Oh, I went to the one you recommended. San Frediano in Cestello."

"Ah, sì. Ma sempre da sola?"

Always alone. I nod.

"It is not a problem? To be so much alone?"

I hesitate. "Well, I have the river. The best kind of friend, right?"

"È vero." He laughs. *"Allora,* Hannah, I must go. Stefano and Sergio wait to train. *Ma, se vuoi,* we have dinner or see something of interest in Firenze. *Insieme."*

"Sì," I say automatically. I find myself saying yes often in conversation, and my many yeses make me feel distinctly un-Italian.

Luca pulls a pen out of his backpack and writes his number on the bar napkin. *"Perfetto,"* he says. "You call if you want—tomorrow, next week. *Quando vuoi."*

I'm supposed to leave on Saturday, take a train to Rome, stay over, then board a plane early Sunday, but still I take the napkin, fold it into my palm.

"Sì," I say one last time. A lot can happen in a week, after all.

Leaving the club, the air is cooler and the sky is beginning to cloud over. My hair is wet from the shower and the breeze is energizing. It feels like rain, so I run for the bus that will take me across the river and down and just catch it. As I board, a man gets up, freeing a seat. This day feels like a victory already. It begins to rain, validating my decision, and fat drops stretch long across the bus's window, break the river's surface into hash marks, and catch in the crevices of the city, pulling familiar smells from the stone and drawing the umbrella vendors out. The rain passes, and by the time the bus pulls to a stop a few bridges down, the sun comes out strong and new scents rise from the city's core, a mix of hot stone, sewage, and earth. The fall in Florence is like this, I've been told. A smattering of rain and sun, cool mornings and hot afternoons that belie that it is nearly October as the city hovers ambivalently between seasons. So different from the climate back home, and I wonder how it affects people here, the lack of hard lines.

I go to my regular café and find it closed. Even this cannot upset the day. Instead, I try the bar around the corner. Its small door hides an interior filled with life, business men and women out for lunch. American music is playing, reminding me of where I've been, of where I am. I order a salad, wine, and water from the tap, and all this is understood. The waiter is friendly but efficient, and the food arrives quickly. I'm hungry and the mozzarella, fresh, is good. I even take a crust of bread, and the waiter returns with oil and salt without my asking. *She might need this.* The choreography of this day is right. The rowing, the bus, the rain, the square salad bowl with its rounded corners, the espresso cups hitting the saucers that line the bar, followed by small spoons. Each thing knows its part. These things, too, add up. These things, too, count. They stack to form a complete whole.

I take out my little notebook and write down what I've eaten, but I don't think about it after I've put it away. I have a new inventory now.

After lunch, I cross the Arno again—how many times have I crossed this river?—and walk to Santa Maria Novella, one of the only churches left on my list. I stand for a long time in the chapel behind the main altar, surrounded by Ghirlandaio's frescoes. They are filled with color and detail, and though they tell the stories of St. John the Baptist and the Virgin Mary, they aren't about religion, not really. They're about Florence, this city that is beginning to feel more and more like home. They're about beauty, bodies, food. The birth of St. John is a footnote to the scene in the Florentine bedroom: the carefully carved headboard, the tufted pillow, the maidservant sweeping in with a basket of fruit on her head, a white gown flowing around her body. *Herod's Banquet* is a glamorous dinner party, the small plate bearing the saint's head an unfortunate hiccup amid all the splendor. And then there's the clothing: heavy brocaded gowns, gold-edged collars, delicate ruched sleeves in deep purples and burnt reds.

As I take in this rich, gilded existence, I feel like a child again, imagining a future in which I am somehow transformed, inhabiting a life saturated with beauty, stability, confidence. My understanding of this future is both visceral and intangible—no hard edges to define it, only a sense of possibility. Maybe I can stay. Because I can't think about Boston, where soon everything will be dying, the grass growing brown, the leaves crumbling to dust. I look back at the baby in the first panel, at the rounded forms of the women. I'm feeling better, eating better, and still I am not full like them, and still I am dry. I feel far from my childhood fantasies then. My hopes for the future are rooted in reality, in the earth, in my body and blood.

"Amazing, isn't it?"

I turn to find Peter staring up at the same panel. I haven't seen him since he passed me on the water—a bird in that silver boat. Squinting up at the wall in his navy blazer, he looks more like a professor than an athlete.

"It's hypnotic," I say. "I had no idea they'd be so..."

"Decadent?"

"*Silenzio*," a guard stationed at the chapel's edge says.

"Exactly," I whisper, leaning closer. "If I had lived then, coming to church would have made me want to get wealthy and sin. And shop."

"Ha! Then it's working." He drops his voice as the guard shoots us another hard glance. "Did you know they were commissioned by bankers? The Tornabuoni family."

"Like the street?" Via de' Tornabuoni is Florence's main shopping street—Ferragamo, Versace, Gucci.

"Yup. Giovanni Tornabuoni"—Peter points to a middle-aged man kneeling at the center of one of the panels—"paid for it."

"That's right. It's funny—I have a degree in art history, but there's so much I've forgotten."

"I'm thinking about changing my major to art history. Or Italian. I'm addicted. Right now I'm taking a class on Renaissance women—I'm the only guy in the class, which is so stupid. The teacher is phenomenal. Did you see this one?" He walks farther back.

Mary and Elizabeth meet in the middle of a city street, three ladies-in-waiting behind them, one of whom stands out—she is in profile, her hair coiled along the back of her head, curls framing her face, her neck long and pale. But it's her gown that sets her apart: doves and sunbursts swirl over a gold background, a brooch at her bust picks up the magenta of her cape.

"Giovanna degli Albizzi," Peter says, following my gaze. "Gorgeous, right? She married Giovanni Tornabuoni's only son. She died in childbirth a year later—I think she was already dead when this was painted."

"That's creepy."

"Well, she's immortalized. Can you even imagine how many people stare at her every day?"

I glance back at her profile. "Still."

"And that's Lucrezia Tornabuoni," Peter says, pointing to an older woman in the birth scene. She is in plain clothes, her head covered. I hadn't noticed her earlier, but her name is familiar.

"She was *really* interesting," Peter continues. "She was a politician and a writer. She also married a Medici, which helped—she had her hand in everything."

"Huh." I examine Lucrezia again. Her face is pinched, her eyes small. A woman beside her is speaking to her with one hand extended, as though she might place it on the older woman's arm, but Lucrezia looks straight ahead, her lips pursed. I imagine her debating, imagine her writing. I'm intrigued, but I still go back to the beautiful stone face of Giovanna, drawn in by the promise that seems to find its home in beauty. Is that how it always was? Is that how it would always be?

He shakes his head and sighs. "I can't believe I'll ever have to leave this city. Listen, I'm going to Orvieto on Saturday. I'm supposed to see at least four other towns for class and one has to be in a different region, so this weekend it's Umbria. Have you ever been there?"

"No."

"Well, you should come. It's just a day trip. I think you'd like it."

My second invitation of the day. And, again, I accept.

Perhaps I've been primed by the inundation of beauty in the art, but on my way home, groceries in hand, I am struck by the light. It escapes an alley and stretches in a rectangle across the street. It cannot be called summer light or autumn light. It is its own. I follow the tunnel of gold to the river, where it becomes a solid beam. The street is ablaze with activity and I am suddenly and completely infatuated with everything: the couple, two on a bike for one, his arms stretched around her to the handlebars; the woman in blue glasses walking a small dog, the end of a gelato—just a triangle of cone—in her other hand; the shop, loud with marble being cut, where I glimpse through the cracked door a young man, bearded and strong; the folds the breeze cuts in the river's surface; the break in the mopeds' hum as a light farther up turns red and the traffic pauses. Even a far-off siren does not ring of death.

I want to remain on this street, but I turn onto my block. I don't think about the future or the crust of bread in my stomach. I think about the feel of my feet on these stones and the warm air that is placed on my shoulder by a passing bus. I don't feel the pull of the scale. I feel instead the sun breaking around the perimeter of my body. My sounds and smells brush up against this city, not changing it but still audible against it, and finally, if momentarily, in tune.

Chapter Eight

Stazione di Santa Maria Novella keeps the pace of the past—the times, tracks, and destinations still flip by on little rubber rectangles, and most of the signs fulfill their original missions: FARMACIA, TABACCHI, INFORMAZIONI. I wait under the departure board and watch the crowds of bleary-eyed backpackers come and go, the haze of this early hour wafting dreamlike through the building. A line of passengers snakes around and around the entry hall. Of the twelve ticket windows, two are open. It is Saturday.

Last night there was a persistent knocking at my door just after I got home. A familiar voice—*Signorina?* Signora Rosa. I remained unmoving and held my breath, though she must have heard me come in, must have followed me up the stairs, and surely she could see the light on. Because it is October now and I'm still here. I changed my ticket again, fees mounting. I wrote Kate—I didn't call, couldn't face her questions. With what money? With what plan? This is now borrowed time. I know the dangers of this type of negotiation. I've done it before, only with food—denials I promised myself I would account for later by eating extra to fill the expanding void. But here is the truth: I was quite comfortable with the void. I felt safe dancing along its edge.

This morning when I woke, I felt, again, the pull of the scale—taunting as though it knew that I wasn't meant to be here anymore.

And I was weak, gave in, trailed down that long hall, dragged its orange body out. I almost stepped on, the certainty it promised filling me, the longing unbearable. Then I doubled over and pushed it as hard as I could. It felt good, pushing it like that. It rattled and rattled and hit the wall hard. Hard enough that it may be broken. *Good*, I thought. *Let it be broken.*

Then I crept out, avoiding Signora Rosa, and headed to the station, thinking all the way, *This isn't wrong.* Just new. Without edges.

The trains are all late, and every minute or so a bell chimes, followed by a stilted recording that echoes, distorted: "*Il treno regionale in partenza dal binario uno da Firenze per Napoli partirà con quarantacinque minuti di ritardo... Il treno Eurostar in partenza dal binario dodici provenente da Roma per Milano viaggia con un'ora di ritardo.*" Forty-five minutes late, an hour late. I look at my watch again. Perhaps I will be alone. If so, I'll go anyway. I am fixed in limbo and this is oddly freeing. The only thing to do is to keep moving. I stop listening to the place names and focus on the repeated words—"*Il treno... in partenza... da... per... di ritardo.*" *The train... leaving... from... for... late.* Then just the stressed words, little punches in the recording—*da... per. From. For.*

"Hannah, hey!" Peter appears and kisses me quickly on both cheeks. He is consciously becoming more Italian. "You okay? You looked like you were in a trance or something. Oh, this is Pam. She's in my program." An American woman emerges from behind him—blond, pony-tailed, tight-sweatered, self-assured. Well-bred.

"Nice to meet you," she says brightly, looking me up and down and then flashing a thin smile, unimpressed, and I suddenly feel like a chaperone at the junior prom.

"You didn't buy a ticket yet, did you?" Peter asks, and, before I can answer, "I bought three. Geez, look at the time. *Andiamo*, kids. Track eight."

"I think all the trains are late," I say, hoping this might give me a reason to back out.

"Not ours—it's an Intercity. Leaves every hour." And he's off, with Pam and me trailing behind him.

"So are you a student, too?" Pam asks as soon as we've settled into the musty compartment, Peter and I across from her. I suspect she knows the answer already.

"No. Just visiting."

"She's got an art history degree," Peter says, barely looking up from his guidebook. "She works for a museum in Boston. I told you that, didn't I?"

"*No*, you didn't," Pam croons accusingly. "He didn't tell me *anything* about you. I don't even know how you know each other."

"From the rowing club," I say.

"You row, too? Maybe I should try that. I mean, all these carbs. I don't know how Italian women do it. What I would give for some good sushi."

"Listen to this," Peter breaks in as the train lurches and pulls out of the station. "Orvieto is built on a hill that's made entirely of *tufo*—this volcanic rock." He pauses, scanning the page.

"And they've got great wine, too, right?" Pam asks. "He promised me a place with good local wine."

Peter nods, then continues. "There's a whole city underneath the city. Built by the Etruscans. Wow. This is going to be great!"

I look back at Pam, who is staring out the window now. Peter's excitement rolls off her but he doesn't seem to notice.

At the second stop, an older man joins our compartment. "*È libero?*" he asks, gesturing to the seat next to me.

"*Sì.*"

He sits down, crosses his legs, and puts a little bag down beside him. INTIMISSIMI, it reads. An Italian lingerie store—"Very Intimate." The bag drifts onto my seat. He shifts, uncrosses his legs, puts the bag on his other side. Then he stands, lays the bag on the overhead rack, and sits back down with a sigh. Pam raises her eyebrows at me before leaning across the aisle to whisper something to Peter. He smiles, but continues reading. *Intimissimi.* I wonder if it's a gift for a wife or a lover. I look past Peter out the window. The colors of the architecture in the towns we pass are changing from the gold-and-green shuttered homes of Florence to peaches and mustards and browns. They are less vibrant, more burnt. I'd love to see a color chart of the homes in Italy, how the stuccoed hues shift.

The sky clouds over and drops line the window. "Perfect," Pam says, but by the time we pull up to the next station, it's sunny again. A young Italian woman gets on and sits next to Pam. She falls asleep almost immediately and her head drops to her side, jerks up, drops down, the ends of her dark curls brushing Pam's shoulder. Pam sighs loudly and inches closer to the window. I close my eyes.

When I wake up, the sun is bright and hot on my face, and Peter is laughing, his body shaking against me. The older man is gone and the woman with the coiled hair is curling out of her seat again, forward this time. Down and then up. She curls and uncurls, curls and uncurls, and doesn't wake, not even with Peter's laughter.

"Welcome back," Pam says to me.

I smile, but I don't know what to say to this woman; I don't have the words to include myself in her world. I remember Luca's question: *It is not a problem? To be so much alone?* Julian had once asked me something similar, though the words were different.

I look out the window at the passing fields, sloping and combed into wide strips. Bales of hay are rolled along their tops. I could go to the top of that hill and push those rolls of hay down one at a time and be perfectly content, watching the light catch first on one side, then the other. One at a time, push them off, and watch them roll down and down and down.

When we pass the sign for Cortona, Pam exclaims, "Cortona! That's where that book takes place!" She leans over to grab Peter's knee. "We *have* to go to Cortona."

"Sure. Maybe on the way back. Hannah?"

I shrug my shoulders. "Sounds good."

She and Peter trade stories about one of their teachers until Peter leaves to find a bathroom. Pam locks her eyes on me. "So what's your story, really?"

"My story?"

"Well, you're not a student. What are you doing here?"

"In Florence, you mean?"

"Yeah." Her gaze is unwavering, so unlike mine, which must look nervous to her, a moth flitting here and there without ever landing. *Look at you.* I wish the sleeping woman would wake. I know what Pam is after. She doesn't know how to place me. But I don't know how to place myself.

"I needed a break," I say.

"From work?" she presses.

"From everything." From the doctor who couldn't help me. From my sister who wouldn't stop watching me. From every corner of the city that reflected back at me my isolation. From all of it. Pam is waiting for me to say more, and what I want to say is that I needed a break from women like her. I hold her gaze and let two beats go by before looking away. We duck into a tunnel and my ears pop. Once we're back in the light, the young curling woman is finally stirring, rubbing the back of her neck. An announcement clicks on—"*Prossima fermata: Orvieto*"—and the train pulls to a stop.

"*Eccola!*" Peter reappears at the compartment's door. "We're here!"

Orvieto is perched on a mass of dry cliff. We take a tram to the top and follow a cobbled road to the center. It feels good to be walking these strange streets on this borrowed time. All the buildings are low and slightly off-kilter, leaning on one another for support. We visit the cathedral first. It is out of proportion, like Florence's, but it lacks the Duomo's uniformity. Tall Gothic archways frame Byzantine mosaics; intricately carved reliefs crowd the doorframes; an army of marble saints encircles the rose window; and on each set of massive bronze doors, angels in flight are half emerging, twisting with joy and agony. It is monstrously impressive.

Peter guides us through the church, whispering lines from his book. "You are not going to believe this," he says, leading us into a chapel at the end of the narthex. I remember the frescoes right away—the apocalypse and resurrection—remember seeing them on slides in a darkened classroom, the images reaching in, scooping me out, leaving me shaken.

"Signorelli," I say. "The artist."

"Yup," Peter says. "This is his masterpiece."

Nude figures and skeletons rise out of the ground, straining to free a leg or torso still buried in the earth. Above them, two angels trumpet and the ghostly figures of infants dance in purgatory. Strange as it is, the scene is tranquil compared with the grotesque fresco beside it, where demons cut down the sinful. The demons' toned bodies are multihued—red legs, purple chests, green heads—like badly dyed Easter eggs, and their scaled wings flap as they torture with indifference, binding hands, twisting limbs, feasting on the ears of the anguished humans, who seem entirely shocked by this gruesome end, their mouths open in protest. A crush of tormented flesh.

"It's disgusting," Pam says.

"That's the point," I say. "He wanted an emotional response."

At the center of the scene, I find an image I remember well. A woman is gripped tightly by a blue demon with a single horn. Her brow is furrowed but she isn't struggling—her head is dropped to the side as though she's sleeping. *Wake up!* I want to shout. *Wake up before it's too late!* But of course, it's already too late and so maybe she has the right idea. It's all borrowed time.

"That's Signorelli," I say.

"Where?" Peter asks.

I point to the horned demon with the lifeless woman. The artist's eyes look out at the viewer with a half-smirk, claiming his prize.

We have lunch on the square. When Peter orders pasta and a meat dish, I feel my stomach clench. I'm getting better, but I am still not like everyone else. I am not normal. I frantically scan the menu for a safe dish. Pam quickly orders a salad, though, and so I order the same, grateful for the first time to have her along. I even wonder if I should try to spend more time with her, suggest to Peter that she join us at the club, on excursions—anywhere where it would be convenient to produce this girl who doesn't eat much and no one seems to notice and so I'm not alone; not eating is what women do, at least what American women do, anyway. The waiter asks if I would like a glass of wine, and I shake my head.

"*Sicura?*" He raises his eyebrows. "It is local. Very good."

"Told you," Pam says to Peter, before ordering a bottle for the table.

After lunch, we visit the subterranean city. The English tour leaves at three o'clock, and at two forty-five we sit outside the cathedral with a crowd of Americans and one German family. By three o'clock the crowd has grown large and there is no guide in sight.

"Always late," Pam says with a sigh, leaning her head on Peter's shoulder and ripping at the edges of her ticket. "I don't know how people live here."

At three fifteen, two Italian women appear and lead us to the wall at the city's edge, where they announce that we need to split into two groups.

"Let's follow her," Pam whispers, pointing to the younger woman with the brightly striped pants and broad smile. "She seems fun."

We join the crowd to the right and follow our guide—"Elena," she introduces herself—through the gate and down into the first cave.

"*Tufo*," Elena says, running a finger along the walls and loosing little clouds of earth. It is the substance that makes up the guts of the hill that Orvieto sits on. Light and permeable, it breaks off easily, fills the air, and I imagine that I'll leave this place caked in the dust of the Etruscans.

Elena has clearly memorized her English tour. Though she knows the history and conveys the overall narrative, the sentences are garbled and she attaches no meaning to the individual words, which hang off her speech at odd angles. It must be what I sound like speaking Italian. Only two phrases are clear and she repeats them with fervor: "But why?" and "Pay attention."

There are layers of history here, she tells us, not continuous but broken. Etruscan homes topped with medieval dovecotes, Renaissance ceramic workshops transformed into olive oil mills and, later, air-raid shelters. All capped with the aboveground city and its massive duomo. A complex warren of 1,200 man-made caves make up the oldest layer. "But why?" Elena asks as we stand in the middle of one of these caves, peering down a vertical tunnel at its center. The *tufo* is so light—"*poo-rus*," she says—that the water ran right through it, forcing the Etruscans to dig down for wells.

"Ninety meters," she says. Lining the tunnel is a row of nooks. "But why?" she asks. Footholds.

We follow Elena up a narrow curling staircase into a larger cave, where a deep window offers a snapshot of the surrounding countryside. It provides the only light, a single beam that cuts across our bodies as we stand in a circle, everyone silent except for the two German children who are playing a modified game of tag, using their parents as obstacles. Along one wall, the earth has been carved into a grid of niches. They look like primitive shoe racks. "Dovecotes," our guide says. Medieval pigeon coops. She points to the back of the cave where a set of crumbling steps leads straight into a wall—each cote connected to the kitchen of a home. Pigeons were ideal because they fed themselves, leaving through the deep windows in search of food and drink, and then returning to be eaten. They remained a staple until the Renaissance, when, our guide says, "the pope orders the windows be closed. But why?" And then: "Pay attention." People were throwing so much garbage over the cliff that merchants were able to enter the city by climbing the trash heaps, avoiding the steep tax at Orvieto's gate.

We follow Elena into three more caves, one a terra-cotta factory, the other an olive oil mill. "But why? Why this ceiling is different from that? Pay attention...But why? Why have to make the oil here? Pay attention."

"She's not exactly fluent, is she?" Pam whispers to me partway through.

"Fluency's overrated," I whisper back, because I like our guide.

In the last cave Elena tells us about Giacomini Nazzarino, a businessman who opened the Quarry of Pozzolana in 1882. He dug out the *tufo* and sold it as material to construct the homes and businesses in the city above. Ten years later, all the quarries were closed.

"But why?" Elena asks, her eyes large. "Pay attention." And even the two children stop their chase. "They dig under to build on top." She illustrates her words with her hands. "Dig under, build on top."

"They were digging out the foundation," Peter whispers. "No wonder."

"The city on top begins to..." Elena mimes the city caving in. "*Allora*, they stop quarrying"—she lays her hands flat, palms down, and then points upward, and we all look up to the ceiling—"to save the city."

Back at the train station, Peter studies the yellowed schedule through fogged glass. "Well, we can stop in Cortona, but we won't have long there. The last train back is at seven forty-five. That'll give us about an hour, though."

"Enough time for a glass of wine," Pam says.

He puts his arm around her and squeezes. "That's right. Your wine tour."

She smiles up at him. "And then I can say I've been there."

As our train pulls into Cortona, an old woman opens the door to the station's coffee bar and turns on the lights. She's opening it just for us—there's no one else here—and she eyes us as she takes a seat on a small plastic chair outside.

Like Orvieto, Cortona is built on a hill, but there is no tram to take us to the town and, according to the schedule, the last bus of the day has already left.

"Figures," Pam says.

"I'm not giving up yet." Peter walks over to a small board with TAXI written across the top. "Wow, these are numbers for individual people. Cortona's five taxi drivers! Who should I call—Pietro or Angela?"

Pam sighs, looking at her watch. "We're not going to have any time. What's the point?"

"Okay, Angela it is," Peter says, opening his phone.

Pam sits down on the curb, her eyes following him. "Nothing gets to Peter." She looks up at Cortona. The city has become a tease. "Doesn't it drive you crazy? Not Peter, I mean. Italy. It's so inefficient. I could never live here."

The old woman has given up and begins to close up the little coffee bar again.

"Waiting all the time," Pam continues. "I didn't even want to come to Florence."

"What are you doing here then?" I ask, pleased to be able to throw her question back at her.

"My parents thought it would be good for me. I think they just like saying their daughter is studying in Italy. Or maybe they wanted to get me away from my boyfriend. It's not like we haven't already been tons of places. But my father says there's nothing like really living in a place, getting the 'full experience' or whatever."

"Guess you're proving him wrong."

"I'm working on it, anyway." She's smiling, though. "Is your family glad you're here? I mean, I know it's not the same. You're grown up."

If only she knew. "My parents aren't really in the picture," I say, and this is true. "My father has another family—kids."

"And your mother?"

"We're really different." *Pull yourself together* is what she would say. Is what she *had* said, in fact, the last time I saw her. In June. She was in town on business and we met in the lounge at her hotel, which, it turned out, was hosting the Mini Miss Patriot pageant, and it felt as though the universe was laughing at me. Girls between the ages of four and six skirted around the halls caked in makeup, striking provocative poses whenever they encountered a mirror. They were towed along by parents, most of whom were overweight and many of whom were angry. I had walked into the lobby to see one of the contestants cowering in a corner as her father screamed at her.

My mother was in a suit, ready for the meeting she had after this meeting, the subject of which was my weight. I kept looking over at her and nodding, but I could not take it in. I nodded when she said "doctor," nodded when she said "therapy."

"Is everything all right?" the waiter asked. My mother waved him off.

I took a sip of my coffee. The lounge looked over the swimming pool, where the tiny queens were children again, their hair wetted back. From where we sat, the water was blue, their faces were white, and the only indication that anything was off were their raccoon eyes, mascara streaming down their cheeks as they bobbed around the shallow end. Up close, I imagined their eye shadow, foundation, blush, and lipstick mixing in the water like a dirty cup holding brushes at the end of a day of painting.

"It's disgusting," my mother said. "You don't expect to see these kinds of things—not here. Do you want to go somewhere else?"

I shook my head. She put her hand on mine, waited for me to look at her. Her face was pained but something else, too—embarrassed? Ashamed? I wanted to look away but her eyes held me. "Honey, you have to pull yourself together. This isn't you. This isn't us."

Us, she'd said. But I'd never been like her. I'd never had her hardness, her resilience, her ability to *just keep going*, marching along with her two daughters trailing behind her, looking back with sadness when we couldn't keep up. She had survived. Why couldn't we? That's not right. Kate had. Kate did. Kate knew how to manage it all.

"Your sister told me she's been trying to help you."

You're not helping.

"You have to listen to her, Hannah. You have to pull yourself together. Are you hearing me? This isn't you."

"We don't speak much," I tell Pam.

But she must hear something else behind my response because her face softens.

"I'm sorry," she says. "Look, I know I sound spoiled—I should be grateful that my parents give a shit. And it really is amazing here. But it's not real." She sighs.

These things are real, I want to say: the ancient tunnels, the *tufo* dust that clings to us, the bar owner trying to survive on a train schedule and a handful of tourists.

"College doesn't even feel real. It's just playing. I'm ready to get on with things, you know? I'm ready for the rest."

I consider this for a moment. She's almost a decade younger than me and she already knows exactly what she wants. She has a clear road map and anything not on the main route is extraneous. My path has become twisted, a series of detours. I'm in a country I should have left in an apartment I haven't paid for. I know nothing anymore, not even what I want. Except maybe to survive. And to move forward, toward... I don't know what.

"It's good," I say, "to be ready for the future."

"Well, I'm only nineteen." Her voice warms a bit. "What the hell do I know?"

"Good news and bad news," Peter announces. "Angela is sick, but her uncle Paolo is coming with his cab. I feel like we already know everyone in Cortona. God, I love this place!"

A few minutes later, a white car pulls to a stop in front of us. Paolo, an older man with a hooked nose and bright eyes, greets us warmly and it feels, oddly, like we're coming home. When he finds out that we have only an hour in the city, he races up the hillside, pointing out the sites as we pass them: two churches, Santa Maria delle Grazie to the south and Santa Maria Nuova to the north; Lake Trasimeno; ancient burial grounds; the Roman walls and, within them, the Etruscan walls; his small house at the edge of town. When we reach the center, it is clear why there are only five cabdrivers. Cortona is tiny, a crush of medieval buildings, and the narrow streets make driving nearly impossible. Paolo crawls along one of the ancient paths, and the people closing up shops or strolling to dinner move slowly out of his way like livestock. He leaves us at the small main square, Piazza della Repubblica, promising to return a half an hour later.

There is magic here. I feel it as soon as I step into the square. Like most of the cities in Italy, the church sits at its center. The sun is too low to reach us here, and already the cafés and restaurants— some at ground level, others in second-story loggias—are lit by candles. Though the tables are filled, the buzz of conversation is overpowered by the shrieks, whistles, and chirps of birds that dive and dance, ducking in and out of the bell tower, circling the scene. I wonder what it is that makes Cortona a magnet for birds.

"Gross," Pam says.

"Extraordinary," Peter replies.

While Pam and Peter have a glass of wine on the square, I wander the side streets. They climb sharply up and then down, curling abruptly one way and then another. If there are people beyond the main piazza, I don't see them. I could be the only one here. I follow signs for the church of Santa Margherita—Cortona's saint, Paolo had told us—but I must take a wrong turn, because the signs disappear. Cortona is a magician, the constantly bending streets hiding what is ahead and what came before. It absorbs past and future, absorbs people, absorbs sounds, except for the continuous calls of the birds. With the fading light, the tan stone buildings are blue. They lean in, their small overhanging roofs like hands curled just at the fingertips. *Poof.* I imagine those hands make me disappear as I round another curve.

Eventually one of the roads leads to the edge of the city, where couples out for an evening stroll, *una passeggiata*, parade slowly along the wall, silhouetted against the setting sun. I join them, the only single body, and look out over the land. The birds are plentiful here as well, climbing up from the countryside to dance across the roofs of this town. To the right is Tuscany and to the left, Umbria.

I strain to see anything that looks like Orvieto, but everything is blurred with the haze of evening. *But why?* our guide had asked. I keep hearing her question followed by her demand. *Pay attention.* I keep thinking about Giacomini Nazzarino and his foolish plan to quarry the undercity: carving out the foundation, building the city with its innards, digging Orvieto its own grave. It gives me chills. Couples wrap their arms around each other and several cameras flash as the sun begins its final descent. It seems to pick up speed once it touches the horizon. This, too, is a trick, and in almost no time, it has disappeared and the crowd has vanished along with it. I find my way back to the central square in the dark.

Paolo is right on time and he speeds down the hill to make sure we don't miss the last train. He even insists on getting out of the taxi to deliver us to our track on foot.

"*A Firenze,*" he says, nodding. Rather than the standard kisses, he hugs us and makes us promise to return. He seems truly sorry to see us go.

"Let's get some wine for the ride," Pam says as soon as he leaves.

"Why not?" Peter shrugs.

"I'll be back."

He follows her with his eyes as she marches down the track toward the little glowing bar, where the old woman is slowly folding up her sandwich board again. Then he turns and smiles at me. We're the only people in the station and, except for the neon bar and the dim lamps along the platform, it is dark.

"Sorry about Pam," Peter says. "She's a little intense, but she's cool when you get to know her."

"I can see that," I say. "Are you two..." I let my voice trail.

"No, not really. Sort of. You know." He smiles apologetically.

"Sure." I give his smile back to him. I'm an almost-thirty-year-old gossiping with a college kid. Who should be sorry?

"You going to the club Monday?" he asks.

"Probably. I've been trying to go every day."

"That's great!" His enthusiasm hangs in the air for a moment before he continues. "Have you seen Francesca at all?" His voice cuts in half, revealing him, and I hear the question he doesn't ask.

"I haven't," I lie. I had seen Francesca a few times in the locker room, but she'd said nothing about Peter. Only talked about her parents who were visiting and insisted on staying with her family.

"She must be busy. Francesca, I mean." He holds her name like a glass sphere, passing it delicately to me in the dark. I remember the power of saying someone's name and of hearing it on the lips of others, and so I say, "Francesca's been nice to me," and Peter smiles.

Francesca. Three syllables rising and then falling. Like the city of Cortona, there is a magic to it. I don't feel lonely, then, but grateful. Grateful to be this single body, untethered and free of that magic, breathing into the dark.

"This was fun," he says. "I'm glad you came, Hannah."

"Me, too." And I am. I could be in Rome right now, about to leave. And instead I'm here.

"*Perfetto!*" Pam returns with three mini-bottles of wine as the light of the train appears in the distance. She links arms with Peter and shivers slightly. "You know, I bet I'm the only customer that woman's had all day."

That night, Signora Rosa and I do our same dance. She knocks and knocks, and I hide and hope that she will not use a key to open my door. She doesn't. Not yet. As if sensing my desperate game, my sister calls. She's been trying to reach me since she got my message. And she's been opening my mail. Do I know how high my credit card bill has gotten? Do I know what my balance is? Of course I know. It's *my* money.

"What will you do there? Do you need me to lend you money?" she asks.

"No," I say, trying to stay calm. But I'm angry with myself as well, because these weeks have distracted me from what I've known since I arrived. Without a plan—a real plan—the only place I'm going is home.

"Well, you'll need to figure something out," Kate says. There is a long pause, and then, "Also, I should tell you..."

"Tell me what?"

"Julian called here—a few times—asking about you." She goes on but I don't hear her.

The seasons with Julian. The hard-edged seasons. The crisp rush of autumn when there was happiness, real happiness, when every corner was a new place to be together and every street that had not witnessed us walking side by side demanded it. My life was full, sated.

But by winter, I felt it already—the old ache returning, the sadness creeping in. And I felt the gulf between us, could see the moment when this would grow stale and I would be, again, alone. Julian asked for words as I folded into myself. *Why won't you talk to me? Why do you keep everything inside?* Was it then that I began to whittle myself down?

By the time spring exploded on the East Coast, he was gone and I was still disappearing. I was carving away the outside, I was carving away the inside.

"Hannah, are you there?" Kate asks now.

"I'm here." I can't go back there. I can't.

"He wanted your number, but I didn't know if you'd want to speak with him. I wish you'd tell me what happened."

"Well, thanks" is all I say. "For not giving out my number. Thanks."

I find the crumpled napkin on the kitchen table. Luca picks up after the first ring.

"*Pronto?*"

"Ciao, Luca. It's Hannah. It's too late?"

"Hannah! *Come stai?*" He sounds surprised, but his voice is warm.

"I was just calling about dinner. To see if you want to have dinner with me." I take a breath in and hold it, but his response is as relaxed and fluid as everything else he does.

"*Sì, certo.* When are you free?"

"Wednesday?"

"*Perfetto.* Wednesday. Five forty-five—it's okay? We can drive someplace?"

"*Va bene.* Do you know where I live?"

"*Sì*, of course," he says. "Ciao, Hannah, ciao ciao."

Chapter Nine

The building looks like a small Italian palace, fortified with caged windows and rough-cut stone. It is right on the river, crouching heavy between the taller structures beside it. As soon as I step through its thick door, I am swallowed in darkness, and I feel as though I'm back in Orvieto, entering a cave, cool and quiet, its edges unknown. Even under my blazer, my skin crawls. I'm in an empty lobby. Another hidden place in this city. I find the staircase and climb the stone steps, daylight growing with each level, until I see plastic letters pressed into felt: BIBLIOTECA SERRONI. An arrow points down a hallway that is open on one side to a courtyard below, the source of this ethereal light. The other side is lined with paintings, all portraits: a man seated high on a horse, a somber child clutching a bird, two more men with matching widow's peaks, and, at the end of the hall, a woman, her face an elongated heart, her hand resting on an open book. She looks straight out with bright green eyes.

"*Buongiorno.*"

My eyes dart around—a large room with high ceilings, shelves and shelves of books—before they land on the source of the voice. An older woman, petite with spectacles. She is tucked behind a wide wooden desk in the corner.

"*Posso aiutarla?*"

"*È*—is this the Serroni Library?" I stutter, breaking my vow to use only Italian.

"Come in. Have a seat." She speaks with a British accent and says this flatly, all business, gesturing to the chair across from her.

Everything about her is smaller up close: her sharp chin, her green eyes, her hands folded on the desk. But she doesn't seem fragile. She is solid, a fortress. A knot of dark hair is perched on top of her head, unmoving. A nameplate—LORENZA RICCI—faces me.

"I'm Hannah," I offer.

"You're American," she says decisively. "Are you a student?" She wears the same expression as the woman in the portrait, aloof but curious.

"No—I mean, yes, I'm American, but I'm not a student. I'm look-ing for work." My voice is too loud and I'm starting to sweat, but this is my last, best chance.

The Serroni Library seeks a motivated individual... This after two days of manic searching and two broken conversations—one in a shop selling bags and shoes, the other in the home of a wealthy family—both with sleek Italian women who spoke quickly as the color rose to my cheeks and I asked them to repeat again and again. *But, signora,* they had said slowly with knowing looks, *the ad said fluency.*

"We do have a position available," Lorenza says, her eyes prob-ing. "But I should warn you that it is temporary—only for this term. And it's nothing glamorous."

"That's fine. I'm not looking for anything glamorous," I say quick-ly, then add, "My degree is in art history. And I worked for a muse-um in Boston."

"Hmm. Good." Her countenance changes, as though I might have something to offer after all. "Well, we need someone to help with cataloging." She says "we," but there isn't anyone else here. "More pressingly, I have urgent travel next week, so we need a per-son behind the desk, preferably someone responsible who knows what he or she is talking about. I had a young woman here who was completely unreliable. I cannot have that again."

I nod.

"Do you have your CV?"

"No. I could try and get a hold of it and come back—"

"Not to worry. We'll do it now." Lorenza opens the desk drawer and removes a pad of paper. I am fully damp beneath my suit. I squeeze my hands together. The first questions are easy: Education. Previous jobs.

"So you've worked with collections, then?"

"Yes." I keep my voice casual as I run through my experience. Everything that I'm saying is true. I was good at my job—at the beginning, I was. And still I fear, in spite of the suit, in spite of my years of experience, that I don't have a professional self anymore, that it may have gone with all the rest.

"That was your most recent employment?"

I nod. How will I explain the months between then and now? Adrenaline courses through me and the deepest, most primal part of my brain emerges. The part that screams *flight*. How have I found myself here again, in a room in a chair across from a person who wants answers, who reveals nothing and asks me to reveal all?

And then all I can see is that past room.

The director called me into his office. The afternoon Claudia found me hiding in the museum courtyard, watching the schoolchildren. It was sometime in May, sometime after I began throwing up.

"It's the third mistake, Hannah." Robert was uncomfortable, older than me. He'd been at the museum forever. He cleared his throat repeatedly while he addressed my slipups. They kept coming now. There had been more than three, I was sure of that.

"It isn't like you."

I nodded. Assured him that I would be more careful.

He cleared his throat, took off his glasses, rubbed his eyes. "There's another thing. This is a little delicate," he said, and sighed. "People have been noticing—"

What people? Who was noticing? Claudia. It must have been her.

"—that you've lost some weight." He cleared his throat again. "Quite a bit of weight."

"I joined a gym," I said.

"A gym..." He nodded. I was doing his job for him. I was making it easy.

The room began going in and out of focus. "And I've been busy —a little stressed."

He nodded again. This was a good explanation. He rubbed his eyes, put his glasses back on, and said, "Don't work too hard, okay? If you need some time off—"

"Absolutely. I'll let you know." I would have to be more careful. And I was more careful. I stayed late into the evenings, going over and over minutiae. There would be no more slipups to reveal me. I began eating publicly, eating more. Defiantly, I ate. I knew people were watching and I performed with confidence. *Yes, I'd love to join you. Yes, I'd love a bite.* And then alone in the bathroom, I'd retrieve whatever I'd put in.

That bathroom. All steel, all echoes. Two doors: a heavy outer door that required a key and made a loud suction as it opened; a lighter inner door. Three sinks. Three stalls. I chose the farthest one. I was smart at first. I waited until after hours, when most of the staff had left. I knew the click of the key and the sound of that outer door opening against pressure and could right myself. When did I get careless? I would go in a little earlier, just a little earlier, each time. Twice I heard that door open and stood up. But someone must have heard, must have told.

A second conversation. He cleared his throat, took off his glasses, rubbed his eyes. He didn't want this. Neither did I.

"Hannah, a few people have mentioned—"

What people? Who? "I haven't been feeling well," I cut him off. "But I know—that I need to take better care of myself, I mean. Make it a priority."

"Yes," he said, relieved. He put his glasses back on. "Take care of yourself. If you need some time—"

"Absolutely."

"And why did you leave that position?" Lorenza asks.

The larger truth I haven't shared sits heavy between us. I look down at my hands. *Please.* Though I can't think that way or she may sense it, may feel the desperation coming off me. No one wants someone desperate. No one.

Lorenza is looking at me oddly now. *You would keep your glasses off, too.*

"It wasn't the right fit."

"I see," she says. "And what makes you think this would be a better fit?"

I look around the room, taking in the quiet shelves, the rows and rows of thick leather spines. "I love books," I say finally. This is true. I used to read all the time—before I stopped eating.

"Mm-hmm." She writes nothing.

"I read that this collection belonged to a family?" I've done my research. I can show her that, at least.

Lorenza nods. "The Serroni. They lived here, in this palazzo. Signora Arcelli"—she gestures to the portrait that had stopped me in the doorway—"married into the family. These books were her dowry. Since the fifties we've expanded the collection to make it more accessible, with books in English as well. But this room and the adjoining room are comprised entirely of volumes from Signora Arcelli's original library."

"That's incredible."

Lorenza nods but remains quiet, waiting for me to say more. Breathe. Be honest.

"My job at the museum—I didn't feel like what I was doing mattered." As I say it, I realize that it's true. "I was good at my job, but it felt... empty." I look her straight in the eye. "A place like this matters. It means something. I think my work would mean something here."

Lorenza's face softens. "Why don't I give you a tour? Give you a sense of what you'd be getting into." I don't know if she's just letting me down easy, but before I can respond, she's up and across the room. She must be a head shorter than me and still I need to move quickly to keep up.

"The library is two complete floors and also this middle level—special interest, specific to region."

I read the labels as we pass them: ARCHAEOLOGY, THE GRAND TOUR, TUSCAN TRAVELS, THE ITALIAN RENAISSANCE, THE MEDICI,

THE GREAT WAR. We take a staircase to the next floor down, where several students, one a version of Pam, sit hunched over computers. She's the only person to look up as Lorenza Ricci says, *"Buongiorno,"* before leading me to the shelves beyond.

"We partner with universities, international programs, make the materials available for a small fee. Don't be alarmed by the number of students here today. It isn't always this crowded."

There can't be more than half a dozen people, but I nod gravely.

"It's almost the middle of the term, so there are exams," she explains. "Not that these programs are truly rigorous anymore. Fewer standards. It's a shame."

I glance back at the girl, who is now whispering across the table to one of the boys.

Lorenza turns with force and leads me back up the stairs. "We also have newspapers and journals on file. And there are plenty of places to work." She walks across the main room and through a set of double doors. "The Arcelli Room, for example, is a lovely spot, even when the children are here."

I realize her speech and her tour are well choreographed. The room we stand in is breathtaking, with long wooden tables, antique books behind glass, and three long windows facing the river. *This,* I think, *is a Library.*

"This is the original reading room. The books in here are for use, too, but not to lend. They're the earliest editions from the Serroni collection. Well, then," she says. "Any questions for me?"

"What makes you interested in this type of work? What makes it—"

"A 'good fit'?" She smiles. "The preservation of history," she says, each word carefully weighed and weighted. "I ought to have mentioned earlier—my father was a Ricci but my mother comes from the Serroni line."

"Really?"

"Sì. I'm the last Serroni—or the last one who cares, I should say. I have cousins who would like to sell this place, profit off the collection. And perhaps they will. But not while I'm living. These books have been here for centuries and survived worse—part of the collection was lost, you know, during the flood."

"The flood?"

"*Sì*. Nineteen sixty-six. You aren't familiar with it? Just a moment." She disappears and returns with a large book. "The images will do it more justice." She sets it on the long reading table and gestures for me to come closer. It feels strangely intimate, standing side by side, our heads bent together, and her reserve disappears as she walks me through the pages. The text is Italian, but the photos speak for themselves. Each scene is a ghostly gray, as though we've caught the images just as they are about to disappear. The opening photos are of the Arno on the morning of the flood. The bridge supports of the Ponte Vecchio are entirely submerged and the shops sit on the Arno's surface like houseboats. In the background, buildings seem to evaporate into fog, the empty ruins of an ancient city. The rowing club is under that water, rapids racing through the cavern where the sculls are stored, filling the coffee bar, washing away the echoes of the locker rooms. The banks where we feed the boats onto the river are disappeared entirely.

"My god," I say.

"And this is only the beginning."

In the pages that follow, the disaster unfolds in real time. Water rushes over the river's walls, pouring into the city, filling the long courtyard between the arms of the Uffizi Gallery, and climbing up the sides of the Duomo and baptistery. Fiats are transformed into makeshift boats, and a bus floats around the square in front of the foundling hospital.

"More than ten thousand works of art damaged or destroyed," Lorenza says softly without looking up. "And I mean all art—sculpture, painting, manuscripts. Including some of our own collection, as I said."

She turns another page and a jolt passes through my body. Water sweeps through the sculptures in the loggia of Piazza della Signoria, swirling around Perseus, Menelaus, and Hercules and reaching up toward the open hands of the twisting Sabine woman. I can imagine the rough current licking at her fingertips. She is drowning.

"How awful."

"*Sì*," Lorenza says. "Though there is a—how do you call it? A silver lining. Thousands of volunteers came to save the art—students primarily. A horrific event, but also a testament to the human spirit. If you can imagine how much more would have been lost. Buried." She shakes her head, then takes a step back, as though remembering herself. I wonder what it is like to be Lorenza, to spend so much time in this place that her ancestors called home, surrounded always by their ghosts. "As I said, the preservation of history. Now, I have some work to do, but feel free to stay and enjoy the books— and take this with you, if you'd like."

Has she offered me the job? Did I miss that?

"You'll begin tomorrow?" she asks, after a pause.

I want to cheer, want to throw my arms around this small fortress of a woman, but instead I just smile broadly and say, "Yes, yes," again the yes-girl, and still—"Yes," and I take the hand she offers me. Her grip, though small and bony, is surprisingly warm.

Later that afternoon, as I row under the Ponte Santa Trinita and look west over the now-quiet Arno, I can't shake the image of the water raging with indifference, the city's lifeblood turning on it without cause or care. The bridge sits high above the water, the streets are dry, and the shops are filled with life. Still, it all feels temporary, perilously so.

On my way home, I decide to stop for an early dinner. I order a glass of prosecco—and why not? I have a job, small as it is. I have the means to stay for a little while longer. I eat my fish and salad and watch the sky grow pink. Things are just beginning. This is a new beginning. Then I take out the book on the flood. In the final pages, I find the silver lining that Lorenza had referenced. Youth crowd into a barely lit hallway, forming an assembly line for the treasures being salvaged from the wreckage of libraries and museums. In one shot, Ted Kennedy acknowledges their efforts. In another, a group sits in the shadow of a column, leaning on one another for support, all mud but their faces. Woodstock in repose. *Angeli del Fango*, the caption reads. *Mud Angels.* In the final images, they earn the title as volumes heavy with water and debris make their way down the human chain and, hand to hand, history is passed out of the ruins and into the light.

Chapter Ten

On my first official day of work, Lorenza Ricci insists that I take notes. She goes over in detail the processes for checking out, checking in, and cataloging books, then walks me through all the library's sections, explaining the organization. It is easy to follow her through the shelves, listening and writing, and I like that these tools—the overly long sheets of European paper with their faint green lines, the generic ballpoint pen a bit narrower than those I'm used to— which are foreign in my hands, have a purpose and will soon feel natural. When Lorenza opens the glass doors of the cases in the Arcelli Room, a thin cloud of dust floats around us. She opens a small drawer to reveal carefully stacked white gloves and puts a pair on before pulling out one of the volumes, impressing upon me the delicacy of the pages and gripping just the very edge of each corner as she turns them. I don't touch any of the books, but I look forward to the time she is away when I might let my fingers run down their rough edges.

By the time I get home, I have to rush to get ready for dinner. Then I lean out the window, waiting for Luca. It is chilly, the sky is clear, and the street below is empty except for a gray cat that darts around in circles and then ducks under a small yellow Fiat. The door of the building across the way opens and a woman steps out.

"Tommaso!" She takes a few harried steps.

My phone rings behind me and she glances up at the sound. Our eyes meet before I duck back into my apartment and pick up the receiver, sure it is Luca canceling.

"Hannah, it's Lorenza Ricci. Can you come a bit earlier tomorrow? Eight thirty? I have an appointment that I'm afraid is going to keep me out for much of the day and I'd like to go over some final things with you."

"Yes, of course, Signora Ricci."

"Lorenza."

"Of course, Lorenza."

I'm employed, I think, the relief hitting me again as I return to the window. The woman is bending over in the street now. I should yell out, disclose the little fugitive's location, but already the cat's plaintive cry has begun, a child both wanting and not wanting to be found. The woman becomes a splotch of white, spreading, as she crouches low by the car. She reaches under and drags him slowly out. She carries him, stiff-limbed, up the block, kicks her door open, and disappears inside. Then the street is quiet.

At six o'clock there is still no sign of Luca, and I'm beginning to think he might not show up at all when his car barrels down the street and pulls to a quick stop. He steps out, looks around, and walks to the door. I don't call out but watch him ring the bell before closing the shutters and putting on my coat. On my way out, Signora Rosa appears on cue with her same look, and I tell her that I will have the October rent to her shortly. I have a job.

In the car, Luca is friendly but quiet. He drives quickly to get us to the restaurant before the sun sets. It is his friend's place in Chianti. "A perfect spot," he says. When I tell him about the library, his enthusiasm fills the car momentarily before we fall back into silence. I begin to feel uneasy and realize how little I know about him.

"So do you do something?" I ask. "Other than rowing, I mean?"

"*Sì. Lavoro in un negozio di sport.*" *An athletic store.* "I am—*come si dice... il direttore?*"

I nod. "The manager. Did you ever row professionally?"

He sighs. "I was for a time on the national team. But it was boring. Training in the country. I wanted to shoot myself, it was so boring."

Soon we're climbing into the hills, Luca's little car working hard. There are few buildings here, only the occasional collection of houses, clotheslines strung between their windows. Otherwise it is all nature—a quilt of hayfields, olive groves, and vineyards, golds and greens cascading down slopes and funneling into valleys. Everything is alive and fertile. I envy the grapevines with their thick, waxy leaves. I envy the hardy olive trees that survive on almost nothing.

Luca points to a sign as we speed by. "A Medici villa. *Li conosci, i Medici?*"

"*Sì, certo.*"

Luca nods. "The wife of Lorenzo stayed there. Clarice. But it is a sad story."

"*Perché?*"

Luca turns down the radio. "*Perché* Lorenzo, he was crazy, you know? Running with women in Firenze. And Clarice remained at the villa—in the countryside."

"All the time?"

"*Sì.*"

"Did they ever see each other?"

"*No, perché* it was a marriage not for love, *capisci?*"

"Arranged?"

"*Esatto.* Clarice comes from Rome. Lorenzo's mother, Lucrezia—"

"Lucrezia Tornabuoni?" I remember the older woman in the frescoes in Santa Maria Novella.

"*Sì.* Lucrezia chooses Clarice. Because she has grand hips." Luca takes his hands off the wheel to show me the size, laughing. Big hips. Good for bearing children. And I wonder again when I will bleed, if I will bleed. I never used to think about this. I always assumed—but how many months have passed? One, two, three. More, I think.

"And also she is from a good family," he continues. "*Allora,* they marry. They have many children—nine, *penso.*"

"Nine?"

"*Sì. Nove.* Lorenzo does not love her. But Clarice, she loves him. She writes, 'I love you,' and 'Come home, *per favore.*'"

Luca is a passionate storyteller, and the more animated he be-comes, the younger he appears. The car begins to feel lighter, and I relax and lean in to better hear him.

"She writes, 'The children wait for you,' e 'I hope to see your shad-ow in the garden.'"

"How sad."

"Sì. But Lorenzo, he stays in Firenze with the politics and the wom-en. *Allora*, Clarice, she knows his favorite food *è la quaglia. Conosci?*"

"Quail?"

"Sì. She writes, 'Every day I watch for you. I save for you the best quail.' *Tragico, no?*"

"Very tragic. But it doesn't make sense."

"*Cosa?*"

"Lucrezia—Lorenzo's mother—was a strong woman."

"*Certo.* Lucrezia was a woman *forte e... particolare.*" He chooses this word carefully. *Unique*, he means, *particular*. Though it also translates to *peculiar*.

"But she didn't look out for Clarice."

Luca turns off onto the road for Radda in Chianti and we climb another hill. "No. But why? Lorenzo was of her blood."

"Well, they were both women. Perhaps they could have under-stood each other."

"Perhaps." Then he glances. "But you forget. Lucrezia is Fiorentina."

"And?"

"Clarice is Romana. *This* is why it is impossible."

"No," I say. "Really?"

"Sì. Really." He laughs.

We ride in silence then. Luca turns the music back up and I watch the landscape pass. I wonder if it was really regional pride that made Lucrezia cold to her daughter-in-law. Clarice, with her big hips and nine children, waiting and watching for a man who did not love her. Saving the prize quail and setting a place that always remained empty.

Finally, I say, "She had it all wrong."

"*Chi?*"

"Clarice. Writing Lorenzo those sad letters. It was stupid."

"Stupid?" Luca laughs. "*Perché?*"

"He probably didn't even read them. Instead she should have gone to Firenze to find some men for herself."

"Men for herself? No. It is not possible." He puts his hand on mine, still laughing.

"Or at least she should have eaten the prize quail."

"*Sì.* That, perhaps." Then he points to a cluster of lights, white shot with red, twinkling in the shadow of the hills above us. "*Eccolo!*"

When we pull to a stop in the small lot at the top of the hill, I realize that the lights are in a garden and the red accents are glowing heat lamps. A chill hits me when I get out of the car, the October air much colder up here than in Florence's center.

"Signor Galletti," Luca says, embracing the owner—an older, rounder man—who meets us at the gate. They converse in low tones before I hear my name.

"*Piacere,*" the man says as he takes my hand, unsmiling now, and looks me up and down in a way that makes me want to cover myself. He nods to us to follow him into the garden. It is all couples and I can feel their eyes on us as we pass. I need a glass of wine. He gives us what must be the prime table right at the garden's edge. Below, the late-day sun pours into the valley like water.

"A perfect spot," Luca says when the owner leaves us to our meal, then, smiling slyly, "I think this place is not in the *Baedeker, no?*"

"Definitely not." I laugh, surprised. "And it's not in my *Lonely Planet,* either."

I take my time looking at the menu, but when the waiter arrives, I'm still undecided.

"No problem," Luca says. "It's okay if I order for us?"

"Sure."

But then the evening turns. Because Luca orders every course. He orders too much. Bruschetta, soup, pasta with mussels, wild boar, dessert. Just hearing the list makes me tense. I curse my lunch, curse that I suggested this evening. I've set myself up. It will be exhausting to try to pick at it all in such a way that it looks like I'm eating. I'm practiced at this—even when my sister began watching me at meals, I was convincing. Still, it will be exhausting.

"We train, so we must eat." Luca smiles. "We are *buone forchette*, no?"

Good forks. The Italian phrase for a person with a healthy appetite. A clean-plater.

"A perfect spot," Luca says again, and I nod.

This is healthy, like the vines, like the olive trees, I tell myself. This is good.

But it's too much. Too much food, too much time, and conversation is again difficult. I drink a glass of wine quickly as we sit in silence. When the bruschetta comes, I cut the bread in half, pick the tomatoes off and eat them slowly, pushing the crusts to the side. Does Luca see this careful surgery? The soup is easy. I press down my spoon, catching only the broth, leaving the beans and pasta stuck to the bowl's base. If I can save enough space I will survive the additional courses.

The sun begins to disappear behind the nearest hill and I'm grateful for the approaching darkness. The waiter lights our candle and the server sets two empty plates and a platter of steaming pasta between us. Dark mussels are nestled in the strands.

Luca heaps pasta onto my plate. I have to say something, to fill the air with words so that he won't notice if I don't eat. But he speaks first.

"So there is someone at home, Hannah? In Boston?"

I shake my head. Not that.

"*Non credo.*" He smiles, twirling his fork, loading it with thick roping. "Many, *no?*"

"No." I look at my plate. "Only me." I pull open a mussel and spear it with my fork, wishing it would disappear at the touch.

"Okay," Luca says. "If you say so—I believe you."

I want something to happen: a natural disaster, a hurricane, even a strong wind to upend our table. I put the mussel in my mouth, chew slowly, put the fork down. A good start, but how am I going to make any headway into these thick cords? They look strong, frightening. I pick up my fork and pry open another shell. Luca eats rapidly with large bites, smiling up at me occasionally. I snag a piece of pasta. Say something.

He takes a gulp of water, sighs, and then says, "I think you are *un mistero.*"

I look up at that. He knows. "A mystery?"

"*Sì,*" Luca says, pleased with himself. He picks up his fork and pokes a mussel in my bowl, which is still nearly full. "Like this. *Un po'*... hard to see."

Or maybe he doesn't know. Either way, I defiantly twirl my own mound of pasta, hating it, hating him. It slips and slips, only one thick strand making it to my mouth. *Take that.*

"*Scusami*, Hannah." Luca looks concerned. What does my face look like? I must seem mad. He knows, he doesn't know. I don't know. I'm spent. "It is not bad—mystery is good, *no? Come un enigma. Un gioco.*"

A game. I swallow. "A puzzle."

"*Sì.*"

He shrugs and returns his attention to his plate, leaving me to my battle. I take a few more bites as he uses his bread to mop up the sauce—he is *making a little shoe,* as the Italians say. *Fare la scarpetta.* He does it with ease. I take two more bites. Then he places a hand on my shoulder and excuses himself. I immediately flag our waiter and tell him we are finished.

I look around the garden—everyone is engrossed in conversation—then slip off my coat and push up my sleeves to examine my arms. I put my hands on my stomach, where I can feel already the pasta growing. I can feel myself getting larger. I need to look.

"*Va tutto bene?*" Luca asks when he returns, sliding into his seat. "You are warm?" He nods to my bare arms, and my face does feel warm as I pull down the sleeves of my sweater.

"I was for a moment." If I could just see myself, make sure that I haven't changed beyond repair, I could get through the rest of this night. I smile at Luca, but his face is going in and out of focus. I need to see myself.

The bathrooms with which I have a history. There were places that were safe and places that were not. At home in my apartment.

Clean—not white and sparse like my sister's, but clean. Light blue walls. One clear mirror. A bright overhead light I would turn off to leave only the soft night-light glowing by the sink. Bent over the toilet, I felt safe. The room would spin when I was done, but it was safe. At work. All steel, all echoes. Not safe, never safe, but still known. And then there was the bathroom in that tall building that swayed and swayed, where Claudia found me. The afternoon when it all came apart.

This bathroom is at the end of a long hall beyond the kitchen. Yellow walls; a floor tiled black and white; a single bulb dimmed behind a ceiling fixture; a small mirror, fogged, above the sink. I try to empty myself as much as possible without throwing up. I will not throw up. I have come too far for that. I can hear the sounds from the kitchen—conversation dipping up and down, the hiss of the stove. I flush the toilet, pull up my pants, and wash my hands. I look at myself in the mirror, which is hung too high. My eyes are dark; they shift side to side. I look crazy. I try to rub away the circles beneath them but they remain. Outside, the laughter of the staff dies as the owner's voice cuts in. I will need to move quickly. I turn the water back on to mute my own sounds, then take off my shoes and pull down my pants and underwear. Struggling to get all that material over my feet, I knock my elbow on the wall.

"Shit." That will bruise. I pull my shirt and sweater over my head and add them to the pile, unhook my bra and toss it on top. The floor is cold under my socks—I take them off, too.

I step back, close my eyes, then open them and look. I wince. I am there in the mirror, or part of me is, anyway, down to just below my breasts. I cannot take it all in at once.

Eyes.

Cheeks.

Neck.

Shoulders and the area in between.

Ribs slightly raised below skin.

Arms hanging out, pressing in.

Breasts limp.

I close my eyes and think back. I begin with the morning.

Coffee. No milk, no sugar.

Toast. Two slices, a thin layer of butter.

Salad at the bar near the library.

Vinegar. A tablespoon maybe?

Mozzarella: two round disks.

A half a slice of bread. Already things are adding up and I haven't even gotten to dinner. My stomach knots.

The bruschetta: a stack of tomatoes soaked in oil, a soggy center of bread.

Broth. Five spoonfuls?

Mussels. Three.

Pasta. Thick ropes—how many? I don't know.

Wine. Two glasses—or was it three?

I open my eyes.

My cheeks look fuller, are fuller.

My upper arms, my breasts—fuller, too.

Below them, fog, and I try to loosen the mirror, but it is screwed in.

I walk back to the toilet and stare into its pool. I feel ill, truly ill. If I throw up, this will be why. I am truly ill. I look down at the floor tiles between my feet. Black squares framed by rectangles of white. Cubic roses, their centers dark pupils staring up at me. I turn around. No seat cover, and so, with a hand on either wall, I step up onto the porcelain lip. Braced, I look to the mirror at the other end of the room. It is too dim and I am too far away, a blur of pink with a patch of dark. I squint. Where are the edges? Nothing, nothing. I can see nothing.

I look down and the tiles stare up. The pattern shifts, the floor blurring. What are they seeing? A woman, grown, knees bent, feet gripping a dirty toilet like an odd insect or an awkward beast. Large bodied, this must be true; I have grown into this larger body. What am I doing up here? It is humiliating.

It is only when I step back down onto the tiles that I realize I'm freezing. I sit on the edge of the toilet, imagining I'm smudging away my footprints, and wrap my arms around myself, shivering. A heaviness wells up in my throat. Not the pasta, though it feels like that, too, might come up. Instead, a sob emerges that shakes and shakes and shakes and threatens never to stop. It is too much. I thought that I was well enough for this, thought that I was getting better, but I'm not. I'm not. I fold into the sobs, waiting for them to slow, trying to steady myself, and still I shake and shake and shake.

A soft tap on the door. It jerks me to attention. A second tap, sharper this time. Then I hear the water running in the sink, the buzz of the lightbulb, the voices in the kitchen outside. I remain frozen, hoping the person at the door will give up, leave, return later when I'm comfortably back at my table. How long have I been gone? I imagine Luca waiting, worried. I open my eyes and see the black and white tiles. I can't. I pick up my head and look at my clothing heaped by the sink. I can't put my clothes back on; I can't go back out there. There is nothing left in me to sit up straight, to smile, to talk. It's too much. Far too much. I wrap my head in my hands. I stare at the floor through my fingers, at the shadow my body casts, at the stain on the yellow wall. If I could sit here for a few minutes more and look at these things.

Another tap on the door. Panic.

I clear my throat and lift my head, my shoulders still shaking. "*Un momento*," I croak.

I can't. How can I face whoever it is that is tapping and tapping and tapping? And to walk from there past the kitchen and all the way back to the garden. To speak without sobbing. How will I be normal? I am not normal.

Another tap at the door. "*Va tutto bene?*" It is a man's voice. What if it's him? I haven't been gone that long, have I? I squeeze my eyes shut. There is a way out of this.

"*Va tutto bene?*" the voice asks again.

This is a puzzle and there is an answer.

"*Chiuda l'acqua, per favore.*"

Turn off the water. Don't think past it. I stand up, go to the sink, turn off the water, and then stay there. Another tap at the door.

"*Scusi, signore, signora. Va tutto bene?*"

It isn't him. The voice doesn't know if it is a man or woman in here taking so long, running the water.

"*Sto bene,*" I say. "*Un momento.*"

I pick up each piece of clothing and dress slowly, not looking in the mirror now, not looking down. I need to keep moving. I reach around to adjust my bra. I zip my pants, button my shirt, pull my sleeves down under the sweater. Pull on my socks, my shoes. When I'm dressed again, I turn on the water for a flash, splash my face, dry it completely. I breathe slowly in and out, counting. Then I turn to the door, unlatch it, twist the knob, and open it to reveal the furrowed expression of the owner, Signor Galletti.

"*Madonna, sta bene?*" he says with concern, though his face says, *It is her, of course it is her,* and his eyes remain narrow. He stares at me, a staccato note in this long hallway. How to get past this small, angry man?

"*Mi dispiace,*" I say. I put my hand on my stomach. "*Non mi sento bene.* It must be something I ate." He doesn't understand.

"*Qualcosa che ho mangiato,*" I say, and he registers this. His eyebrows go up and he is immediately apologetic.

"*Mi scusi, signora.*" He hurries off to the kitchen, and I feel guilty as I hear his sharp voice begin the investigation.

I weave through the dark garden, my legs gaining more strength with each step. No one looks up at me, only Luca when I arrive back at the table. I preempt any questions with a smile.

"Sorry that took so long." I sit down and force the quiver out of my voice. "There was a line."

Luca looks concerned, but he nods as though it is all perfectly logical. My nerves sit on the surface of my body, my skin crawls with the breeze. Luca has already placed hunks of meat on each of our plates and his portion is almost gone.

"*Scusami,*" he says. "I waited for a time. I can ask to have it made warm again."

I look at the pile of boar in front of me and I'm surprised at how easy it is to say, "It's okay. I'm not hungry anymore."

He lifts up the wine bottle and raises his eyebrows. I nod and he fills my glass.

I feel wrung out. My eyes ache. I need to speak, to stay alert.

"Do you do this a lot?" I ask.

"*Cosa?*" He looks confused.

"This." I gesture around the garden. "Dinner."

He shrugs. "Not so much."

"There are many, *no*?" I attempt a smile.

Luca chuckles but it is hollow. He pauses, takes a sip of wine, then says, "Now, no."

"And before?"

"When I was young—*sì. Certo. E poi* there was one woman. For many years, we would start and stop, start and stop. But... *non lo so*. Italian women are difficult."

"Difficult?" I echo, my surprise obvious. I'm awake and feel suddenly quite sober.

"Very jealous," Luca explains.

"What about the men?" I ask, since we're speaking in generalizations. My rawness has hardened me and there's a meanness in my voice. I can hear it when I say, "Aren't the men difficult? Aren't they jealous?"

"*Scusami*," Luca says. "I speak like an idiot. But this woman, she was jealous all the time."

"Of what?"

"Of nothing. There was no one else. When we were together, there was nobody else." He is adamant. "*Capisci?* She was crazy."

I nod but don't say anything.

Luca puts his fork down. "I think you don't believe me. Why not?"

"It's too easy."

"*Cosa?*"

"To call her crazy. Anyway, I think you can tell when there is someone else."

"*Ma davvero*, Hannah. There was nothing. She was crazy with these ideas."

"I've been called crazy. I wasn't crazy." I'm not sure of this.

"Who said so?"

I ignore his question, keep talking fast. "Maybe I was crazy. When you care enough about someone—or something—maybe it does make you crazy."

"Ah, okay," Luca says, "but this is the problem. She was not crazy with love. She does not love me, *non credo*. I loved her. She was for me the only one. She was saying always she knew of this lady or that lady, but there was no one. *Dopotutto*, I think I was the crazy one, to not understand that she did not want me. I wanted her. I wanted marriage. I wanted children."

"And now?" I ask after a moment. "Do you still want those things?"

Luca looks out over the dark landscape, his eyes catching the candlelight. The entire valley is in shadow. We are surrounded by darkness. We are a single light in all this darkness. It feels as though everything else is slipping away. It makes me sad, as though I'm slipping away, too.

"Maybe it was my fault," he says. "*Non lo so.*" And with that, a door closes.

"I'm sorry. I didn't mean to—"

"*Non fa niente,*" Luca says, his eyes coming back to our table. "You do not know me so well. I understand."

"It's not that. It's not you. It's... I've had a bad time myself." I can't finish. I look down. Don't cry. You have survived the bathroom. Don't give the rest away now. Don't be the woman crying in the middle of the restaurant, the woman who needs saving. You don't need saving.

"*E poi?*" Luca says gently.

"Or maybe it was me that was bad." Because who else was to blame? *Leave me alone*, I'd growled at Julian. Pushing him, pushing everyone, away.

"You, bad?" He pauses, deciding, then says, "*No.*"

"Well, you didn't know me then." I force a smile.

"That you were bad? *Non è possible.*"

I stare at the candle, pulling things back to center. I won't cry now.

"*Allora.*" Luca ducks his head down to catch my eye, his face bright again. "Too serious, *no*? We need something. Something sweet?"

I shake my head.

"*Un espresso?*"

I nod, grateful, as he calls for coffee.

On the ride home it begins to rain, and I watch Luca, who is no longer a stranger. He concentrates intently on the dark road ahead. The radio is tuned to a classic rock station and Bruce Springsteen is singing. *Il Boss.* You'd think Italy had more of a claim than New Jersey. His voice is everywhere—in the shops and cafés, at sporting events, in clubs and bars. All the associations I have with the music enter fleetingly before they are lost to the passing night. It is too distant, too difficult to try to incorporate old memories into this moment. The rain picks up, rushing toward us with force. Through it, I see the lights of Florence.

"*Che pioggia,*" Luca says. *What rain.* He speeds as we descend into a valley and the city disappears again. "*Povero* Argo."

"Argo?"

"My cat." He smiles.

"Oh. You have a cat."

"*Sì.* Argo. Like the dog of Ulysses."

"Is your Argo as loyal?"

"He is a cat, *allora,* more independent. But tonight, for sure, he waits by the door. Crying, *penso.* The rain—I did not expect it. He is outside."

We climb up another hill and seconds later we're approaching the Porta Romana. The streets are almost empty and the few figures we do see are hunched over without umbrellas. It feels cozy in the car and I don't really want to go home, but then we're at the river, crossing the bridge, and turning onto my street.

"*Eccoci,*" Luca says, pulling to an abrupt stop. We sit staring ahead as though watching a film projected on the rain-splattered windshield, a kaleidoscope of light. I can hear the bass thumping in the bar.

"So," I say finally, "thank you."

Luca's jacket brushes against his seat as he swivels, and then we are kissing. I lean into him, awkwardly bent in front of the gearshift. After a moment, we part, inhaling the warm air between us, this new atmosphere.

"What do you want to do?" he asks.

"I don't know. What do you want to do?"

"I would like to kiss you more," he says matter-of-factly.

I put my hands around his neck and lean in to meet his lips again, slightly parted and surprisingly delicate on the outside, his tongue rough within. This is not a tunneling, but it is something. I remember, I remember, I remember.

He pulls back and looks at me, serious. "I respect you."

I nod.

"*Davvero*," he says, "I respect you. It is important."

"I respect you, too." I try to match the graveness of his tone but I can't help smiling.

"Oh, I sound stupid." He looks out the window.

"No!" I say, putting my hand to his face. "Not stupid. It's good. It's nice to hear." I examine the crevices of his cheeks and neck with my fingers until he finally looks back at me.

"You are a woman *particolare*," he says.

I don't know how he means it. *Unique. Peculiar.* Before I can ask, he pulls me in and I stop wondering. I don't know if this is moving backward or moving on, but it feels good, it feels earnest. I kiss the rough skin around his collarbone, feeling freer, feeling not myself.

"Poor Argo," Luca says between kisses. "He must wait *nella pioggia*. In the rain."

I laugh and finally pull away. "I have to be up early," I say.

"*Va bene. Allora, vai, vai!*" He grins, then leans over and gives me a kiss on each cheek. "But only if you say we see each other soon. Tomorrow? At the club?"

"Okay," I say, climbing out. "Until tomorrow."

"*Povero Argo*," Luca hums as I close the door. "*Povero Argo nella pioggia.*"

Chapter Eleven

I was closer to something, I thought proudly. *I was closer to something they couldn't see.*

Until I saw.

One afternoon in a shop window on Beacon Street, in a sliver of glass for a sliver of time, I saw. Everything was written across me in spaces and hollows.

Boston hurried around me, cut through me as though I were no longer there. And I was no longer there. It was someone else in the window. She was alone. And she was disappearing. She was almost gone.

Just before lunch the next day I find St. Angela.

I'm reshelving books, grateful for the redundancy of the task, for the appearance of a new subject in my mind with each text as I slide it into place. In the daylight, the previous evening is unreal, me naked in the bathroom as impossible as the intimacy in Luca's car. I had survived the night, more than survived it, yes—and still.

And then St. Angela appears. I'm not looking for her, and if I were, I wouldn't have looked here. *The Book of the Blessed Angela of Foligno*—a slim volume sitting on the shelf at eye level as though waiting for me. It doesn't belong in this section. Someone had been careless. Lorenza would be horrified. I pull the book out. It is old, yellowed, and as I leaf through it, the pages seem as though they might disintegrate in my hands. The back cover is gone, the last paragraph ends midsentence, and there are no numbers on the binding. I flip through, looking for any other markings, and a phrase jumps out at me—

I stripped myself of everything.

—just a flash of words quickly lost to the turning pages. I flip back in the opposite direction, and then reenact the first motion, the crumbling paper fanning out behind my thumb, until I find the phrase again.

I stripped myself of everything. Of all attachments to men and women, of friends and relatives, and even my very self.

I read it and then read it again. The words find their way in, settle somewhere deep. And they do not settle gently.

I stripped myself of everything.

Last night, shivering and sobbing in the bathroom, the panic mounting.

Even my very self.

And then this morning, fear. Even before I remembered its cause, it was there. The knowledge that I had slipped, that past woman reemerging, violent and biting at my heels.

And there is something else, something beneath the slip, beneath the impulse that drove me to the bathroom, drove me to my knees, stripped of everything, again, as it had so many times before. *Even my very self.* It is the feeling that it inspired. The familiarity of being in that place, even with the tears and panic. The certainty it promised, alone but not alone. *I stripped myself of everything.* I'd been eating better, sleeping better, thinking about it less, and still it had reappeared. The thing that says, *This isn't behind you,* as though it would never be behind me, its hooks too deep in me to loose, and already I can feel its draw, can feel my old friend waiting, that friend for whom I'd lost everything before and for whom, I fear, I would gladly lose it all again. *I stripped myself of everything.* It is the last year of my life. It is every moment in every bathroom. *Even my very self.* It is every lie I told, every person I lost, every piece of myself that I let fall away—though the truth is that I didn't just *let it fall away*, a passive onlooker. I stripped it away, actively, violently, proudly. All of it. *Even my very self.* It is as though St. Angela has reached out to me from the past and placed a hand on my heart and a hand on my throat. *I stripped myself of everything.* It compounds and compounds and compounds.

And so instead of returning St. Angela to her improper spot and meeting Luca at the club as I'd said I would, I lock the library's door, carry the book to the Arcelli Room, and settle in by the sunlit window. There is a brief introduction. Born into a wealthy family, Angela married young, and her transformation came only after tragedy—the death of her children, husband, and mother. She entered the Third Order of St. Francis and, like St. Catherine, she experienced a mystical marriage to Christ. The rest of the volume is Angela's account, or the account recorded by her confessor, a Franciscan friar, and the translation is archaic. It opens with "Treatise I: Of the Conversion and Penitence of the Blessed Angela of Foligno and of Her Many and Divers Temptations." The pages that follow are the eighteen spiritual steps that led to her conversion. The many ways Angela had sinned, the tests that she endured before she was saved. Then her instructions on how to live according to the controlled existence of faith. All solemnly penned, all carefully measured.

But even though the writing is restrained, St. Angela's devotion is not. When her mother, husband, and children die within months of one another, she grieves but is also grateful—the loss answers her prayer that she be freed of all earthly things. What kind of woman is grateful for her family's death? *I stripped myself of everything.* And when Jesus appears to her, the images are grotesque: Christ shows her his wounds—the hairs plucked from his eyebrows, every spot where his body has been scourged—and instructs her to drink from the gash in his side. *What can you do for me to match this suffering?*

The cadence of the words, the repeated language of love and pain, becomes hypnotic, lulling me.

Until I reach step eighteen. *I forgot to eat,* Angela confesses.

I forgot to eat. I'd said that phrase—used it—so many times. It was an easy cover, especially at the beginning. I wasn't alone—

women say it all the time, with pride, with pleasure. *Oops! I was too busy. I forgot to eat.* Though it is innocent, there is a challenge in it, too: *Try to prove me wrong.* Angela's fasting isn't unique, especially not for a devoutly religious person in the Middle Ages. Food is just one of the earthly pleasures she is stripping away. What is strange isn't the fasting, but what it inspires. Because it is in *forgetting to eat* that Angela first experiences an ecstatic vision: *The fire and fervor of such divine love in such a degree that I did cry aloud.*

And there is something that is missing, a gap between the loss of sustenance and the onset of visions. I reread the section—it is only a few lines—two, three, four times, looking for some acknowledgment of the connection between the denial of food and the moment of ecstasy. But there is nothing, no explanation for why these two experiences occur together in this final and, presumably, most vital step of Angela's conversion. No sense that they are connected at all. They simply exist side by side. *I forgot to eat. I began to have visions.* The gap remains, unacknowledged. And it is this that gives me pause. Why? I am not Christian, am not enamored with the love of God that fills Angela. But there is something in it that I know, that is mine.

"Hannah, you can't forget." This was the mantra of the doctor I saw at Kate's insistence, waiting each week in a roomful of women much younger than me, some of them with their mothers, and I wondered if they were all waiting for my daughter to arrive. It was June, I was jobless, I was alone, and so my only task was the assignment she gave me: to keep a journal of everything I ate.

"Everything?"

"Everything."

I looked not at this doctor but at the photos over her shoulder of the smiling women, all younger, who must have been the lucky ones. Healed.

One yogurt.

One coffee.

Two teaspoons of milk.

It wasn't hard. I'd been doing this for months already in my mind.

One salad, no dressing.

One apple.

One piece of cheese.

There was something about seeing it on paper, though, stripped down to its parts, that made it more expansive, even as each week this woman looked at the journal and looked at me:

"And dinner?"

"I forgot."

"Hannah, do you understand what will happen to you?"

Three sticks of gum.

One glass of wine.

"This isn't enough."

But it was more than enough, my bloated list a permanent re-minder. It was too much for me to look at, though I did look—be-fore our sessions I read over the words again and again, hoping they would suffice, like the people I used to see on the train each morning, hunched over tiny Bibles with their lips moving silently as their fingers traced the lines, the passages read and reread so many times that the pages wore thin and the ink smudged, one word bleeding into the next.

In the Arcelli Room, the clock chimes one thirty, and outside on the river, a boat passes. Four bodies I know, Luca in the second seat, his features indistinguishable but his movements undeniably his own, and I almost duck before I remember that he cannot see me, the sun's reflection off the windows hiding what would only be a tiny pinpoint of a figure to him. The boat disappears under the bridge and I keep my eyes on the water until it reappears going the oth-er direction. Then I return to my reading. When the clock chimes two thirty, I unlock the library's door, return to my desk. The men will be having lunch at the club, chuckling as Luca recounts our evening and confesses, perhaps, that I'm odd, sad, *una donna parti-colare.* Or maybe he won't tell them anything. Maybe he is instead waiting for me to appear. When the clock chimes three, I imagine him leaving, confused at my failure to arrive.

A few hours later, I lock the door behind the last student and return to my seat by the window, the river now dark and silent. As St. Angela describes her visions, I have again the sensation that this woman who lived so many centuries ago is here in the room with me. In ecstasy, she sees herself *without a body and without a soul, as she had always wished to be... as if she no longer existed.* I knew that feeling. I had felt something of it. I had disappeared, too.

Where are you?—Julian on our last night together, when my mind kept drifting, when I couldn't stay with him.

How did you get to this point, Hannah?—Claudia after it all came apart.

I defended myself to them, but I was lying. I was always lying in those days. I didn't know where I was. And I couldn't remember anything. I was somewhere else. I was someone else. I was gone.

I am continually in this state, St. Angela writes. *It seems I am no longer of this earth. And when I am in this state, I do not remember anything else.*

I arrive home to my phone ringing.

"Ciao, Hannah. It's too late to call?" As soon as I hear his voice, I remember his kindness the night before, the quiet way in which he coaxed conversation, the edge of regret he let show.

"Ciao, Luca. No, no. It's fine."

Then the warmth of his hands, his lips smiling when we kissed, and I crave him and want to believe that there is hope in this. That he won't witness that other woman, the woman who lies.

He asks about the day and I talk about work, though not about St. Angela. Then, finally, it comes: "So for this you did not go to the *canottieri?*"

"Yes," I lie.

"Oh," he says, "I was looking for you." There is no accusation in it, only a bit of sadness. "*Allora,*" he continues, recovering quickly, "when do we see each other?"

"Tomorrow? This weekend?" I say, and then feel foolish for being so completely available.

"*Sì.*" He pauses. "Tomorrow I cannot, but Saturday, *sì.* In fact, there is a festival. We can go."

"A festival?"

"Yes," he says, the vowel bending. "For Santa Reparata. I explain Saturday, *va bene*?"

After I hang up, I try to hold on to his voice, to the hope, to the things that are real in this, my new beginning. But the day has changed me. St. Angela has changed me. *There is in my soul a chamber in which no joy, sadness, or enjoyment enters,* she wrote. And who would not defend that place that is for one's self and only for one's self, that cannot be touched by the criticisms of confessors, by the insistent pull of earth, by the sharp blows of existence? It is isolation, but it is also ecstasy. It is both and all. *My soul languished and desired to fly away.* It is the last thing I read before I drift into strange dreams of burning flesh, blinding light, eyelashes raining from the sky.

Chapter Twelve

Is there any saint who can tell me something of this passion which I have not yet heard spoken of or related, but which my soul has seen, which is so great that I find no words to express it? Saturday afternoon I'm reading, still, this book on St. Angela, tucked into the corner of the Arcelli Room during lunch. But it is past lunch when Lorenza Ricci's voice shakes me from my reading. Lorenza, who will be leaving me in charge beginning on Monday.

"I'm sorry. I didn't realize how late it was."

"What are you reading?" is all she says.

I hand her the small book and remember the feeling of ceding my journal to that doctor, who wasn't old enough to be my mother, but still I felt like a child, caught, as I do now.

If Lorenza registers my discomfort, she doesn't show it. "Sant' Angela—are you familiar with the mystical saints?"

"I've read about St. Catherine."

"Of course, but there are hundreds of others. Come."

She leads me down a level, past the section where I had found this book that I now clutch as though it is my last possession, and around a corner where a small sign reads SPIRITUALITY AND MYSTICISM.

"The other half of the church," Lorenza says, pointing to the spines: *Between Exaltation and Infamy*; *The Dark Night of the Soul*; *The Order of the Poor Clares*. "Santa Caterina was mainstream, but some of the others..." She pulls out a book on Margaret of Cortona, her arm shaking against the weight, and hands it to me. "...less so. Women you've likely never even heard of. Don't be mistaken. In their era, they were celebrities. Untouchable. In fact, Florentine families had a strong connection to the saints, particularly the local ones, like Caterina de' Ricci"—she smiles over her shoulder at me—"my ancestor. Florence has always been a city of women—though, perhaps, not always *for* them." She runs her finger along the shelf and stops at another book. *The Life and Doctrine of Saint Catherine of Genoa.*

"What happened?"

"What was holy became heresy." She raises his eyebrows and turns a book over, opening it to the title page. "Santa Maria Maddalena de' Pazzi."

I remember the small plaque to her in San Frediano in Cestello.

"People like Maria Maddalena became dangerous."

"Why?"

"That is for you to tell me," Lorenza says, turning to me with a smile. "Not now. Read first. *Allora*, back to work?"

Before leaving to meet Luca at the festival, I look up the saint he'd mentioned. There is only a single, small entry: *Santa Reparata: Early Christian martyr and patron saint of Florence.* That's it. The city's patron saint and I've never heard her mentioned. I turn the page and find a second entry: *Santa Reparata. Original cathedral of Florence, the ruins of which now lie under Santa Maria del Fiore.* Under the Duomo. So she and her church were buried and Florence given a new idol, the Virgin Mary.

When I arrive at the Duomo, the piazza is already packed with bodies. Bikes zigzag through the crowds, and *carabinieri* troll the perimeter, sweeping out the acrobats, magicians, and musicians who fill their cups here. Near the cathedral, people wait in a slowly crawling mass. The cafés on the piazza are filled as well. Luca had mentioned a specific place but it could be anywhere, and the sun is glaring, masking everything in light. I cup my hand over my eyes and try to make out the names until I hear my own name.

Luca takes my hand with a broad smile and greets me formally—two quick kisses. "We have good seats, no? Front row." Among the sea of small tables in the café behind him I recognize two men—his rowing companions, both there the evening I blacked out danc-ing—and the adrenaline goes straight out of me. I've misunder-stood something.

"Everyone comes today," Luca continues, putting an arm around me and leading me toward them. "Our friend Enzo marches for Santa Croce. *Allora*, we come to cheer." He puts his hands in the air, shakes two fists, and I want to wrap my arms around him, but not in front of these other men.

"*Ti ricorda di* Hannah?" Luca asks, and they rise with deliberate formality. "*Ecco* Sergio." The man with red hair and large teeth smiles shyly. "And Gianni." The tall, bearded man. They greet me with kisses and a chorus of *certo, sì,* and *ciao, bella,* overly friendly. I feel as though I'm wearing armor or a halo. Either way, I'm protected.

"So what is going to happen?" I ask once we're seated.

"*In realtà,*" Luca says, "it is not normal that we come for this day— you see there are many tourists. All tourists. But we come to see Enzo."

"And instead, I should be watching the game," Gianni cuts in.

"Big game," Sergio says. "Fiorentina *contro* Milan."

"And Carlo?" Luca asks, and they are on to a new topic and I still don't know what to expect, and this, too, is so Italian. Nothing de-fined, only suggested, and the evening stretches vaguely ahead of us. I cannot follow their conversation, though I recognize the tone as different from the usual banter—it is anchored now, serious.

"*È molto triste,*" Luca says, turning to me. "*Lo sai?*"

I shake my head.

"Carlo is separating from his wife."

"Divorce," Gianni says. "It's very bad."

"In America, it is also bad?" Luca asks.

"It's common."

"Do you know many?" Sergio says this as though referring to celebrities or lepers.

"Many. My parents." Naming them, I feel suddenly displaced —"my parents" doesn't belong in this piazza.

"*Davvero?*" Luca asks. Sergio and Gianni are looking at me as though I'm the leper now.

"They are not Catholic," Sergio states.

"No. Not even close. They—well, my mother, anyway. She isn't anything."

Sergio nods, and Gianni flags the waiter and orders a round of espresso and some sweets. I see a flash of gold on his finger and wonder if he'll make any reference to his wife this evening. I rarely hear the men talking about their own families, as though their lives don't exist beyond the club's boundaries.

"To not believe in God, this I understand," Luca says. "But divorce? No. This I do not. This is about people. The 'God' is not important."

I'm surprised by his rigidity and want to ask him more, but a loud *"Ragazzi!"* interrupts us and there is Carlo, tall and broad. Sun glints off his dark shades. I remember him from the evening at the dance club. Drunk, like me. He's as gracious as the others now, though, removing his sunglasses and taking my hand with an exaggerated bow. "Hannah di Boston," he says, before pulling up a chair next to Gianni.

With Carlo, the conversation is again buoyant. It fluctuates naturally, dipping into comfortable silences before rising. Meanwhile the line outside the cathedral grows. Before entering, people stop at a statue tucked into a niche near the door, some taking pictures. It must be Santa Reparata. Every day she must watch people enter this cathedral that used to be hers, and on every day but this one, she is probably not given a second glance.

When the coffee arrives, the conversation pauses as though for prayer, and there is only the sound of five small spoons stirring espresso, then the *tap tap tap* of metal on china before each man sets his spoon down and takes his coffee whole. I refuse the cookie that Luca offers and sip my espresso while the men's conversation resumes. I spot Peter and Pam then, across the piazza, part of a group of students following a small Italian man who holds a red umbrella above the crowd, gesticulating wildly as he burrows in so that the umbrella swings side to side.

"Che succede?" Luca asks, following my gaze. "Ah. *L'Americano.*"

The barrage of commentary begins, each man trying to best the others, and I have to concentrate to follow.

"The boy from the club?"

"Yes, the *other* American." And for the first time, I realize that they see me as half of a pair—*the Americans*—though right now they don't seem to see me at all.

"Have you ever spoken to him?"

"No, but he's arrogant, I think."

"He rows alone. Always alone."

"In *Borea*."

"He's not so bad, no?"

"No. He's good but—"

"*Sì*, for an American, good."

They all laugh.

"We only joke," Luca says, breaking into English.

"The blonde looks good," Carlo says then. "More than good."

"Yes, cute little blonde." Gianni nods.

Luca smiles at me warily, but he and Sergio say nothing as Carlo and Gianni lob adjectives back and forth. By the cathedral's entrance, Pam and Peter stare up to where the umbrella-waver is pointing.

"Cute," Carlo says, "but not little, not *too* little. Not little everywhere."

"I think we should invite her to join us, yes?"

I wish that Pam would disappear. I wish that I could disappear. *There is in my soul a chamber.*

"*Bionda*," Carlo sings in her direction. "*Biondiiina...*"

"Carlo..." Luca begins.

"What? I'm only friendly."

"*Sì*," Gianni says, turning to Luca now, "we are only saying the blonde looks good."

"Yes," Carlo agrees, nodding. "And maybe she—"

"Carlo, *scusa*," Luca says sharply, glancing at me.

Carlo shrugs.

"You know the Americans, Hannah?" Sergio asks quietly.

"A little bit. Not really," I lie.

"*Allora. La bionda*, you know her?" Carlo asks.

All eyes on me.

"Pam."

"*Sì*, Pam, Pam," Carlo echoes. "Of course."

"And the boy?" Sergio asks quickly.

"Peter."

"He's very young, very handsome, Luca," Carlo says slowly and pointedly. "*Fai attenzione.*"

Luca no longer seems to mind their game. He turns to me with a grin and asks, "Should I be jealous?"

It feels like an old childhood game—Truth or Dare, and either one would land you in hot water. I always wondered why Flee wasn't an option. Truth or Dare or Flee. There is no right answer.

"Maybe," I say finally, igniting cheers from the others.

"*No!*" Luca feigns shock, placing his hand on his heart as the men's laughter circles him, and I feel like there is some other woman in my place, sitting beside this man and laughing along with his friends. She is the woman who flirts with a man she doesn't know very well in another country, and even though she does not know him very well, she still wants to please him and appease his friends. I'm afraid, though, that she might also be the woman who props herself up against this man, abandoning everything else, and begins to mold to him, adjusting to his temperature, adapting to his desires, bending into the woman who is maybe not the one he asked for but is certainly the one she thinks he asked for, until she is gone entirely and there is only him and the stranger beside him. I'm not sure which woman I am, but as I watch Luca consumed by his friends' mockery, I know that I want to shoo their laughter away from him. I can protect, too.

"He is very handsome," I continue, "but..."

"*Però?*" Luca raises his eyebrows and puts his hands up in the air. "*Silenzio, ragazzi, silenzio,*" before turning to me expectantly, his smile still wide but his eyes serious, as I'd seen them a few evenings before.

"Continue," he says, his hands still up. "He is very handsome, but..."

"But way too young," I say, "and also not as handsome as you," which ushers in skeptical groans from everyone except for Luca, who gathers my hands in his and gives me a kiss before turning to the men.

"You see?" he says. "*Allora, basta. Un aperitivo, no?*"

At exactly four thirty, following the bells of the Duomo, drumming begins in the distance and all the men rise. The *carabinieri* shepherd people away from the piazza's center to create a path to the cathedral as the drumming grows louder. Luca takes my hand and pulls me closer to the sound. Parading up the street are people in medieval garb. A hush falls over the crowd until there is only the rhythmic beating of the drums.

"The procession of the Republic," Luca says.

The parade snakes slowly into the piazza and trumpets join in. Luca nudges me and points to four men who look like politicians, each one wearing a dark suit with a distinct, brightly colored sash—white, blue, green, and red—across his chest. "The color"—he draws his hand across his own chest—"is for the area: Santa Croce, Santo Spirito, Santa Maria Novella, San Giovanni." The four quarters of the city, the four major churches. One of the men holds a garland woven with ribbon. "The *bravio*," Luca explains. "The prize for the *calcio storico*. A kind of football match."

"There's a game today?"

"No, no," Luca says. "It happened already. In the summer."

After the politicians there is a gap in the procession, and then cloth flutters in the wind as flag throwers step into the piazza. The fabric spins in different formations like brightly colored birds. The drums grow louder. Around me, everyone is speaking English.

"What is it for?"

"It sounds like a dirge."

"It must be for a visiting cardinal."

"A random Saturday in Florence. Who knew?"

Even on this day that honors her, Santa Reparata is invisible. The malleability of history, the ease with which she has been erased, is chilling. The crowd erupts into cheers and whistles as men in medieval uniforms appear behind the flag throwers. They are all young with strikingly muscular legs and sober expressions. Four rows of five. Twenty solemn faces.

"*Eccolo* Enzo," Luca says. "With the flag for Santa Croce. Last summer, it was Santa Croce that won the *calcio storico*—Enzo plays for Santa Croce."

"Very serious," Carlo whispers, imitating Enzo's stone expression.

"*Sì*," Gianni says, and laughs. "Very different from last Friday."

"Enzo!" Carlo shouts, but their friend keeps his eyes on the flag he's carrying. Behind the athletes are men and women in period dress. At the end of the line, four children decked in the colors of each quarter play small drums. When the last child has disappeared into the Duomo, the *carabinieri* form a half-moon around the entrance.

"And now," Luca says, "we wait *perché* they must give a blessing to the *bravio*."

The sounds in the piazza return to full volume and we return to our table in the café.

"Francesca and Marco," Gianni says.

Francesca and an older Italian man are stopped in front of the baptistery. They are speaking quickly with a flurry of gestures.

"*Attenta*. Trouble," Gianni says, setting off another wave of commentary.

"Where there is Francesca, there is always trouble."

"Where there is trouble, there is always Francesca."

"She *is* Milanese."

"If she was my wife—"

"Maybe Marco doesn't know."

"You think? He's a smart guy."

"Yes, but remember last year—at the regatta."

"True, true. They weren't fighting then."

"But, Sergio, one time—what does that mean? We never see him. At the game, for example."

"The regatta? Wasn't that the time Nicoletti showed up?"

"Yes, the idiot. Like coming to one race would fool us into voting for that buffoon."

As they talk, Peter and Pam reappear around the side of the cathedral. I glance at the men, but they have moved on from their dissection of Francesca and don't see as Peter almost collides with her. Francesca's intense frown shifts to a look of surprise and then—so quickly that it is almost imperceptible—fear, before she recomposes herself. She is calm, glowing. If her husband has registered anything, he doesn't act like it, though Peter's enthusiasm is glaring. Maybe the men are right and Francesca does what she wants. And so what if she does? Her husband points in our direction and they turn to us. Peter squints and I give a half-wave. Then Francesca says something to the group that makes them all laugh before she and Marco split off. It is only when they're almost upon us, the sun edging their silhouettes in gold, that Luca and his friends look up. Francesca's face is impenetrable as she greets them and presents her husband to me.

"Marco, you remember the American I told you about—Hannah."

He grips my hand tightly. His irises—deep blue—are rare in this city of dark eyes. He holds my hand and my gaze for a second too long, and in that second, there is no one else at the table. I am certain, in fact, that we are the only two people in the piazza.

"Nice to meet you," he says. "I'm glad Francesca has another woman at the club."

His mouth turns up at the corners, and I cannot tell if he's making a joke. He is all charm and I can see how Francesca would have fallen for him. How anyone might.

"So you got dragged along, too?" are her first words once she's seated next to me. Marco has pulled up another table and sits by Carlo, leaving the women to themselves. "It's all ridiculous, if you ask me. Do you see any other Italians here? But Enzo is marching, so here we are. *Scusami*—Marco, *un bicchiere di vino, per favore.*"

Marco nods but continues talking. Francesca sighs and rolls her eyes.

"Do you know anything about her? Santa Reparata?" I ask.

"She was an old saint—before all of this." She waves her arms around at everything in the square before turning to the men. "Santa Reparata?"

"She was the patron saint of Florence," Gianni says.

"Why?" I ask. "What did she do?"

"She was burned alive," Gianni says.

"*Sì*," Sergio agrees, his forehead wrinkled. "*O forse è stata decapitata.*"

"Decapitated?" I ask.

"*Ma dai, ragazzi,*" Luca exclaims. "You make things up!"

"She defended Florence from barbarians," Carlo interrupts.

"Well, this city's still full of them if you ask me," Francesca says.

The waiter arrives and Francesca orders a wine and then digs around in her bag, producing lipstick.

"Honestly, I can't keep up with all these saints," she says after blotting her lips. "Everywhere you turn, it's another one. It's too much. Will you still be here at Christmas?"

"I'm not sure." Christmas is over two months away. Will I be here? I have no idea.

"If you are, you'll get to see the craziest thing—the Display of the Virgin's Girdle."

"Her girdle?"

"Yeah, like her belt. Apparently, she dropped it as she was ascending. And it made its way to Prato, of all places."

Prato is one town over, Florence's "little sister."

"You can't make this stuff up," Francesca continues. "Anyway, a few times a year you can have an audience with the girdle. Hey, Luca." She reaches across me and grabs his wrist.

"*Sì?*"

"You're a good Catholic, right?"

"*No,*" he says.

"But you know the story of the virgin's girdle? *La cintola?*"

"*Certo.* She gave it to Santo Tommaso," he explains, speaking slowly to include me. "Because he did not believe she was the mother of God."

"Doubting Thomas," I say.

"*Sì.* She gave him *la cintola* from Heaven—as proof."

"Thank god for hard evidence," Francesca says.

Here Marco jumps in, his voice cutting the air, clear and resonant. Like Francesca, his English is flawless. "No, it's about faith. The belt was around the womb—the immaculate conception. It is the beginning of all belief. St. Thomas doubted, but the belt was a gift of faith, not 'evidence.'" Whatever our beliefs, Marco has a way of speaking that makes you want to listen, want to believe, or at least want to believe in him.

"Glorified pornography, if you ask me," Francesca says. "And why does Prato have it?"

They shrug.

"Why not?" Carlo asks, before drawing the men back into discussion.

"*My* question," Francesca says to me, "is why all the men are running things in this country if they think women are so important. Nothing changes, does it? They can tell you what to believe, but it's just that. A lot of talk."

The waiter returns with their drinks and Francesca raises her glass to Marco, who doesn't acknowledge it. "See what I mean?"

I want to ask Francesca about how she and Marco met, but there is a commotion by the cathedral as the bells ring five o'clock and the sound of a drum announces the return of the procession, the prize now blessed.

"*Allora, finalmente!*" Francesca says.

The *carabinieri* clear a path and the drummers emerge, followed by the rest of the participants. We all stand as they wind through the piazza and around the baptistery.

"*Vai, Enzo! Vai! Vai!*" the men shout when he passes, and a small grin creeps onto his stone face. The parade moves out of the piazza, taking with it some of the spectators. Luca tells me they will do a loop through all the major squares, drumming and singing.

"And then?" I ask.

"And then nothing." He smiles. "Then the festival is done. But we stay for a bit to take something to eat and to see Enzo maybe, *va bene?*"

We stay until the square grows dark. Portions of the crowd disperse while others set up camp on the cathedral steps or squeeze into the few open spots in the cafés. At our table, the men order pasta.

"Francesca, what do you want?" Marco asks.

"Nothing," Francesca says, pulling out a cigarette. "Another wine."

"*Va bene.*" Marco shrugs, then says to Carlo, "She is a bird."

"We'll all have wine," Gianni announces, ordering a bottle.

When the waiter looks to me, I order a salad.

"Another bird!" Marco cries.

But Luca puts his hand on mine and says, "Hannah can share with me. I'm not very hungry."

"For the first time!" Carlo says.

When the pasta arrives, I reach my fork over and have a few bites. Luca doesn't look at me, but he puts his hand on my back for a moment, smiling. With the wine, the conversation begins to swell, more animated but less focused. It swings from politics to rowing to the football season and the scandal the Fiorentina are involved in—*will they or won't they be viable this year?* and an argument erupts as Sergio disappears inside to check the score of the game—to the upcoming Florence marathon to Marco's trip to Geneva to the conference on Calvino to ranking the best Italian authors, operas, actresses—here another disagreement ensues, with Carlo's argument resting mainly on breast size—and then on to restaurants and what Marco claims is the *only* place in the city for pheasant, though Sergio counters and Gianni negates them both in favor of a small trattoria outside of Florence. Luca says we'll try them all.

Francesca is silent through most of it, quieter than she ever is at the club. She throws in a comment here and there or feeds me asides, but she mostly watches Marco. I watch Marco, too. When he is in the conversation, he is utterly focused on the speaker, and when he's the speaker, no one interrupts. When he pulls away, he watches the square, his eyes catching on any woman who passes before he brings his gaze back to the table.

After the meal, Francesca excuses herself to call her daughter and disappears. Carlo's eyebrows shoot up, but no one says anything or asks about her daughter when she returns twenty minutes later.

"*Andiamo,*" she says to Marco.

"You're leaving?" Sergio asks.

"Francesca, *tranquilla,*" Marco says. "We'll finish eating and wait for Enzo to come."

"*Sono tranquilla.* I'm going. I'm tired. Do you have the keys?"

There is silence at the table. Marco holds Francesca's gaze. Then he reaches into his pocket and pulls out the keys, dangling them in front of her.

"So go," he says. "Carlo can drive me."

Francesca looks almost pained, but her face hardens and she takes the keys, and with a "*Grazie. Ciao a tutti,*" she's off into the night and I am, again, the only woman at the table. A lull settles over the group. The men stick to safe topics now and the conversation doesn't regain its previous pace or energy. Sergio checks the game and returns to announce that Florence has just lost.

"Again, Milan." He sighs, throwing down money.

"At least Francesca will be happy," Marco says, his tone unreadable.

Luca yawns and turns to me: "*Andiamo?*"

I nod, and he stands and announces our departure.

"When you see Enzo," Luca says, "tell him we celebrate Monday at the club."

The men rise, all formality again, to kiss me on each cheek.

"You should join us for dinner one evening," Marco says, before releasing my hands. "Francesca would like it." Then, glancing at Luca, he adds, "*Tutti e due.*" Both of you.

Luca has parked near my house, so we walk back together. As soon as we're alone, I realize that I'm exhausted—from the wine, from keeping up with the conversation, from having my defenses up for hours. I link my arm through his and listen to the echo of our feet on the empty street and the soft swishing of Luca's jacket.

"I'm sorry," Luca says, "that it was not only for us."

"It's okay. They're your friends."

"*Sì.* Sergio and Gianni—always. Marco? He is hard to know, I think. Carlo—yes, but different. I am sorry for Carlo. He is sometimes strange now. Angry and also embarrassed."

"Because of the divorce?"

"*Sì.* But Carlo always has trouble with women."

"Women don't like him?"

"No. He likes too many women, *hai capito?*"

"He sleeps around."

"*Come si dice?* 'Sleep around'?"

"Exactly. So his wife asked for a divorce?"

"No, Carlo wanted it. She did not."

"She didn't know about the affairs?"

"Yes. But also she was with another man. And Carlo discovered it—and then he wanted the divorce."

"You're kidding."

"*Cosa?*"

"He was okay with having affairs, but as soon as she does, it's a problem?"

Luca shrugs. "It's different."

"Why? How is it any different?"

"I don't know."

"Do you think it's different?"

"*Non lo so.* A couple is two people. Not one. You cannot just point at one. I would not be happy if my wife—*come si dice?* 'Sleep around'?" I nod.

"But also I would not 'sleep around,'" Luca says matter-of-factly. "*Allora*, I feel sad for them. For both of them. It is shame." I don't know if he means *a shame* or *shameful*.

We step into Piazza della Signoria, almost empty except for couples who, like us, are walking slowly, delaying the evening's end. Luca points to where people have gathered around a vendor selling glowing tops. When wound, the tops spring high into the air, spinning disks of light. The crowd watches, heads thrown back with an "ooohh." The vendor keeps sending them up as we approach, and as he launches another one, I let go, too, imagine that I grab hold and the orb pulls me up and up until we are one form, a distant glowing circle against the sky. I feel light but still here, and I slide my arm around Luca's back as we watch in silence.

"Do you want to come over for a bit?" I ask when we arrive at my building.

"To see where this famous woman lives?" Luca grins. "*Ma certo.*"

"Okay," I say, pushing open the heavy door, clicking on the hall light, and taking my first visitor by the hand.

As always, the door on the landing creeps open and the bleached head pops out. She glares at Luca, but he bows deeply and says with great deference, "*Buonasera, signora*," and for the first time, Signora Rosa smiles. She nods, pleased, before shutting her door.

"What kind of magician are you?" I whisper.

Luca keeps up his act when we enter my apartment, surveying the space soberly. "Okay," he says, nodding with exaggerated interest, and I follow him down the hall and into the living room. "Nice, not bad, not bad. Good windows. So this is where you are all these days?"

He stops and smiles before bounding up the steps to the kitchen. He spots the wine bottle on the counter and raises his eyebrows. "*Posso?*"

"Of course," I say, digging out the corkscrew for him.

He pours us each a small glass, then opens the doors to the balcony with a "Wow-wah. Very good, *sì*."

He points down at the old woman, still at her window. "You know her?"

"No!" I whisper, grabbing his arm. "Come back inside."

A phone rings and the woman looks up. It's my phone.

Luca raises his eyebrows again. "Another friend?"

"One minute." I head to the bedroom as the shrill sound continues. It could only be my sister at this hour. Why? I already wrote her about my job. I watch it ring two, three, four more times, and then lift the receiver and place it back down. I don't want her here. Not now. I take a few sips of wine, count to ten, and then walk back to the living room.

Luca is standing by the window, looking out at my favorite view. "*Che bello*," he says.

"It is." I stand beside him and he puts his arm around me without speaking.

I look at the tower of the Palazzo Vecchio, now lit gold from below, and think about the many mornings I've stood alone watching this city gathering light. *There is in my soul a chamber*. But it's not right. It can't be right that I must always be alone. And so I put my arms around Luca, his body already growing familiar, and begin kissing him. He pulls me closer, his hands running under my shirt and around my back, and I think about that other woman, the one who disappears into the man beside her. But this doesn't feel like disappearing. It feels like not being alone. And then I stop thinking, and just feel his hands and lips, and feel my own body waking up, returning as though from a long absence. And it's true. A part of me has been absent for months.

"Do you want to stay?" I ask, surprising myself.

Luca is surprised, too. "Do you want me to?"

"*Sì.*" But I hesitate.

"*Sicura?*"

"I do," I say, trying to sound certain, wanting to remain with him, wanting to remain in myself. And still the doubts creep in. Because if Luca stays, then he might see me, really see me. See the broken scale, my many lists, the controlled details of my controlled existence. See in my violent tossing and turning my violent dreams. And see the body I haven't looked at for months.

"Don't worry," Luca says, squeezing my hands. "I would like to stay, but maybe not this night, okay?"

I nod, feeling both relieved and foolish.

"I think maybe it should be," he continues, "*non lo so*—we can have a nice dinner or something, *no*? You think I'm crazy?"

"No, I just think maybe you're not Italian."

"But I am not Italian. I am Florentine."

I can't tell if he's joking. "So you're a *real* Italian, the *best* Italian."

Luca drains his glass, then pulls me in with a smile. "The best Italian? *No.* Not better. Different. *A Roma, a Napoli, in Sicilia*—in truth, people are different."

"Don't you think that's a bit of a stereotype?"

He looks down at me, considering this. "Maybe, but—" He stops himself. "*No.* I think really we are different."

"I don't believe it. People are not only where they're from."

"But"—Luca puts a finger up—"in this way, you think all Italians—all the men—are the same. All wolves, *no*?"

Touché. "Only some of them."

"*Va bene.*" He smiles and kisses me quickly and definitively before setting down his glass. "And now it is time for this very *gentle*, very kind Fiorentino to go home. Because you will make him crazy now if you continue to kiss him." He offers me his hand and I take it, keeping hold as we walk to the door. "Thank you for this grand tour. If you want, I will make a dinner, *va bene*? The week is very busy, but Friday is okay? We meet at the club and then we go to my house. I will cook."

"What about Carlo?" I ask suddenly.

"Carlo? What Carlo? I'm not cooking for him."

"*Sì*, Carlo. He's a wolf. A Florentine wolf. What about him?"

"*Esatto!*" Luca is laughing now. "Carlo is not Florentine. Where Carlo comes from, the men are wolves, *hai capito*?"

"That's ridiculous."

"But it's true." He wraps his arms around me, still laughing, and the sound reverberates deep through his body and shakes mine until I'm laughing as well. "*Da dove viene lui,*" Luca says, catching his breath, "*ci sono più lupi che stelle.*"

Where he comes from, there are more wolves than stars.

Chapter Thirteen

Lorenza leaves for Milan—"Estate business," she says with determination—and I work full days and don't go to the club in the afternoons. I won't see Luca until Friday, and so it is a solitary week.

I spend my evenings with the mystics. As soon as I start reading about them, I cannot stop. I am hungry for words. On the surface, they are all very different. They lived centuries apart in different regions of Italy and came from different social classes. They joined different religious orders—Dominican, Franciscan, Carmelite—or founded new ones. St. Clare of Assisi was born into wealth but gave up material goods for the ascetic life of the Franciscans, then created her own order, the Poor Clares. St. Margaret of Cortona, born decades later, was impoverished and followed a path of sin until her conversion. They had disparate methods for practicing their faith, for proving their devotion. St. Agnes multiplied loaves of bread for the poor. St. Margaret could detect the difference between consecrated and unconsecrated hosts. The evidence of Clare of Montefalco's sainthood came after her death, when her Augustinian sisters opened her corpse to find carefully arranged in her heart the crucifix, whip, and crown of thorns.

They were virgins or widows or devoted wives who never left home. St. Catherine of Genoa was a model "holy housewife." Trapped in an abusive marriage, she never entered the convent. She served the sick during the plague without falling ill herself. They were political figures, like St. Catherine of Siena and the Blessed Lucia of Narni, famous for her political prophecies; and they were recluses, like Maria Maddalena de' Pazzi, the Florentine mystic whose church I had visited weeks earlier—intensely private, she had visions that left her bedridden.

They were pure, precocious naïfs and hardened, penitent sinners. They were from Tuscany and Umbria and Emilia-Romagna. They were rich and poor and everything in between. It is as though any woman, whether born in the 1200s in Cortona to peasants or the 1500s in Florence to nobility, had the potential to cross that elusive threshold. As though that first apparition of the cross or God or Satan was there waiting for whoever might stumble upon it—Catherine in Siena or Angela in Foligno or Clare in Montefalco. *This is where it starts.* But there is no consistent starting point, no predictor, as these women, one after another, fell into sainthood.

There is something alluring about their behavior—Margaret cutting down to the bone when flagellating herself, Angela drinking from the sores of lepers, Maria Maddalena licking the wounds of her ailing Carmelite sisters and punishing her own body with burning and icy water—and I'm not disgusted but curious. As with St. Angela, there is a longing, an intense desire that simmers and ultimately explodes into feverish visions, and I witness, again and again, them straining away from a world that can no longer sate them. Life is torture, existence a punishment—

Living, I seem to die in pain—St. Catherine of Siena.

I wish to die a thousand times a day—St. Margaret of Cortona.

The visions provide the only relief and they are addictive—once they begin, the single, consuming desire of these women is to lose themselves in ecstasy. I don't want their isolation, don't want to be always alone with my silent mornings, don't want to flee this life that I am, little by little, constructing. I'm looking forward to seeing Luca, to rowing on the river, to letting go of some of the rituals, the counting, the precise and precarious balance that has dictated my life for so many months. But still there is something magnetic about the saints.

The eyes of my soul were opened.

Outside of my body.

Wholly true. Wholly certain. Wholly celestial.

When St. Angela describes arriving at ecstasy—her soul separating from her body and revealing truth—her words echo St. Clare's and anticipate St. Maria Maddalena's. *I have reached the summit of perfection. I comprehend the whole world.* There is such confidence—confidence in an absolute truth and one's place within that truth, even when confronted with doubt, with a confessor or sister who might say, with suspicion, *She did not seem to be the same person,* and I wonder again how this is possible, that you can be so sure of your clarity of sight and self even as people tell you that you are blind, crazed, a stranger.

This isn't you.

Where are you?

Look at you.

As their actions become more extreme, they're accused of being sick. But they don't try to appear normal and do not trust those people who attempt to change their habits. *Priests cannot preach it,* Angela says. *They do not understand what they preach. They babble.* And, in truth, their behavior must have been celebrated—what is recorded is not evidence of illness but proof of saintliness.

Stop watching me, I'd said to my sister. But I was asking for witnesses all the time. Was it just about the audience? *How do you cut so close to the bone?* They were a part of it at the beginning, before it became something else. Something with teeth in it.

When I stopped eating, I didn't have any of the illuminations, understandings, or visions that the mystics describe; I didn't feel a connection to God. But I had something not altogether different, something that I didn't want anyone to see because it was mine alone, and that I didn't want to talk about because I didn't have the words to describe it. *I know more, I see more; you don't know, you don't see.* You just had to *know* it, and they couldn't possibly know it. *This vision is not tangible or imaginable,* St. Angela writes, *but something ineffable.*

While not every saint was celebrated in her lifetime, each woman who entered that celebrated state—Catherine or Clare or Margaret—inevitably gained followers, cults and convents springing up in her wake as women, young and old, flooded the cloistered communities or practiced in the clandestine privacy of their own homes, in Genoa or Mantua or Perugia, the miraculous behaviors and rituals for which the mystic had become known. Few might ultimately wear the mantle of saint, but there were hundreds trying to inhabit that sacred space, and so the rituals, behaviors, and practices—from Angela in the thirteenth century to Maria Maddalena in the sixteenth century—gained traction and spread, fast as an epidemic.

All week the saints circle my thoughts, informing my memories and insinuating themselves into my dreams. In the evenings, I row, but I don't see anyone I know, and without the reality of conversation, there are only their voices. Even when Luca calls one night, I have trouble connecting—his voice sounds far away and my own, unfamiliar, and I remember that feeling of disappearing, when all other voices became distant until there was only one voice, urging me forward, prodding me on.

And then there are the reminders. They are everywhere in Florence. In the streets named for these women, in the bells that ring continually on the hour and half hour, in anything that catches my eye and drags my gaze up. In the mornings, I take a longer route to pass the church where Maria Maddalena de' Pazzi practiced. The tall gates of the adjoining convent are closed as always, and I stop to look up at its walls. It was here, in this place, that she starved herself to death. And she was not alone. Fragmented references to food appear throughout the accounts, tossed off casually as a part of the denial of earthly things, riches and sustenance given equal weight. *We must fast every day except Sundays,* St. Clare says when establishing her order. *My delights have heretofore been bodily and vile, because I am a body*—St. Angela. And always the gap between the denial of food and the experience of ecstasy. Some confessors suggest that meals simply slipped their minds. *She forgot to eat and drink, as if her spirit did not exist in her corporeal body.* That phrase again: *I forgot to eat.* But there is more to it. Their fasting is not weak or forgetful—it is an all-out war. *Let the tongue of the flesh be silent when I seek to express my love for you,* St. Clare cries in a moment of ecstasy. *Strip yourself of self,* St. Catherine demands. *Do not ask me to give in to this body of mine,* St. Margaret pleads when urged to eat. *Between me and my body there must be a struggle until death.*

Of all the mystics living in Italy in the Middle Ages and the Renaissance, most denied themselves food, and many spent portions of their lives bedridden and died of the complications of malnourishment. Only Catherine of Genoa avoided extreme fasting, and she became famous for her insatiable appetite.

My rituals. What I ate, when I ate, counting and categorizing, teasing apart a plate to pull out the acceptable bits, returning to one of the many bathrooms when they became unacceptable. I built my day around these rituals, cut loose any plans that interfered. By June, I no longer accepted invitations to meals, but soon anything in the evening was out because I grew exhausted immediately, could not hold my wine, could not hold my attention, could not keep defending myself—*I forgot to eat*—against questions and suggestions.

I was seeing, still, this doctor. Handing over my journal with its too-spare lists, knowing she would say, *You can't forget.* So I edited, padded the entries with items that I surely *would* have eaten if I hadn't forgotten to eat. In this way, I believed that the account was honest.

Still she said, "It isn't enough." Over her shoulder, the parade of healed girls smiled at me as she prescribed one can a day of liquid supplement, a sweet, viscous substance that tasted of metal when I took it as a single shot, pouring it into my throat without thinking, wanting to gag it back up but keeping it down. She congratulated me on this, on keeping it down, as though it were a triumph. It wasn't a triumph. It was a defeat. It forced a crack in the balance; it threatened to topple the whole.

"It's good," she said.

I didn't trust her. I didn't trust her or her vats of liquid or her waiting room filled with younger women who had nothing to do with me. She was trying to bury me with her labels, to trap me with her words. But she was speaking the wrong language. In the end, all she did was disrupt my rituals—counting and categorizing, dividing the day into consumption and expulsion, dividing my body into parts I could look at. These were the things she didn't understand. This was where I put my faith.

By July, I'd stopped seeing this doctor. I collected my severance. I made my own plan. I left her behind with everyone else.

"*Scusami*, Hannah." Friday morning. I'm on the phone with Luca, who is canceling our plans. Because I've been so distant? But he says, "I must go to Arezzo, to visit my father. He is not well."

"Will he be all right?"

"*Sì, sì*," he says, but he doesn't sound certain and he continues speaking quickly. "*Allora*, I return tomorrow. I meet you at the *canottieri*? *Scusami ancora*, Hannah."

I nod into the phone before I say, "Of course. It's no problem," because it isn't his fault that I have no one else, and I realize how dependent I was on seeing him now that I can't. I call Peter but there's no answer, so I leave a message inviting him to join me at Piazzale Michelangelo this evening. "And Pam as well," I add.

The day passes slowly. The sun is out and only two people, one in the morning and one in the afternoon, visit the library. I've finished the work Lorenza left for me, so I'm reading St. Angela's letters, which are filled with love, the eroticism of her language so common to these women. *The Word entered into me and touched me throughout and embraced me, saying, "Come, my love, my bride."* In one of the oddest visions, she is in a sepulcher with Christ. She kisses him, places her cheek on his. *He, in turn, placed his hand on her other cheek, pressing her closely to him.* I close my eyes, try to understand the comfort that such a morbid image could provide. It makes me feel my solitude more acutely. No word from Peter. Luca gone. I slip the book into my bag and decide to make an evening of it on my own.

I'm planning on going to the *canottieri* but it begins to drizzle. It isn't the right weather, either, for Piazzale Michelangelo, set up on a hill. But maybe the rain will let up in time for sunset. I stop at a bar in the meantime, where I drink a glass of wine and continue to read about Angela's experience with love, which is inseparable from suffering. *Love took the form of a sickle.* But her suffering is not bodily. It is the pain of stretching away from the earth and from herself to arrive at that moment of ecstasy, which, once experienced, produces its own pain—the anguish of leaving that heightened state, of returning to the earth, to the body. Then the pain of having known that pleasure and living perpetually in its echo. *I am continually in this state.* But that isn't right. To be always in that state is the wish—the reality is something other, something that leaves her wanting. *She was filled with love and inestimable satiety, which, although it satiated, generated at the same time inestimable hunger.*

I watch as the rain grows lighter and lighter, until it is only a mist and people return to the street. It is Friday evening and I am alone, but now I don't let the melancholy take hold. I finish my wine and then walk along the river for a ways, the storefronts becoming residential and the street growing quieter, until I reach the steeply ramped steps that curl up to the overlook that is Piazzale Michelangelo. As I climb, I pause at each level and watch the city grow smaller, farther away, comprehensible.

When I make it to the top, it is almost sunset and the piazza is full. The romance has not been lost on the visitors or the locals, who line the perimeter to look out over the city. There is an openair café that I know will be overpriced, but I sit down at one of the small tables. The waitress arrives immediately to wipe away the remaining raindrops. I order a wine—and why not?—and then watch as the sun sinks and couples frantically pose and re-pose for the kind stranger to whom they have handed their camera, hoping to capture, really capture, the light of this moment, the reality of their love. I look down at the city, where the forms of the buildings fade until it is too dark to make out the disparate colors but too bright for the lights to break through. One of the people by the wall looks like Luca in profile and my heart catches. It isn't him, but once I think it, I imagine him everywhere in this city with another woman—maybe the one who had broken his heart before, now returned—the convenient excuse of a sick father keeping me oblivious. I remember then his description of his ex's irrational jealousy. Is that the type of woman he attracts? Is that the type of woman I am? *There is nothing in the world that I hold as suspect as love,* St. Angela said, *for it penetrates the soul more than any other thing,* and as another passing figure becomes Luca, I begin to suspect love as well, or at least my decision to open myself up to anything like it.

I order another drink, but when it arrives, it looks daunting. What was I thinking? I'll just finish this drink slowly, very slowly, and then go. I pull the candle closer, returning to St. Angela's experience with love, which is really a continuous cycle of elation and pain that leaves her entirely full or entirely empty, and when she is empty, her only desire is to suffer enough to return to that place of satiation. *I will leave you in such great love of Me,* she is told by God, *that your soul will always burn with it.* It echoes and echoes and echoes. *He withdrew so very gently and so very gradually. I lost then that Love that I bore in myself.*

"Hannah, you're freezing," Julian said our last night together. The radiator clanked and clanked as though there were a small drummer boy at the heart of it. We were on the cusp of May, but it felt like winter, as it always did to me then. I kept trying to wind the covers around us, to lower the goose bumps that covered my body, to warm my legs, my arms, my lips, my heart, which felt full but also numb, too tender then, like my nerves, too raw.

Even as Julian pulled me into him and I could feel the heat coming off him, I felt cold, unable to absorb, even, his physical warmth. We touched and kissed, and I tried to stay with him, but my mind kept drifting.

"Where are you?" Julian asked, because he could tell.

Still I kept returning to my ever-growing list—everything I'd eaten, which was more today in an attempt to keep myself from unraveling—to Julian's bathroom, which was just off his bedroom, too close, and so I would remain heavy tonight. I tried to stay with him. I could see him seeing me, could see him touching me, and when I looked down at my new valleys, I felt surprised, happily so. I took it in as someone might a painting, before I was drawn back to the heaviness in me, and then to that other being always with me now.

"Where are you, Hannah?" he asked again, and I grew more aggressive to compensate, kissed with force, moved with force on top of him, as if to say, *I'm here, I'm here, I'm here,* willing it to hurt just to feel—I never orgasmed anymore, my body refused, and I felt empty even as I moved violently so that he might feel my pain until he cried out into the darkness.

I could not imagine a death vile enough to match my desire, St. Angela writes. But it wasn't Julian that filled me and emptied me. It was that other thing that I clutched close. I loved it and it hurt me. Both were true. But had I loved it because it hurt me? I don't know. But I understand the profound joy and loss in Angela's plea: *Who would not be set afire with such love? What heart could keep from breaking?*

It is almost dark when I hear my name. I look up through the fog of alcohol to find Peter crossing the piazza, his light coat bright and bleeding into the air around him.

"I just got your message," he says, taking a seat. "This is nice. Romantic."

Again the waitress appears immediately.

"*Whisky con ghiaccio,*" Peter says quickly. He looks different, hardened, as though there are more edges to him—in his face, in his voice—and his eyes shift side to side.

"I'm glad you came," I say, once we're alone.

It takes Peter a moment to process this and I wonder if he's heard me at all. "Oh, yeah."

I ask him about his classes and he shrugs. So I tell him about the reading that I've been doing, describing in some detail the history of the mystics, their language, things that would normally interest him, and it feels good to be sharing them with someone, especially him, but he doesn't pick up any of the threads, just swirls his drink and lets me speak, his eyes still shifting, shuffling down the figures on the wall, and I wonder if he's looking for someone, too. Below us, Florence is blazing now, a sea of lights swimming around towers and domes, the Palazzo Vecchio a great ship sailing toward the Arno. Peter looks down to the lit city, up to the lit sky, before interrupting me.

"Have you spoken with Francesca at all?" he asks, having waited what must have seemed the appropriate amount of time. He's on a mission. It is the reason he has come to meet me.

"At the festival last weekend—you were there, remember?"

"Oh, right, so you met *him* then, too."

"Marco? Yes."

Peter almost visibly flinches at the name. "He's arrogant, don't you think? He completely ignores her. How could anyone ignore her?" He pauses, perhaps waiting for validation.

"I don't know, Peter," I sigh. I think I see Luca again, this time in the figure of a man in the distance who becomes a woman when she passes our table.

"It's messed up. Why would she marry someone like that? God, it drives me crazy."

"Neither of them seems happy." I pause. "But we don't know the whole story. We don't know anything."

"Well, I *know* he's a prick." His voice is too loud, the word doesn't belong to him, and his face twists up like a small child's, rage rooted in disappointment. "And if you heard what Francesca had to say about him, Hannah, you wouldn't be defending him. Trust me."

"I don't doubt it."

But he keeps going, laying out the charges against Marco, one after another. Then he moves on to Francesca's in-laws, their friends, the men at the club, everyone who has wronged her, ignored her, misunderstood her—and who am I to say they haven't? He could be right. Of course he could be. I've heard the men at the club; I understand the problems of being a woman here—up on a pedestal one moment, up on a stake the next. Peter could be right about all of it. And still it wouldn't change the fact that he's coming apart in front of me. I keep nodding, waiting for a break in the stream of spite. I remember my meal with Claudia so many months ago. *You have a problem.* I put my hand on Peter's—he tenses but lets it rest there.

"I'm not defending him," I say, trying to bring us back to center, to this table, to this night, which is suddenly and speedily unraveling. The alcohol is wearing off, my head is clearing, and, for a moment, I think that I can do it, can pull him out of the clotted sludge, can balance us both. "All I meant is that we don't know the whole story."

Peter pulls his hand away. "She's right," he says pointedly. "You can't trust Italian men. *You* should be careful."

"What are you talking about?"

"Aren't you dating one of the guys?"

"Who told you that?" I'm angry, even as I can feel myself taking his warning to heart.

"Francesca said—"

"Francesca doesn't know anything about me," I say sharply, and Peter seems to see me for the first time since he sat down. He remains silent.

I drop my voice. "I'm sorry, but she doesn't. She's an unhappy woman in an unhappy marriage. I'm not surprised that she doesn't trust anyone but that doesn't have anything to do with me. I'm sorry I snapped at you—I don't like being talked about."

"You really think her marriage is unhappy?" He's heard nothing else.

"Yes, I think she's unhappy. And I feel badly for her. But I'm not sure anyone is in a position to fix it," I say. "The night of the festival, when you saw her?"

He nods, leaning in so as not to miss a word, looking in his eagerness so young again.

"She disappeared for a long time and then she left dramatically. It was strange. And, yes, I think Marco could be more attentive, but there's more to it, Peter. She was making a statement. She practically announced that she was going to see someone else. You, I assume."

Peter looks confused, so I add, "She said she was going home to her daughter, though. I'm sure she was only making a point."

"She won't talk to me," he says then. "But that's typical, right? I mean of someone in an abusive relationship. She can't help it." He drains his drink in a gulp and sets down the glass hard enough that the couple at the next table looks over.

"I'm so sorry, Peter."

"Whatever. It doesn't matter. She might seem unhappy to everyone else, but she's not unhappy with me. She'll realize that."

"She's married. Anything outside of that—she's only trying to survive."

"You don't believe she's happy with me? Well, she is."

"She has a child. She has a husband. You can't change that."

"You don't understand." Peter gets up, shaking his head. "You don't understand her at all. You don't understand anything." He fishes money out of his wallet, then looks back down at me with disgust. I can't do either of the things that would help him. I can't deliver Francesca to Peter and I can't bring Peter back to himself.

"I'm sorry."

"What kind of person are you, anyway?" His words hit hard, and there are many eyes on us now. "You would leave her for dead because she's married? Just because she made some bad decisions?" He puts money down on the table, shaking his head again. "Congratulations on the job. Good luck."

And then he's gone, disappeared into the darkness of the piazza, and I am, again, alone. What kind of person am I? I don't believe that we have to resign ourselves to our bad decisions. I do believe that we can grow. But I also know that Peter isn't seeing the situation for what it is. The waitress returns to ask if everything is all right, and I can hear whispering at the other tables. Let them whisper.

By the time I leave the piazza, I'm sober. The visions of Luca in the crowd with another woman feel silly when compared to Peter's situation—his pain protects me from my own. And when Luca calls later in the evening to confirm he'll be back the next day, I feel more grounded in myself, more present on the phone.

I don't think of Peter again until the following morning, when I'm passing the church of San Frediano in Cestello and the bells begin to ring, and I remember the story I'd read about Maria Maddalena. Her ecstasies—or her *raptures*, as her sisters called them—could last for days on end, during which she would roam the convent like a somnambulist, physically acting out what she was experiencing. On one of her late-night wanderings, she found her way to the church's tower—in a *state of hysteria*, her sisters wrote—where she began to ring the bells, the same bells that stopped me here, ringing ceaselessly, evenly, stubbornly chanting, *Love itself is not loved*, each tone intoning a word of that repeated phrase. *Love itself is not loved*. She said it again and again, in rapture but with clarity, hysterical clarity. *Love itself is not loved*. I think of St. Angela—*to love and to wish to suffer for one's love*—and then I wonder if Peter is any different from them, reaching for a person who can only hurt him, losing himself in the process.

I listen to the metallic clanging and clamoring of the bells, filled with the sound and then empty in its echo, until they begin to resemble weeping. *Love itself is not loved*. I close my eyes. The sound licks at my skin, pulls me up, and the words change form, become *Are you searching for? Are you searching for?* and for just a moment more, the bells, the words, the cloistered voices of all those pallid virgins cry within me.

Chapter Fourteen

"*Boh*," Gianni says, looking up at the sky.

Late Saturday afternoon. I'm in my rowing gear and ready to take out my own small scull when I find Carlo and Gianni evaluating the weather. It is clear and the sun is bright, but Gianni points to clouds, more gray than white, far off in the hills.

"A storm, maybe."

Sergio appears, gives me a kiss on each cheek, then looks up as well. "*E poi?*"

"*Boh*," Gianni says again. *I don't know.*

I jump at hands on my waist and turn to find Luca.

"*Ciao, bella*," he says, and the imagined Lucas of the evening before disappear. "You came this time!"

"Your father?" I ask.

"Okay, okay. Not so good, but okay. *Allora*, you row? So do we."

"*Boh*." Carlo sounds doubtful.

"Maybe better inside," Sergio says.

"Gianni?" Luca asks.

"*Boh*. It might rain."

"*Boh, boh, boh!*" Luca exclaims, throwing his arms up. "These guys know nothing. Look at this sun!"

"*Va bene*." Gianni shrugs before disappearing inside with Carlo, who must be rowing for Stefano today.

"*Allora*," Luca says, "after, we have dinner? No other guys this time."

"Sounds good."

"*Amore*, let's go!" Gianni calls from behind the body of the boat.

I find Correggio to help me with my scull, but when we carry it into the sunlight a few minutes later, the four-man boat hasn't moved from the dock.

"Alessandro!" Luca calls for their young coxswain.

"*Aspetta*," Correggio says, and sighs, gesturing for me to lay the scull down. There is no getting into the water until the men leave.

"Alessandro!"

"Alessandro *non c'è*," Correggio says, walking down to the dock, his hands on his hips.

"*Non c'è! Ma perché?*"

"*Perché* it is going to rain," Gianni shouts from the back of the boat.

"*Madonna*," Luca says to me, "what a bunch of babies, *no*? *Allora, ragazzi*, what do we do? A beautiful afternoon, four strong men, a good boat, and no Alessandro."

It takes only a few traded phrases before someone says, "Hannah!"

"Hannah?" Carlo asks, skeptical.

"*Sì*," Luca says, already laying down his oar and stepping out of the boat. "*Perfetto!* You can be Alessandro for today!"

I know nothing about coxswaining, but as Luca takes both of my hands, his face is filled with such confidence that I say, "Okay," and follow him down to the dock. Sergio smiles at me enthusiastically from the second seat.

"*Allora*," Luca says, helping me step into the boat one foot at time. I feel the wooden body shake, but the men have a tight grip on the dock and the frame remains upright as I lower myself onto the small seat in the back of the boat facing them.

"*Grazie*, Hannah," Carlo says, "our savior," and if he's being sarcastic, I can't tell.

"*Brava*," Luca says, maneuvering his long body around the oar and settling into his seat in the first position, his legs tenting up like grasshoppers. Two ropes run along either edge of the boat and encircle me, meeting at the rudder in the water behind me. They course through two wooden handles beside me.

"You hold them like this," Luca says, gripping the handles tight. "The boat is straight. You move..." He pulls the right handle, which pulls the rope, and so the rudder. "A little bit only, the boat goes this way. The same with this." He moves the left handle.

I take the handles from him and dig them into my waist. Each man has a single oar and they alternate—Luca's to the left, Sergio's to the right, followed by Carlo's and then, in the last position, Gianni's. Now the oars rest on the boat's lip as they wait.

"And the calls?" I ask. Luca looks confused. "*Uno, due, uno, due,*" I say.

"Ah, don't worry." He smiles. "I will do it." He pats me on the knee and then, in unison, they push off and take a few small strokes away from the dock before aligning the boat with the Ponte alle Grazie so that I'm facing the bridge and they have their backs to it.

"*Ciao, ragazzi!*" Correggio calls from the shore. "*Buon viaggio!*"

I adjust the handles until the rope is again taut, the rudder straight, and the nose of the boat comes to a rest.

"*Aspetta,*" Luca calls to the men. He looks over his shoulder to the bridge. "We want to go..." He whistles and gestures. "*Dovete scegliere un punto,*" he explains. *Choose a point.* "Then imagine a line between yourself and the point. Keep your eye on the target and steer to hold the line."

Choose a point. I choose one of the streetlamps on top of the bridge, imagine a line connecting me to it, grip the handles tight. It is not much different from the visualization I do when steering my own boat, only this time I'm facing in the right direction.

"*Tutto a posto?*" Luca asks.

"Yes," I say. "I'm ready."

"*Pronti!*" he calls sharply. "*Via!*"

We begin to move slowly as the men row with just their arms. After a few strokes and with no instruction to do so, they add their legs so that we move a little faster, like an engine slowly revving up. I keep my eyes on the lamp, and when the boat begins to strain away, I pull just slightly on the rope, returning us to center. When we near the Ponte alle Grazie, I adjust the rope so that we cut a diagonal. Then the men pause. Luca and Carlo dip their oars, pulling against molasses, and Sergio and Gianni make small strokes until we're facing the opposite direction, the Ponte Vecchio ahead of us. Again we come to a full stop.

"Hold on," Luca says to me, then, "*Pronti... Via!*"

There is no warm-up this time, and in one breath, we are a fast-moving body, carving a path in the water. My back beats against the wood in time and I keep a tight grip on the handles, trying to hold a straight line. This is entirely different from the quiet solitude of my small scull. The power and speed create a new animal, wide hulled, that pushes the water out of its way rather than tracing a narrow path through it. I tuck my legs farther under the seat as Luca's hands almost brush them. Except for his calls, the men are silent, moving with great force but such precision that the boat does not waver. I steer us under the middle arch of the Ponte Vecchio, then pick a new target on the Ponte Santa Trinita.

"*Uno! Due!*" Luca shouts faster, as we pick up speed between the two bridges. The calls are barely necessary. The men are seamless. Years of training have ingrained the movement in their joints and muscles and they act as one body, sliding forward in time, pushing back hard, snapping the oars into their chests at the end of each stroke. They could probably do this in their sleep, slowing down and speeding up, not a single oar out of tempo. Only I am not in synch, off-balance in the boat, gripping the handles tightly to keep us straight as we churn a hard line toward the second bridge.

"*Brava,*" Luca says, as we dip into its cool shadow and then emerge on the other side, and I focus on the second arch from the left on the longer Ponte alla Carraia ahead of us. Except for the distant clouds, the sky is unblemished and the sun bakes my shoulders. People line the bridges and cameras flash in our direction— we will be the strangers in someone's album. Four oars dig into the water with a deep *whoosh*, and four red-and-white-striped palms appear and skip lightly over the river's surface as the men slide forward, the oars catching in the metal U-rings each time with a satisfying click before they slide back with another *whoosh*. Most of the time, Luca's head is down, his hair brushing his shoulders, his face concentrated, but he smiles up at me occasionally. I understand his elation—it is thrilling to be racing up the Arno.

"To the right," Luca says between strokes, as we approach the ledge that interrupts the river just before the Ponte Amerigo Vespucci. Water spills over it unevenly, and sunbathers stretch across its dry patches. I slacken one hand and pull with the other. The men do not stop, don't look over their shoulders to see where I'm carrying them as I pull harder, letting the rudder turn the boat. As we approach the river's wall, they finally halt their strokes and then dip the oars into the water, bringing us almost to a stop.

"*Bionda!*" Carlo calls between heavy breaths to a petite blonde in a black bikini sunbathing on the ledge. She looks coolly his way before returning her attention to her tan with a blank expression, unembarrassed, and the men laugh. Gianni and Sergio take quick strokes together to bring us back around. Once I'm facing the direction we have come from, the men again dip their oars, ready to make the trip back, but all of a sudden Luca is yelling at a dead fish, bloated and floating on the river's surface, shouting at it in Italian to wake up and get moving. Then, in a flash, he's serious again.

"*Pronti!*" he shouts. "*Via!*"

Gianni and Sergio continue to chuckle, and the boat again comes to a halt.

"*Ragazzi! Ragazzi!*" Luca groans. He rolls his eyes at me. "A bunch of babies!"

The boat reverberates with a boom of laughter, shaking until Luca gives a second "*Pronti! Via!*" and we are off. "*Tutti insieme!*" he calls. *All together.* We cut back under three bridges until we pass the club and arrive at the beginning of the course. Trying to stay centered, I make minor adjustments as we again trace a path under the three bridges and back. With each bridge and each lap, I am more a part of the whole, my individual self disappearing into the larger body that carries us. *I stripped myself of everything.* But it doesn't feel like whittling down or losing myself. It feels like becoming a part of.

In the middle of the third lap, all the men close their eyes. Oars smack the water in time as the boat moves forward at full speed, and I am the sole pair of eyes left to navigate the reality of bridges, other boats, and fallen branches. The night watch. I feel a lightness that I haven't felt in a long time, and the voices of the previous weeks—Peter, my sister, even the saints—fade. I listen to the *whoosh* and slap of the oars, feel the chill under the bridges, the occasional breeze, the wooden seatback gripping me. I focus on my targets and hold our course.

"*Brava*," Luca says quietly, his eyes still closed as we pass under one bridge and then another, before they all open their eyes to turn the boat around for another lap.

It is Sergio who feels the first drop when we emerge from under the Ponte alla Carraia. His oar knocks the boat as his head snaps up.

"Rain!" Gianni calls. "I knew it!"

Drops begin to fall consistently, and there is no speaking while the men concentrate on getting back to the club—still three bridges away—ahead of the weather, but by the time we reach the Ponte Santa Trinita, the rain is falling steadily. Above us umbrellas bloom along the river's wall and the lights on the Ponte Vecchio blink on as the sun disappears behind a growing fortress of clouds.

"*Via! Via!*" Luca shouts, his calls faster as the drops fall heavy and closer together. "*Uno! Due! Uno! Due!*"

I hold tight, try to keep us straight, but my hands, wet, begin slipping. The wind picks up, drawing waves across the water and blowing me side to side. I remember the photos of the great flood, remember this river's volatility. It is one thing and then it is something else.

"Have courage, *ragazzi!*" Gianni shouts. "Have courage, Hannah!"

I dig the handles hard into my waist to keep them from moving. We're flying now, barely a breath between Luca's calls, and the men become a blur as the rain intensifies. I keep my eyes on a single light on the Ponte Vecchio, the only visible point through the slanting drops. I tug slightly on the right rope to keep us aligned and then hold steady as we pass under the bridge. I can see two figures at the end of the dock.

"There are people there," I say.

"Who?" Luca asks between breaths.

I squint. "Correggio and Stefano."

"*Madonna*," Luca says.

"Stefano! *Stiamo arrivando!*" Carlo shouts over the wind.

"*Forza, ragazzi!*" Gianni yells, the laughter still in his voice. "If I am to die now in the waters of the Arno—" He stops, the effort too great to continue.

They are all straining now, we are soaked through, and a thin layer of water has collected in the bottom of the boat, which is working against us, protesting our efforts to steer it home. I hold the left handle tight and keep my eye on Stefano as the men pull—*one, two, one, two*—and the boat turns slowly inland, the choppy water slapping at its sides and spilling over, the base becoming a tub. Sergio and Gianni lift their oars as we approach. The nose of the boat hits first, clanging loudly against the dock, announcing our awkward landing. Correggio guides us in, then offers a hand first to me and I almost fall as I stand, my legs asleep. Stefano is angry and shouting, but as soon as the men are out of the boat, he falls silent to help grab its body, turning it over to let the water pour out. He and Gianni bear it on their shoulders into the club, and the rest of us run up the ramp behind them as the rain begins to fall harder, Luca and Sergio with their arms in the air as though they have won a marathon, my socks slap-slapping at the bricks.

Inside, we shake off and look out at the water through the blurred glass doors. In spite of Stefano's anger, everyone is smiling, children caught playing too late and too long. Gianni throws his arms around Luca and Carlo, patting each of them on the cheek before raising his hands in the air again.

"*Grande!*" he exclaims.

I'm shivering and Luca wraps himself around me. "*Bravi, ragazzi,*" he says.

Even when Stefano returns from storing the waterlogged boat, frowning at the sight of us, their spirits remain buoyant and Gianni slaps a wet arm around him, too.

"*Capo,*" he says, "we have returned from a grand *odissea,*" shaking him until the manager smiles as well, though he says, quite seriously, "Don't let it happen again."

In the locker room, I peel off my clothing, my body racing with the adrenaline of our adventure. And as I let the hot water beat at my chilled skin, I remember something I almost lost in the excitement—the moment when the men closed their eyes and the boat was entirely silent except for the sound of the oars. The moment when they trusted me to see.

After espresso, the men disappear to their Saturday evenings, and we decide to go to Luca's house in Fiesole, though he has warned me that because of his trip he is not prepared for the feast we had planned. It is dusk as his car climbs the winding roads into the small town above Florence. We take a sharp corner, and the city appears below us, a jumble of forms, as though the buildings had slid down the hills and collided in the bowl to create the chaotic mess of streets. From here, the cathedral is a caricature of itself, the bulbous red dome jutting up out of scale. We pull in through a narrow gate and onto a pebbled drive flanked by a high stone wall and several connected homes. Luca comes to a slow stop where the land drops off.

"Life," Luca says, gesturing to the city. "And death." He points in the other direction to a cemetery in the neighboring valley, where a collection of tombs are stacked like shoeboxes, each with a candle glowing faintly in the fading daylight. Ashes upon ashes in that white marble cloister, and I think of the mystics and then of all the corpses that fill this country, and I wonder at Luca's ability to face death every day and smile.

Luca swings open the door of his house exuberantly. He's excited to have me here, proud of what he has created. His home is one story but cavernous. White walls stretch up to high ceilings and the doors between rooms are overly tall. Luca, who is usually crouched over in his car, in the boat, in a city constructed for smaller people centuries ago, must feel finally comfortable in a space like this.

"It's a home for a giant," I say.

"*Sì,*" he confirms seriously, setting down his keys. "Argo," he calls. "Argo! You see? Argo is never waiting. Argo speaks only Greek. *Solo greco.* Also, he is a great artist. But very private, yes?"

"Like most artists."

"*Sì.* Okay, no Argo today. *Allora,* you are hungry?"

"A little."

"*Andiamo.*" He gestures and I follow him to his kitchen, which is narrow but still tall. Beyond a small window are the surrounding hills, faintly lit; they are green brushed with orange in this late-approaching fall, loping like the great bellies of men sleeping below the earth.

"Let's see, let's see," Luca says, opening his refrigerator and then looking through several cupboards. "I am *un po'* bachelor. *Mi dispiace.* I would have prepared a grand meal."

"That's all right, I'm not that—"

"*Aspetta!*" He raises a finger in the air and brushes by me. He returns with a half a leg of prosciutto, grinning. "I forgot this!"

"Impressive," I say. "You are a magician."

"*Certo!*" he says. "*Allora...*" He puts the leg down on the counter, opens a cabinet, and hands me a small bottle of olive oil, then opens the oven and pulls out a paper bag, which he places in my arms. "Bread," he says. "*E poi...*"

He adds to my load a tomato from a dish on the counter and, as an afterthought, a jar of oregano that he nestles between the other items.

"Instant meal!" he says. "What do they say—a magician?"

"Tada!"

"Tada!" He pushes me out of the kitchen. "*Allora, va'.*"

Luca's living and dining area is meticulously clean and sparse except for several pieces of heavy antique furniture. I set our provisions on the dining room table and Luca follows with napkins, plates, wineglasses, forks, a cutting board. He lays all of these items out and then leaves and returns with a bottle of wine.

"*Bop!*" he says, pulling out the cork and filling our glasses before toasting: "To our new team member!" Then he cuts us thick slices of bread and shaves the prosciutto into thin strips.

"*Questo* prosciutto we won—"

"You won?"

"*Sì*. For a race. In Milano. With Sergio, Gianni, *e* Stefano."

"This was the prize?"

"*Sì. Aspetta.*" He brushes the crumbs off his hands and disappears again, returning with a photo—four men and a woman I don't recognize, all in rowing gear. Luca and Gianni grip the prosciutto between them with large grins.

"You see," he says. "When we eat this prosciutto, we taste the victory."

"I can't wait," I say. "Who's that?" I point to the woman at the end.

"Mariella," he says. "She is *il timoniere*—like you today! Only when we are in Milano. In Florence, we have the boy."

I feel a bit jealous, but before I can say more, Luca exclaims, "*Allora, mangiamo!*" and places the prosciutto slices delicately onto a plate beside the stiff unsalted bread. He pulls out one of the large chairs for me and then seats himself across the table. I like this simple meal, so much more manageable than our last dinner together, and we take our time drizzling oil on the bread, laying the prosciutto over it, slicing the tomato on top.

"Victory tastes delicious," I say after the first bite.

"Yes, always. Like today. This was a victory."

"I don't think Stefano was happy."

"It's okay. He only does not let himself be—he cannot."

"Because he's the manager?"

Luca takes a sip of wine, considering this. "No. He was always this way. Since we were children," and I'm reminded of how far back their roots reach. "Saturday night," he says, and sighs then. "*Finalmente.* Tomorrow—no work!"

"Do you like your work?"

"*Sì.* Enough." He shrugs. "It's not so interesting, but okay. Anyway, I have the club. I have my home. It is a good life. You think it's good?"

I nod, looking around and smiling. "A very good life. Some people would say that you're living the dream."

"Living the dream," he echoes, with a hum in his voice. "And your work, Hannah? How is it?"

"I like it. It's quiet. And, honestly, I spend most of the time reading."

"What do you read?"

"Right now, I'm reading about the saints. The women."

"*Le sante,*" he says. "*Interessante.* Caterina, Teresa, Chiara..."

"There are many."

"They interest you, why?"

"I guess I understand them in some ways. Not that I'm religious, but..." I pause. How can I explain it? There is so much that I can't tell Luca. For a moment there is only the sound of the rain outside and Luca chewing and waiting. "I admire them," I say finally.

"*Perché?*"

"Well, they were able to do more than many other women at the time."

"Ah," Luca says, pouring us each another glass of wine. "Because it was not necessary that they marry."

"Yes, but not only that. They were in control of their lives."

"And they were very famous."

"But they didn't ask to be. They were famous because of their faith."

"Also for the mystical visions. *Erano molto sensuali, no?*" Luca asks, raising his eyebrows with a wicked grin. "It is for this that you like them?"

"For their erotic visions, yes." I smile.

"But what do you think—of the visions? They were real or created only?"

"Do I think they made them up?"

Luca nods.

"Well, I think they believed what they were experiencing."

"But *you*—what do you think?"

"Do I believe they were in the presence of God?"

"The big question, *no?*" Luca smiles.

"I'm not sure it matters. I think their belief is what matters. The reality? It seems beside the point."

"Many Catholics would not agree with you."

"But what we believe is real *is* real." I stop, unsure of how to proceed from this position. "*I* don't believe they were in the presence of God. But I think they did. Or maybe they just wanted more than what they were offered, and they kept searching for it. Real or not."

"*E poi?*"

"I understand that. I respect it."

There is a pause before Luca says, "*Ho capito.*"

"What do you think?"

"I don't believe it."

"You don't believe what?"

"God. Heaven. More life after life. *This* is life, I think, this only. Only this." He looks down at his hands, large and blistered from years of rowing.

I jump as something brushes my legs, and Luca leans under the table and reappears with a bundle of gray. "*Ecco* Argo!" He raises the cat above his head. "You thought he was a spirit?"

"No," I say, and laugh. "Well, maybe."

He sets Argo down and the cat is gone in a flash. "You see?" he says. Then he stands and stretches. "Finished?"

I nod, and he leaves and returns with a roll of foil.

"Do you think you'll always work at the store?" I ask as he collects the newly cut slices of prosciutto, wrapping them together.

"*Forse.* It is enough money for me. And I am the manager, so I can do as I want. I would change only if..." He stops here, folding the edges of the foil and tearing a new sheet. "I thought, when I was young, I thought... *non lo so.*"

"You thought what?"

He sighs. "I thought to have children."

"But you still can."

"*Sì*, maybe, maybe. But not only this. I thought..." He pauses. He is at war with something, too. With the things he can't tell me, perhaps. Or the life that has failed to present itself. It ripples across his face and then is gone. He gives me a smile but it wavers. "*Niente.* This is life, *sì?*" And I realize for the first time how different his life is from the other men at the club. They never speak about their families, but they all have families.

Luca carefully seals what remains of the bread in foil, as if perfectly content with these small things that have been left to him, of which, I suppose, I am one. But I don't feel small, and for the first time in months, I feel like I'm not just taking—pity, charity, anger. And so I don't wait for him to find his expansive smile. Instead, I walk to him, put my arms around his stooped figure from behind until he turns and leans into me. I take in the smells and tastes that are now growing familiar—detergent, shampoo, salt and wine, and, from somewhere deeper, a scent unique to him. We kiss for a long time standing there, and then move to the couch, the aluminum parcels forgotten.

"It's okay? You want to stay?" Luca asks. The room is dark except for a small lamp in the corner, and in this light I can see how he must have looked years ago, smooth-faced, perhaps laughing less than now but believing in more. I feel so safe, so in control for once—a control that has nothing to do with food—that I nod, decisive. And as we continue kissing and then make our way to his room, there is not a small part of me that imagines that with each kiss, I am replacing something spoiled with something fresh, something healthy, something new. *It is good,* I think, glad for the weight of Luca on top of me. There is no fumbling here, though Luca moves slowly, and I can still say and mean *it is good.* Good to be with this person, good to have this other form growing familiar.

But when my body is exposed and I feel his hands on my skin, something shifts, as though I've been abruptly awakened, and I become sharply aware of lying in this room, my body almost bare, my body that I haven't looked at, really looked at, in weeks. And then I'm not in control, not at all, and though I try to remain in this room, in this body with Luca close to me, I feel the moment break, the change so rapid that I don't even have time to cry out, to say anything. It is as though I'm outside of myself, watching everything from above. *For when love is pure, you see yourself as dead and as nothing.* I can see the forms in the room and hear the sounds: birds beating their wings above the rafters, the wind blowing hard at the exterior walls, Luca's breathing growing heavy. I can see and hear all these things, but I can't feel them. *There is in my soul a chamber.* Why alone? Why always alone? I don't want that, don't want to be always alone. That is not what is meant for me. There are these things that I can be with other people. I know that there are these things that I can be. *I could not imagine a death vile enough.* I see Luca's hands sliding up and around my back but don't feel them, and I see myself kissing him but my lips are cold. I can't feel anything. I am a body in a tomb, I am without a body, I am a mind, a set of eyes floating, and I want someone to pull me down, back into the bed, back into my body, back under the weight of him, just to feel the weight, just to feel something. It is only when I'm fully naked that I feel anything at all, and then it is pain. *I could not imagine a death vile enough to match my desire.* My body is laid out there below me and I cannot look at it. I don't recognize myself. It is too much to take in. I close my eyes.

Luca stops. I feel his body tense, hear his voice. "Hannah, *stai bene? Che è successo?*"

I touch my face. I'm crying.

"Hannah. Look at me."

I open my eyes. Luca is looking at me with concern, his head in his palm. "You are okay?"

I shake my head.

"What is it?" He softly runs his hand up and down my arm, that arm that I cannot look at.

I take a breath in and I can feel a door opening as I say, "I'm embarrassed."

"*Perché?* Because you are crying? Crying and still beautiful—that is not so tragic."

"I don't feel beautiful. I don't know." The tears continue to roll out. It is ridiculous, humiliating, and still I can't stop. I shouldn't have come here.

"*Madonna!*" Luca cries then, sitting up on his knees with his arms raised, and even through the tears, I smile at the sight of him, so easy in his nakedness, comical shock on his face.

But when he says, "Regard yourself. *Look,*" I shake my head. *Look at me.*

"*Davvero?* Only for one moment?"

I keep my eyes on him, a pit of dread in my stomach. "Let's turn out the light," I say.

"Definitely not! *I* would be embarrassed to turn out the light on such beauty. *Aspetta...*" He drops down beside me so our faces are close. I remember my body in that fogged mirror. I remember myself in many mirrors. What would he say if he knew about that? He sees the beauty in everything, it seems, but what would he say to the reality of me naked in a restaurant bathroom?

"An idea," he says, rolling onto his back so that he's lying beside me. He holds up his hands above us, his index fingers and his thumbs meeting to form a circle.

"Look, *per favore*," he says. I follow his hands as he uses the little window he has created to frame the lamp, the beams in the ceiling, a stack of books, and finally—sitting up and bringing his hands to his face—his eye, sparkling with rough skin folding around it. He takes the little window he's made and places it in front of my cheek. Then he shifts the frame to kiss the spot before moving on to my eyes, my lips, my chin, making me laugh.

"Now look," he says, moving his fingers down my arm, each framing echoed by a kiss and a soft *bella*. I follow with my eyes, willing myself to trust him, looking only at the image between his fingers—a breast, my ribs, my stomach, a knee, each one met with a kiss. And I find that I can do it, can look at these parts without flinching, can look at one piece and then the next and the next. When he's made his way all the way down to my toes, climbing off the bed to do so, he looks up at me with his eyebrows raised, and I look all the way down the length of my body for just a moment, and only for a moment, but in that moment I do not feel pain. I smile at him and gesture for him to come back up to me. And when he begins to kiss me again, very slowly, I stay with him, feel his kisses, feel his hands on me, and feel my own hands on him.

"It's okay?" he asks.

I nod.

"*Sicura?*"

"I'm sure," I say. And I am.

It is a quiet kind of lovemaking, none of the violence of that last time with Julian. And though the calm is punctuated with moments of uncertainty, this time I do not float away.

Chapter Fifteen

I wake up in a bed not my own, to a new place with its own early-morning sights and sounds. I hear the persistent call of a bird before my eyes open. On the wall is a perfect square of light, pink—a temporary painting of shifting hues—and I wonder how long it has been there, ignored by our sleeping bodies. I get up and walk to the window, lean my head against the pane with my hand on my stomach, feeling it rise and fall, and look out at the bright garden and, beyond it, valleys and valleys. I remember all the mornings that I have woken to stand alone by my own window. My own window, somewhere far below and empty this morning, its view unseen. I look back at Luca, hidden except for his face and one hand that curls over the edge of the mattress, and I feel a rush of affection—it is exhilarating to feel this again. My breath spreads and retreats off the glass. I wait as the pink square traces a path across the wall and evaporates, and the sunlight turns a pale orange, biting at the ends of my lashes. I'm startled by a movement: two birds, one after the other, knock at the window and then fly off. I watch as they disappear before returning to bed.

When I open my eyes hours later, Luca is still curled away from me, his breath whistling lightly. I turn over and meld myself around him. He shifts, his body beginning its slow ascent out of sleep. He twitches, rolls over, sighs, and looks at me with fogged eyes. His brow furrows, but the concern passes and is replaced by a small smile. He squeezes my arm.

"*'Giorno,*" he says finally. Then he grins fully and pulls me in. "*'Giorno, bella.*" His hand makes soft circles on my back and I can feel his body growing heavy, but he sighs and says, "*Mi dispiace.* I have to go," and pulls away. "You stay. Rest here." This is Luca in the morning. Short sentences.

"Go where?" I watch him cross the room, hunched a bit. He looks out the window where I had stood earlier, stretching his arms high above his head now, pulling his back smooth, before turning around with a smile.

"I go to my sister's. It is Sunday." As though that explains everything.

He disappears into the bathroom, and I pull up the covers and remain stiff as I listen to his choreography. The ease of it. He whistles, hums, any of the fears that I had witnessed in him the night before now shed. Where is my place in his bright morning? As though reading my thoughts, Luca comes back into the room and leaps onto the bed. He's fresh from the shower, his body fragrant and warm, and his wet hair drips, little droplets hitting my cheeks.

"*Madonna,*" he says, smiling down at me, "I wish I could stay." He burrows into my neck and plants a few wet kisses, making me laugh.

"*Allora,*" he says, "I will go but take with me this picture." He closes his eyes tight and then opens them. "And I'll see you very soon, okay. Tomorrow? We go to a movie?"

"Sounds great," I say.

"*Sicura?*" he asks, dubious.

"*Sì.* No games."

"No games," he echoes. "I like that. No games. *Perfetto.*" He gives me a few more wet kisses before hopping up. "*Va bene.* I go."

After he leaves, I take my time showering and dressing. In the kitchen, I find a note with the number for a taxi company, a promise to call, and "*un bacio,*" followed by Luca's signature in smooth script. I make coffee and pace the living room as I drink it. My body is tired, depleted, and now that I'm alone, there is an edge of melancholy.

The whole day stretches out before me without the promise of interruption. The club is closed, the library is closed, and there is no one waiting for me down in the city, and so I decide to stay for a bit.

I find a pack of cigarettes on the bookshelf and take one and smoke it out in the garden and think back on the night. My panic before the calm. St. Angela's words: *There is in my soul a chamber.*

Were their ecstasies real? Luca had asked. *There was no intermediary between God and myself,* Angela said. She was so certain. Not fearful in her raptures. Even as she disappeared, consuming nothing, consumed by love, her confidence in that singular truth didn't falter. I think of my refusal to look at my body, the impossibility of letting go of my own truth even as Luca gently asked me to consider a different one. Would it always require such coaxing?

I'm reaching for another cigarette when I hear ringing inside Luca's house—not the sharp shrill of a landline, but the manufactured tune of a cell phone, the melody unfamiliar. The ringing continues for what seems like a long time before it cuts off abruptly. I wait in the newly thick silence. Sure enough, the tinny tune begins again. I go back into the house, where Luca's phone sits on the dining room table, forgotten. I watch it until the tune plays out. It would be intrusive to pick up, but who calls with such urgency on a Sunday morning? A few seconds later, it starts up again and I pick up the phone quickly but don't say anything.

"Luca, dove sei?" A woman's voice, fast and confident, a sharp point of business in this slow morning. I say nothing, my face growing hot. A woman. Of course.

"Luca, stai arrivando?" the voice continues. *"Silvio deve partire alle due oggi."*

"Pronto," I say, as if I've only just answered, my voice rough from the cigarette and catching in my throat.

"Luca?" The voice is confused now and the quality changes, as though the caller has taken the phone away from her cheek. *"Ma questo è il numero di Luca. C'è Luca?"*

"No." I explain, brokenly, that it *is* Luca's phone, but Luca isn't here, he's just left.

"Ma chi parla?"

"Hannah. *Un'amica di Luca.*" *A friend of Luca's.* Take that, whoever you are.

"*Oh?*" The voice lilts up, light but laced with judgment, and suddenly I can see this woman, can see her eyebrows raise before her mouth settles down into a frown.

"*Allora,*" she says then, speaking quickly in Italian, though she must know from my poor accent that I'm American. "This is Simona, Luca's sister." His sister. "We are expecting him for lunch. *If* you see him..." She pauses as though I've been lying to her, as though Luca is right here in the room with me, both of us naked and giggling at our little joke. "*If* you see him, Hannah," she repeats, saying my name in a way that makes me wish she didn't know it, "tell him that he's late and we're here waiting. *Di nuovo.*" *Again.* With a *ciao, grazie,* she hangs up, and I feel as though something has been lost. As if with that single word swinging upward—*Oh?*—she has taken something from me, from us.

When I leave Luca's house, the streets are empty and the piazza is silent except for music muffled by the doors of the church. I don't call a taxi—I need to walk. The hills around Florence are threaded with roads, and there must be one that will deliver me back to its center. My body is buzzing with an excess of energy as I imagine Luca driving toward his sister's house, where I've now made myself a presence. I pass through town quickly, stopping at a small bar for a bottle of water that I slip into my bag with my rowing clothes. I take one road until it dead-ends, then make my way back to the still-empty square and choose another road that curls out of town. Almost immediately, stone walls rise on either side of me. I eye the flowers and ivy that spill over their tops and imagine the beauty on the other side: olive groves funneling into valleys, green oases of cypresses, and, farther below, Florence trapped under the haze, where the shops are now closed but tourists are still tracing and retracing the city's bones. I can imagine it all, but I cannot see any of it. The view is saved for those who live behind the walls, and the non-member is left to wander the negative space.

A number of roads cross the one I'm on, but none look promising: the smaller ones are too risky—narrow and dark—and the larger ones hold their own dangers because of traffic. So I keep to my chosen path. It is level, and though I'm not going down yet, I'm also not going up.

It is so quiet up here, an absolute silence I have not yet experienced, not even on the river. There is only the occasional cry of a bird and the wind moving through the cypresses. Nature finds its way in, and with it, the evening before, the awkward phone call, even the image of Luca arriving at his sister's, become as distant as the city and dissolve into the solitude of my steps. Dry leaves dance, scratching the ground. The sun emerges full from behind the clouds, and for a moment there is nothing of me but my shadow.

Rounding a bend, the path levels to reveal an intersection and three figures. A family: a man, a woman, and a boy. Their bikes are propped and they are looking at a sign that reads VILLA ALBA. They nod as I pass but don't say anything, the young boy following me with silent eyes. Family. A concept so distant now, though I can remember being that boy's age—frustrated by the imposed interruptions on any given outing, the adults always needing to stop, take a break, reassess. And I tethered by that invisible cord, unable to break free and make my own way. It was a time when I had, still, that feeling of invincibility so specific to childhood, when I didn't think about my body, when it was nothing more than the necessary vessel I used to navigate the world. I wonder what Luca was like at that age, if his eyes ever looked so solemn as that boy's, if he waited impatiently, tethered, too. I can only picture him smiling and charging ahead.

I round another bend and the walls shrink, tapering until they reveal a stretch of land, a villa spreading yellow into the hill. Across the property a smattering of olive trees pitch away from the building, diving toward Florence, and I realize I've cut a long curve around the city without having made much progress toward it. If I continue in this way it will take me days to wind my way to its center. I need a faster route.

The family bikes by me, the boy ringing his bell once before they disappear, and I am, again, alone. I follow their path, hoping this road doesn't end around the next bend—because this home was a destination, must have been *the* destination, the long road I've taken only its driveway perhaps. But the family doesn't reappear, which gives me hope, and after a few minutes I come to another intersection. Via del Rosario disappears up into the hills on my left. I take the road to my right—Via Virgilio, not too wide and not too narrow—and begin to descend.

The sun is high overhead by the time that I stop. On the side of the road, the strong, twisting roots of an olive tree have created a jagged gap in the wall, splitting the stone. It is a mouth smiling sideways, welcoming me. I should keep going—I have no idea what time it is—but this opening beckons. Maybe it was seeing that young boy that urges me on. The freedom in knowing that there is no one here now to make me pause, rest, reassess; no one to tell me who I am or am not. And so I place my foot on the broken stone and, using the craggy roots as handholds, step up to find a large olive grove stretched out before me, a valley beyond it, the rise of another hill across the way. Ducking under branches, I creep in, staying low as though someone might leap out and cry, *Trespasser!* But there are no buildings in sight and these olive trees are not in use. They are overgrown, shrubs and weeds crowding their trunks. And unlike the pruned grove across the valley, the pattern of this field is invisible.

I stand up straight, walk to the edge of the grove, and take a seat on the dry grass. Ahead of me is a familiar view. I'm on the other side of the horseshoe from Fiesole—I have come farther than I thought. The hill hugs the town and the sounds of Sunday echo across the valley and make their way cleanly to me—the crunch of gravel, a woman's voice calling. Below is Florence, and I recognize the towers of each of the city's churches, read them left to right, the length of Santa Croce ending in a triangle, the mast of the Bargello, the ballasted Palazzo Vecchio with its small lion unrecognizable but visible, the cap of the Duomo shrunken from here.

In Fiesole, bells ring the quarter hour. A large jackrabbit runs by and two cicadas call back and forth. The sun is so bright that it cuts through the leaves and everything sways, everything moves.

I have the sense that this place has been waiting for me to arrive on this day at this hour, each step of my journey funneling to this spread of sky. Involuntarily I let out a small, soft "Oh," not rising like the *Oh?* of Luca's sister, but level and filled with air and wonder.

The bells ring short on the half hour and then again fifteen minutes later. Still, I don't leave. I love this messy grove, love the rebellious tree that granted me access to it and the overgrown trees that now hide me, and I feel, again, centered. *Wholly certain.* Is this how Angela had felt? *No one could convince me otherwise,* she wrote. *Even if the whole world were to tell me otherwise, I would laugh it to scorn.* I knew that feeling, I knew that conviction. I'd held tight to it. And for what? *I lost honor, dignity, peace,* Margaret writes. *I lost everything except faith.* Was it all for faith? For the heart of Christ that Catherine felt beating in her chest, for the ring that was visible only to Clare, for the body Angela lay beside in a cold sepulcher? And always left wanting. I remember, then, St. Margaret's words as she begged to be admitted to the convent, pleading in that voice that would not be sated. *I have fled from the world... I have changed my life. Is it not enough?*

It is only when the bells begin to ring on the hour, echoing across the valley, that I realize that I haven't eaten. I haven't eaten all day. It is three o'clock and I haven't had anything aside from coffee and a cigarette. For a moment, I feel flush with it, light. I used to do this—hold out until I couldn't hold out anymore, triumphant as I became dizzy, high on my emptiness, the air around me vibrating with it, objects and people glowing through the fog. Right here in this moment I could give in to it, give in to the ease of it, ride it out, see where it goes. But I know where it goes. I know where it goes and I cannot go there. I cannot not eat, because there is this other path now that I need to see through. *I will wait until the quarter hour,* I think, *wait until the next set of bells and then go.*

But then I decide to leave right away, knowing how even the most solid of bottom lines can become flexible and slide. I leave the grove with speed, propelling myself forward, pausing only to take care as I climb back down through the break in the wall. It feels as though I'm exiting a fairy tale, the modern world distant, the only darkness the silhouetted trees as I hop down onto the road, the only sound my feet hitting the pavement, loud. I am filled with the magic of the afternoon, changed by it. And in that instant I have again the sense of being ahead of myself, far in the future. Only this time I'm not afraid of that future woman, who would look back on the younger woman whose journey was more difficult, covered in sharp edges and dark crevices, finding her way for the first time to this place, uncertain of which way she would pitch or how she would emerge. I don't look back then but walk quickly ahead before anything else takes hold. I leave the saints and their insatiable ecstasies, leave that lost woman. I walk quickly toward the city, toward food, toward all the things that are just beginning to grow.

Chapter Sixteen

"*Ciao, cara,*" Luca says, when I approach the club the next evening. It is almost dark and he is waiting outside the green door. We're going to a movie and it feels like an oddly American thing to be doing.

"*Allora,* you spoke with Simona," he says with a smile as we stroll to the theater. "*Mi dispiace.* Simona is *un po'—come si dice?*—in charge?"

"Yes," I say, relieved. "My sister, Kate—she's the same."

"She is older, your sister?"

I nod.

"Ah, then we are both the babies," he says knowingly, drawing me closer.

The city is emptier than it has been, and a lone saxophone plays "Autumn Leaves" in the Uffizi courtyard to almost no audience, the sad melody slowly rising and falling. But I'm not sad now, walking with Luca. I'm full—not with saccharine elation but a sort of glowing calm.

The movie is a second-rate American horror film poorly dubbed into Italian, and still we gasp at the arrival of each apparition—"My heart is in my throat," I whisper to Luca.

"*Anch'io,*" he says dramatically, his eyes wide, before grabbing my arm tightly and huddling close.

He walks me home after the film, comes upstairs, and this time, when I invite him to stay, no voices stop me. I'm not as self-conscious as we undress, and we take our time, learning each other slowly. St. Angela doesn't reappear.

For the next two weeks, my life takes on an easy rhythm. With Lorenza back, I'm able to spend lunch hours at the club with Luca and the others, some days acting as coxswain, other days rowing alone. When it is sunny, we are out on the water. When it rains, we train indoors. After we train, I eat with them on the embankment below the ivy trellis that Correggio prunes every few days. I am tired, hungry, and eating becomes easier. Conversation is easier, too. There are few women here and the men are different—there are none of the side comments. They discuss politics, soccer, pick up a small detail and argue it loudly, every disagreement a sport. And Luca creates space for me. He is more comfortable at the club as well. The things that set him apart from his friends, the things he doesn't have—the family, the overt machismo—don't matter here. The men have the same conversations they had before wives and children and mistresses and divorces. They train together, eat together, spend every afternoon this way, the rest of the world dropped away. They're well into their forties, but on the river, in the gym, on the banks of the Arno with a bowl of pasta between them, breaking off pieces of the bread that Luca arrives with tucked under his arm each day, they are thirty, they are twenty, they are teenagers around a table they have shared for years.

I'm not a part of their history, but I am, more and more, a part of their present. And though no one states it directly, suddenly and without ceremony, Luca and I are a couple. Couplehood suits Luca, and when he turns to me midstory with a broad smile and puts a hand on my arm, I feel I'm witnessing him in his most natural state—as though he is more *Luca* when he is one of two. Am I more *Hannah* with him? I don't know. I don't feel like I'm slipping away. I don't feel lost in Luca. But when I watch him bustling around his kitchen or observe him quiet, his face content, before he wakes, I cannot imagine tiring of these things.

Evenings without Luca, I cook for myself and climb into bed early to read. At Lorenza's suggestion, I've taken out books on art history to revisit the works I'd studied years earlier. On Sunday, when Luca goes to his sister's, I take my walk down through the hills, stopping at the grove to let the afternoon drift for an indeterminate amount of time.

I write Kate consistently, but no one else from back home. Not even Claudia when I receive a second e-mail from her that promises "good news!"—I delete it without reading on. When I think of my life before this, it seems further and further away. So distant that when I'm out on the water in my small scull, I can imagine letting it go, a leaf lost to the current. I don't think of the past and don't think of the future, but try to live as Luca and his friends seem to, always in the present.

During the second week, the rain arrives. It rains consistently from one day into the next and the men agree, with long sighs, that the rainy season is here to stay, and now we spend each afternoon at the end of the boat-lined hallway in the training room. I arrive on Friday to find the room empty, all the men running late—being late is a given when it rains in Florence, I've learned. I choose my usual rowing machine, strap in my feet, and reach forward for the T-bar, pulling it back against resistance. By the time Gianni waltzes in singing, I'm exhausted. I nod at his reflection in the wall of mirrors and he continues humming with a smile. Behind me is the raised rectangular tank of water. Four oars float on its surface like the splayed legs of a water bug. Gianni settles onto the first of the four sliding seats at the tank's edge, grips the oar beside him, and warms up with slow strokes.

A vent near the ceiling provides a partial view into the Uffizi courtyard. Feet go by, and some days I've seen faces appear, trying to locate the source of the club's sounds—the whirring of the ergometer belts, the deep suction each time oars scoop water in the tank, the voices that echo through the hallways. On these rainy days, even two or three men bantering sounds like a crowd. Today it is too loud outside, though, windy and raining steadily, and no one takes the time to peer down at us.

I hear Luca's voice before I spy him crouched behind the rack of oars near the entryway. He peeks over it, then runs up behind me, and I laugh and pause to give him a quick kiss.

"You're late," I say.

"*Certo.* It's raining," he says with a smile.

Sergio arrives with Stefano, and once everyone is seated, they begin making slow waves in the tank. In the training room, Gianni leads, and after giving the signal, he goes hyperspeed, grinning as the rest try to keep up, before settling into a regular pace. I miss acting as coxswain. When we train indoors I'm not really a part of it, even as I try to match their rhythm. I glance at Luca in the mirror. Under these harsh lights—his face concentrated, his hair stringing wet, each stroke sapping the last ounce of energy in his body until, miraculously, he musters the next—he looks older again. Thunder shakes the walls and I hear Correggio shuffling up and down the hallway outside, preparing to take the dock up onto the shore in case the rain becomes heavier, as it looks to this afternoon. Another round of thunder and the lights go out. The oscillation of the tank's water stops as the men come to a rest. The only sound is the exhalation of my machine, the belt winding and unwinding. Then there is another sound above it.

"Hannah..." Luca moans, and the others join in, a chorus of ghostly wails. I pause and grin into the darkness until the lights hum back on. Then we hear shouting.

"Stefano!" Correggio's panicked voice ricochets up and down the hallway. "Stefano!"

He appears in the doorway, words flying from his mouth. In a beat, the men are up and out of their seats, while I fumble to release my feet. I run after them down the hallway, past the boats and coffee bar, through the glass doors, and out into the rain, where I am immediately soaked to the skin. We join the crowd gathered along the brick steps, looking out toward the river. Stefano is at the end of the dock shouting, his face haggard. The sky has turned dark, and through the slanting sheet of rain I can just make out a figure in a small scull at the base of the Ponte Vecchio, stuck, his rowing useless against the wind.

"Who is it?" I ask.

"*L'Americano*," Luca says.

Peter. I remember him in Piazzale Michelangelo, the hardness in his face, the determination. Was that weeks ago? Has so much time passed?

All around me, voices are carried up by the wind: "Why is he out there?" "Doesn't he know better?" "Just like an American." Peter, once a bird in that boat, is struggling to make it back to shore. The raindrops pierce the water like sharp needles, turning the river a muddy brown, and the wind counters his efforts, inspiring more comments: "He'll never get to the dock." "The boat will be ruined. Look at Stefano—he'll kill him." "But why doesn't he take the speedboat to help?" "Too dangerous. Why ruin two boats?" "Just like an American."

"Don't worry," Luca says, putting his arm around me, "it will be okay." I don't see how it can be, though. There is nothing okay about this. The wind shifts and I'm blown backward, but the change helps Peter and he begins to make progress, his red shirt shining like a beacon, growing larger as he approaches the dock. Stefano tries to catch the edge of the scull, but the angle is all wrong and his fingertips just graze the lip and then slip off it at the last moment as he throws his balance back to keep from toppling into the water. The scull drifts out and I glimpse Peter's face, pale and furious. Stefano flails his arms in a circle and shouts to him to turn around. He will have to make another lap and try again. All the men groan in disbelief and Peter rows back in the direction of the Ponte Vecchio. There is a small flash of light from the bridge—someone snapping a picture. Then another flash and another. I want to run up there and snatch the cameras out of their hands.

I look around at the faces, all streaked with water, all angry except for Luca, who gives my hand a squeeze and turns to speak with Gianni. Then Francesca glides out through the glass doors. She makes her way down the steps as though walking through a painting of her own creation—which it may be, in fact—her eyes bright with excitement.

"What's going on?" she shouts to me.

"Peter's out on the water. I don't know why. He knew the weather was bad. I don't know why he'd do this." But I do. Sometimes you need to escape and there's nowhere to go. And the next thing you know, you're a spectacle in a storm.

Francesca purses her lips and watches him. "He's a stubborn boy, isn't he?"

The rain turns to hail, large bits of ice chafing at my frozen arms, bouncing off the dock like thunderous applause, and likely drumming on Peter's boat and body with an intensity that must be maddening. He has made the turn before the bridge and is again pulling toward us, the boat teetering from side to side. He is no longer using his legs, only his arms as he tries to keep the scull balanced. If he can get back on this lap, if he can get back now before there is too much water or too many hailstones weighing down the boat, he will be okay. I squeeze my hands into fists, my nails digging into my skin. Behind me Luca and Gianni are arguing, and, with a final flourishing shout, Luca comes to stand beside me and places a hand on my back. He's concerned, and now I am more so. Francesca turns and raises her eyebrows, but a moment later, Luca hurries down to Stefano and begins speaking urgently. Then he plants his feet firmly and, with both hands, grips Stefano's arm, allowing his friend to lean all the way out over the water as the scull comes within feet of the dock. Peter forces the right oar into the boat and pulls frantically with the left to get just a little bit closer. The voices around me go silent as Stefano's fingers slip and slip and finally hook over the scull's lip. He drags it in with great effort until Peter is close enough to reach his hand out and grip the dock. For a moment, none of them move; they only breathe. Behind me the men applaud, though not for Peter, I know.

Correggio runs down and takes the oars, and Luca helps Peter out of the boat, slapping him on the back with an encouraging smile. Peter is shaking, and his face is covered in red splotches and dripping—with tears or rain, I cannot tell. Stefano says nothing. He and Gianni lift the boat slowly, hail and water pouring down their backs and onto the dock as they mount it on their shoulders and carry it into the club.

"Whewwww," Francesca whistles next to me. "Crazy, huh?"

The club members begin to head inside, the youngest ones still talking heatedly, the older men shaking their heads. Luca stays, speaking quietly to Peter, who has his hands on his knees, his head down, breathing hard. He looks up then, as though registering the crowd for the first time, and his gaze locks on Francesca. I wait for her to acknowledge him, but she says, "Well, show's over. Coming in?" and turns to follow the crowd. It seems cruel. But, of course, she still has something to lose.

Peter's head drops, and Luca puts an arm around him, urging him up the steps, still talking. Peter does not raise his eyes as they approach me, even when I begin to speak, and so I let them pass and wait in the rain for a minute longer. By the time I get inside, the club has returned to normal; the tables in the bar are already filled and I can hear weights clanging in the training rooms. I don't see Peter, and Luca tells me later that he didn't even change, just grabbed his things and left.

That night, I call Peter a few times but there is no answer. I'm worried, but I also feel relief. There is relief in not always being the person slipping off the edge, sliding into that fog. Relief in being here now, curled into Luca, listening to the hammering of the rain. And though my future is no more visible than Peter's, the present seems no more dangerous than Luca's quiet breaths against the back of my neck as I drift to sleep.

Chapter Seventeen

The first of November. I wait by the club in the early morning. It is a day off in Italy, a deep intake of breath. Many businesses are closed, but the markets are still open, enticing people to begin purchasing, already, for the holidays. Luca is picking me up for "a little vacation." I haven't seen him in a few days. His father is sicker than he's let on, and he's been with him in Arezzo. He hasn't spoken about it, not directly. I know how it feels to be pushed too early, too hard, and so I haven't pushed him at all.

October has come and gone. *You lose time here*, Francesca had said. She's right. It's impossible that I've been here three months, and indirect but pointed references to the future have been creeping into my sister's e-mails. I've been careful to withhold the details of my life from Kate, but one evening, after a few glasses of wine and provoked by her comment that I must be lonely in Florence, I said, "I'm not. I'm not lonely at all. I have a job. I have friends. And I'm seeing someone."

"Who?" Kate jumped on it, and I regretted my admission immediately.

"Someone from the club."

"Is he Italian?" she asked, as though the possibility had only just occurred to her.

"Of course."

She sighed, a sigh that suggested that I was doing this to get back at her.

"What?" I could feel anger edging in.

"Nothing. Just be careful. Don't get too involved, okay?"

Then, "I don't want you to get hurt, Hannah."

Then, "And, anyway, where can it really go?"

"I can handle it, Kate."

"So what's his name?" she asked after a minute.

The lie came easy. "Antonio."

Luca said that I would not need overnight clothing but would need a swimsuit and, if I had them, goggles. It is cold and I'm not sure how I'll have the opportunity to use either, but still I stand by the club, both items in my bag, and I feel the customary jump in my stomach when I see his car round the corner. He pulls up beside me, smiling and already leaning across to open the door.

"'*Giorno*," he says, pausing to kiss me. "I missed you." Then "*Pronti?*" as when he's directing the boat, "*Via!*" and we are off across the bridge.

We're leaving early to avoid the masses that will arrive later, and as we dart through the empty streets, Luca explains that we're going to thermal baths south of Florence. It is the best time to go, he says. Even in this November chill, the baths will be warm. I draw my coat tighter and watch the city waking up. The ghostly stucco buildings are blue in this light, the streets bare, except in the piazzas, where vendors are preparing for the sales this holiday promises. The streetlamps break the fog, and the faint glow in the gray is comforting. The promise of warmth, the promise of home. This could be Boston at this time of day. But it is Florence, and I wonder for the first time in weeks if it is right to feel so untethered and to be so at home with it.

Luca squeezes my hand. "*La nostra piccola vacanza.*" *Our little vacation.*

"The baths—are they near Bagno Vignoni?" I ask.

"*Sì*," he says, surprised. "You know them!"

"St. Catherine—her father brought her there. To heal her."

"*Sì*," Luca says. "And?"

"It didn't work."

"But we are not saints," Luca says, and smiles. "Wait—you are not, are you?"

I shake my head, laughing.

"Good. Then we can be healed in the waters."

"Yes," I say.

He turns on the radio, and I return my gaze to the window as we rattle out one of the city's gates. A few minutes later, we pass a station in a small suburb, where stooped figures wait on the platform, and I remember my solitary visit to Siena and then my trip with Pam and Peter—Peter on the dark platform at the night's end. I feel guilty. But why should I be the one to look after him? Because we are from the same place, because we're not from this place? I suspect that if the situation were reversed, though, he would do more for me, if only because he might still believe that with enough will, we can persuade others of our own happiness, our certainty that everything will, after all, be fine. But I know that isn't true, not when a person has slipped so far down that she can't see anything beyond her own hands clawing to make it past the next immediate hurdle—getting up in the morning, having a conversation, breathing—each exhaustive victory too minute to be called progress. The happiness of others is a feeling forgotten; it cannot be imbued. *Why won't you talk to me?* Julian had asked. But what could he have done? I don't believe that I can do anything for Peter, but the guilt remains.

I look over at Luca. He's humming along with the radio, tapping the steering wheel to the beat, but without his usual small smile. When I ask how his father is, he says, "Okay, okay, *grazie*," with a conviction that prevents me from saying more.

The car is quiet then except for Luca's low humming and the radio, and I slip in and out of sleep, lulled by the drone of the engine and the classic rock songs wailing high and then low. When I open my eyes, we're passing another train station, and I wonder at the frieze of families—they must be families, the tight clusters of old and young—some gripping packages, others holding flowers, their stone faces outside of time. The only solitary figure is a young girl. She has broken free of the crowd and stands near the end of the platform clutching a bouquet, the bright blossoms exploding from her hands. All this in an instant, and I think that I'll ask Luca about it, but I fall back asleep and by the time I open my eyes again, the chalky landscape has drifted into soft pink and we're in the province of Siena. As the yellows and oranges of day triumph, I cannot remember if I'd dreamed the vision, the scene displaced in this new light.

"You sleep well?" Luca asks, giving my hand a squeeze before pulling off the main road into a small town. "*Allora, un caffè?*"

The little coffee bar is packed. In the front, people are sipping espresso and speaking loudly, and a long line has formed at the pastry counter in the back. Luca maintains his easy smile, his hand clasping mine, as he creates space for us at the bar.

"*Due caffè!*" he says, catching the young barista as she passes. I look around at the animated faces. It feels like a holiday. Luca puts an arm around my waist and slides me my espresso.

"What is happing today?" I ask.

"*La festa di Ognissanti.*"

"All Saints' Day."

"*Sì.* And tomorrow, *il giorno dei Morti.*"

The Day of the Dead. Of course. At home, people would be recovering from Halloween, and Thanksgiving displays would already be appearing in store windows. I'd seen none of that here. No costumes, no pretend, no pushing of sweets except, perhaps, for pastries in bars like this one.

"What do people do for it?"

"Some go to church, maybe, but it is not only religious. Some bring flowers for the dead."

The mirage on the train platform becomes clear—grave visitors. "A day of remembrance. It's the same everywhere, *no*?"

"*Forse.* But it is not sad. To remember, yes, but not to think only of death, not to stay..." He draws his lips down with his fingers, an expression I almost never see on him. "It is to celebrate life."

And, indeed, the mood in the bar is celebratory. If Luca is fearful or sad, it is no longer apparent—he is glowing warm, too. He puts his hand on my arm with a quick *"aspetta"* and calls out to the barista. A minute later, a small plate appears in front of us with two round cookies, dusted white.

"Special for the holiday," Luca says. *"Ossi dei Morti."*

"Ossi?"

Luca traces his finger on my forearm. It has more flesh, but I remind myself that the flesh is good, it is good; I am here.

"Bones," I say. "Bones of the Dead."

"Brava," he confirms, handing me one of the cookies with a smile. It is hard and the crunch reverberates in my ears. All at once, I remember the feeling of my own bones, the points of them touching any surface I propped my body against, the realization of how I must have looked then emerging now. The memory isn't frightening, though. It makes this moment full. Taking a bite of his own cookie, Luca smiles, seemingly content to be munching on death.

Once we're back in the car, I watch with interest the changing landscape and the isolated towns—Isola d'Arbia, Quinciano, Torrenieri—until Luca turns off at the exit for San Quirico d'Orcia and pulls to a stop.

"Eccoci!" Luca smiles.

I expect the baths to be large stone pools where Romans might have lounged between conquests, but the sole remnant of the original structure is a colonnade that surrounds an algae-covered basin. We stroll the perimeter of the old bath before entering a building that wraps around a modern pool, complete with artificial waterfalls, where water is piped in from the hot springs. We're each handed a soft white robe at the desk, and when I step out of the locker room to meet Luca, I can't help laughing at the picture of us, shivering in our matching robes.

"Allora," Luca says, "it is too cold to be still—*andiamo!"*

The baths are divided into two sections, one cold and one hot. We shed our robes and, still shivering, I follow Luca down the stairs into the warm section, our splashes echoing. Luca pulls me to the end and we rest with our arms on the edge, looking out. The pool is perched on an incline, and all around and below is the countryside, layers and layers of hills as far as we can see, unbroken by human creations. Orange and red rake across the landscape. The pools are modern, but this must be the same view that Catherine saw when she was forced into the thermal waters. They may not have cured her, but they still brought her what she wanted. Freedom.

I relax into the heat. I'm glad to be here now, beyond the realities of both home and Florence. Luca, too, is more relaxed. The pools are empty except for a couple who have been entwined since we arrived and an elderly man seated by the water's edge reading. He's dressed in an old-fashioned red bathing suit that runs from his neck down to his knees and, with his white beard, he looks like Santa Claus. I tell Luca, and he laughs and then grabs my hand and pulls me toward the artificial waterfall. We stand under it side by side, and the water beats hard on my shoulders, pummeling them with heat until the muscles are almost numb. Luca lets out a loud sigh and says something I cannot hear over the sound of the water. I wade closer, facing him, finding his body with the same hands that have found it for weeks, my fingers tracing the outline.

"It's okay? You like it?" he asks.

I take his hand under the water and squeeze it. "*Sì*. It's perfect. Healing." I grin.

We stare at each other for a moment, hands gripped, as though right at the edge of something and about to leap. Then Luca steps back until he is veiled by the water. His face blurs as he reappears, rivulets tracing his cheeks. He smiles and moves closer, his eyes large and shining.

"Okay," he says, the word lifting and stretching. It's a sound I've come to love—*oh-kai*. Then he puts his hands on my waist and his lips on mine only for a second before I feel myself being lifted and he carries me over the ledge. I cry out as we spill into the cold water, then put my arms around his neck, my legs supported by his hands, and we float as a single organism. He nuzzles my nose and then kisses me, small quick kisses, his features going in and out of focus.

"Like little fish," he says between pecks. "*Piccoli pesci* boiling in the water."

We dance from the hot pool to the cold, together and then separate. I swim laps while Luca stretches out on his back, drifting on the water's surface. Then we both rest our heads on the ledge, hands together, and stare at the sharp blue of the sky. By the time we look around, the pool is empty. Free of spectators, we kiss until I begin to shiver in spite of the warm water.

"*Andiamo*," Luca says between kisses.

I take my time in the locker room. After I shower, I moisturize my whole body—my skin is dry and flaking from the spring water. I feel content, in a warm fog. Somehow this feels like our first date again, and I dress slowly and wonder where we'll go next. I stand under the dryer for a long time, running my hands through my hair, which still has a faint odor of sulfur. When I step outside, it's colder and the baths are closing up for the day. I see Luca, his back to me, pacing where the parking lot drops off into the valley. I feel enamored with the shape of his shoulders and the slope of his arms that have become so familiar.

I catch up and walk just behind him, smelling the sweet, clean fragrance coming off his body. He is thinking intently and doesn't hear me. Finally I reach out and grab hold of his sleeve. He turns and a smile, almost apologetic, stretches across his face as he comes out of his trance. He reaches into his pocket and pulls out a bottle of water.

"It is very important to drink now, *sì*? Otherwise you become sick."

"Dehydrated," I say, taking a long sip.

We stop at a walled medieval town not far from the baths. It is perched on a hill, and the buildings stand crooked where the ground has sunk. It is desolate except for several old women who sit outside on folding chairs, and children whose voices echo but whose figures we never see. We take a table outside the one open bar.

"A sandwich?" Luca asks.

"*Sì*. And also a coffee."

"*Americano?*"

I feign insult at the offer of regular coffee. "*Un caffé normale!*"

"Okay." He smiles, the word lifting and stretching again, before he ducks inside.

Across the street, the late-afternoon sunlight pools on the uneven windowpanes, and in the alley between buildings, floral-patterned sheets blow in the breeze, forgotten.

Luca returns, followed by a very young waiter who smiles shyly as he sets down our sandwiches, coffees, and a small plate with two powdered pastries—more bones of the dead.

"For the holiday," he says to me, his English stilted, and hurries back into the bar.

"Very nice," Luca says.

We eat the sandwiches quickly, hungry after hours in the water. While Luca is paying, I take my espresso as a shot and then eat the bone cookie. When he reemerges, he's on the phone, and he waves to me and holds up a finger before walking in the opposite direction toward the end of the street where the hill drops off. It seems like there is nothing beyond this place, the day's vistas a false memory. I watch Luca's back as he approaches the edge of town, imagine that he might just keep going into that nothingness. I wonder what shape he would leave in his wake. It has a shape to it, loss. The contours of the missing, the angles of absence. When my father left. With Julian. And then with myself. Less distinct with my father, the lines softer, broken by his brief appearances. With Julian, it felt inevitable. But the loss of myself was something altogether different. *Where are you?* he asked. But even as I could clearly see my own edges changing, the flesh falling away, I didn't feel loss. I had that other thing with me. It became a part of me, in the way that people do. They bleed into you, stay with you even when they've gone, the shape imprinted. Like Angela after ecstasy, the absence acutely present, palpable and growing.

Luca returns without saying anything but leans over to wipe some sugar from my lip, followed by a kiss.

"Is everything okay?" I ask as we walk back to the car, our arms brushing lightly.

"*Sì,*" Luca says. "This was my uncle, Silvio. I have a dinner with him."

"Tonight?"

"We must speak. To decide some things."

"About your father?"

"*Sì.*" He pauses, clears his throat. "Tomorrow he goes to the coast, so it must be tonight. I forgot." He squeezes my hand. "The water made me crazy, *no*? *Mi dispiace. Allora*, I will take you home. I would invite you..."

"Of course not. It's your family."

"Also, Silvio is a little strange." Luca speaks quickly, as though he's been waiting to say this.

"Strange? How?"

"*Lui è molto tradizionale. Capisci?*" He looks at me, concerned.

"Traditional." I put my hands in my pockets and watch my feet.

"*Sì.* He would not understand..." He gestures between us.

This. He would not understand this. Because I'm younger? Because I'm foreign? Because I don't quite fit here? I remember his sister's *Oh?* And in Luca's silence now I hear it—that absence that keeps returning.

The bells of the town's crooked church start ringing, and he puts his arm around me. "It's okay?" he asks for the second time today.

I don't answer but slide my hand around his waist. I'm tall compared with most of the women here, but he is taller still, and we walk the rest of the way out of step. He pauses after he opens my door, taking in my expression.

"Why would you tell me that?" I finally ask. "What does that mean? That you want to end things?"

"No! No." He takes my hand, but I pull it loose.

"Or is it some sort of warning? That this can never be anything more than... whatever this is. Jesus, I'm not asking for anything more."

Luca sighs and looks back up at the town. "*Non lo so. Mi dispiace.* I don't like that Silvio is like this. But sometimes I think of it. I think of the future." He looks back at me. "I try to imagine what it would be. Because I like being with you. But my family—they are not easy. Not even for me."

"It's okay. It doesn't matter."

"No, Hannah. It's important. Really. For me, this is good. Isn't it good for you?"

"It is." I sigh. "It is good."

"And what do you think? Do you think of the future?"

"Of course."

"*E poi?*" Luca asks, waiting for more. But I don't know what to say. He knows so little about me. If he knew who I was—who I really was—would he still be speaking about the future? I feel far from him.

"I'm tired," I say. "It's okay, really. I'm not upset." I duck under his arm and climb into the car.

"*Va bene,*" he says softly.

We don't speak for much of the ride home, the radio tuned to the same station, and Luca hums along softly as Bruce Springsteen cries about dancing in the dark.

"*Cazzo,*" Luca says when we pull up to my building. "I am an idiot. We had a beautiful day. It is a holiday. We should not end it like this. I will call Silvio from home."

"Are you sure?"

"*Sì. Sono sicuro.* Silvio wants things only one way. But we can speak on the phone."

And minutes later, we're climbing the hills back to his house.

Chapter Eighteen

Time picks up. Each day, we lose a minute of light, and now there is the suggestion of winter, arriving later than it would have at home, but still it has arrived, the air cold as soon as the sun goes down. I feel the wind shifting, carrying with it the smell of chestnuts from the vendors who are roasting the seasonal treat in all the major piazzas, anticipating the revelry to come—and in this, there is a question. Where will I be when nature takes another turn, cycling and recycling, and winter sets in for good? Because this is no longer the Florence of my arrival, but it is also not the city of the previous weeks, autumn holding on and on.

When I sit out on the balcony in the morning sipping my coffee, I wear a coat and hat. Across the way, the old woman still stands guard, but the scent wafting from her apartment has changed—I smell meat and, occasionally, something sweet and light. The shifting season, the shorter days, the approach of the holidays that I will or will not participate in, all make me feel I need to come to some sort of decision. And my other life, the one that runs on a parallel track but miles away, reasserts itself. Claudia writes me again—"Hannah?"—and again I delete the message. But the messages from Kate I can't ignore: Will I be home for Thanksgiving? For the holidays? Where will I be when the decorations go up, and the club closes its doors, and the Duomo and every other church fills, and... and... and... And then there are the questions about

Luca. Though our routine has remained unchanged, and Luca is the same, I imagine more often that world to which he is attached in which I don't belong, and the questions about the future crowd in, crowding him out.

I respond by digging into my life here. I take a longer route to and from work. I begin ticking things off an invisible checklist. I buy a cookbook and try out Tuscan specialties. Bread and tomato soup, stuffed calamari that leaves my apartment reeking of fish. *"Buona,"* Luca says, smiling through the stench.

I'm reading all the time now about the art this city holds, going deeper than I ever did as a student. I seek out the pieces I haven't yet seen. Lazarus miraculously raised from the dead on the walls of the church of Santa Trinita. The frescoes tucked away in the Brancacci Chapel of Santa Maria del Carmine. In one, Masolino's wooden Adam and Eve accept the apple with hollow smiles. In a mirroring panel, Masaccio depicts their expulsion from paradise, bodies melting, faces horrified.

And a week after our trip to the baths, I go to the Uffizi. The last time I visited was in August, on my second day in the city, jet-lagged and delirious. The museum was packed and it was impossible to get close to any of the art. But now it is November and an hour before closing, and so there is no wait and little noise except for the sad song of the same lone saxophone. The museum has thousands of works from the thirteenth to the nineteenth centuries, but I don't make it past the 1400s on this trip, spending most of my time in one of the first rooms with three different versions of the Madonna enthroned. Two are flat, sober Marys, elongated heads tilted down at odd angles, arms stiff, corpse-pale hands clutching an equally alien child. They are both seated before the gold backdrop of Heaven, outside of place and time. It is the third painting that holds my attention. Up close, I understand, for the first time, its power. Because out of these solemn Madonnas—and all the virgins on all the altarpieces before them—this Mary, Giotto's, sways sensually into the world, her eyes wise, her royal-blue cloak falling away to reveal her breasts, two globes shining beneath the soft folds of her white shift. She is framed by the architecture of the day, and the angels, drawn in perspective, reach toward her with bright hands, and at her feet are vases of flowers, real flowers, the kind of flowers that come from the earth. Mary holds the rotund child with love but without concern, in the same way that she is unconcerned about the veil slipping back off her head, and her not-so-sorrowing almond mouth approaches a smile. Giotto has created a marvel. She's the first real woman since antiquity—and she knows it.

I've made it to only the fifth room, where an altarpiece depicting the life of my old friend Santa Reparata has stopped me, when a guard arrives to announce the museum's closing. And so I move quickly through the rest of the galleries, taking in the bodies growing into their humanity, the repeated female faces looking down at a child or glancing with fear at an approaching angel, Venus on a shell and, centuries later, stretched across a bed, knowing.

"You need at least three full days in the Uffizi," Lorenza tells me the next morning. "Did you see Alessandro Allori's Isabella de' Medici?"

I shake my head.

"A beautiful portrait, but a tragic story—she was killed for adultery. Strangled. Just awful. Did you see the Lippis?"

I feel inadequate, as I sometimes do around Lorenza. I cannot remember all the specifics, only bodies and eyes. "I don't think so."

"There are two. Filippo and Filippino, father and son. I prefer the father's work. He was a monk, but he painted beautiful Madonnas—always the same woman. A nun." She pauses for effect. "His lover."

"Really?"

"There are plenty of sordid details in that museum if you know where to look. They ran away together—Filippo and the nun—it was a true Renaissance romance."

Later I find the paintings in the oversized reference books. The pieces done by the Lippis—both of them—are ethereal. Allori's portrait of Isabella de' Medici is disturbing, though. The young woman with the pouting lips and ivory neck is so far from the accusations, real or created, that would end in the strangling of her older self. How did such events get set in motion? When did she realize things were out of her control?

I cook and eat and read and observe and kiss and make love as the days grow darker and the air grows colder, and suddenly it is mid-November and holiday lights are creeping up—it seems every night there are municipal workers perched on ladders to string a star, a basket, a lit canopy, along another cobbled street. And I think, *Already?* and then, *Where will I be?*

I run into Pam on a Friday afternoon. I'm leaving the library as she enters with a group of girls. She waves them on and stays to chat with me, exuberant until I ask about Peter.

"You haven't seen him? He hasn't been in class, and when he was there, it was like he was a ghost or something. Maybe he went home. Do you know what happened?"

I shake my head—it's the least I can give him. "He hasn't been at the club, either."

"Huh." She looks at me with doubt.

"Only one more month of class. You must be excited. Back to real life, right?"

Pam shrugs and pulls her scarf tighter against the wind. "I don't know. It's funny—I'm really starting to like it here. I kind of can't imagine leaving now."

"I know what you mean," I say, and I want so desperately all of a sudden to ask her advice, this woman who is so much younger than me, but she's already on to the next thought.

"Yeah, well," she says, smiling, "it helps that I have an Italian boyfriend. Anyway, good luck. Say hi to Peter for me if you see him, all right?"

On Sunday, Luca leaves for his family's and I return to the grove. As soon as I climb through the break in the wall, time collapses, as though nothing has occurred between my last visit and this moment, as though my existence in this place is a continuous line, uninterrupted. I settle in the brush overlooking the city and stay for a long time. I look down into the valley and think of home, valleys and valleys and a sea and then an ocean away. I examine the twisted gnarls of the olive trees and the parched grass that is always so dry it is hay. Why is it that the grass never grows while the olive trees flourish, absorbing all the nutrients, all the life? Why is one supported and the other not? And then I think of my old life and wonder if I was just in the wrong place, like these low-lying grasses.

The sun drops, painting the tips of the leaves. The colors and sounds are different from last time. There are evening insects now, and a crow calling insistently. On the other side of the valley, the scene washes out with the twilight. It grows lavender, blue, and then gray as the sun leaves it in shadow and Luca's town fades into the monotone of the hillside, a blank canvas for whatever might appear the next day. The crowing and buzzing rise and then pause as the sun descends. Just before it sets, everything is still, even the wind, as though anticipating the night ahead. And then Florence comes into focus, no longer hidden under the sun's bright eye. Its own lights twinkle on and claim the evening, beckoning. I look at my feet, sloping down, toes pointed toward the city as though I've mounted a sled, the light fading and fading around me. I exhale into the view. And then I decide that I'm not ready to leave. Not yet. There are things to be done. There is something to be done. There is something I've forgotten to do. I wait for the last bit of light to disappear before making my way down my familiar path in the dark.

"Will you be home for Christmas?" Kate asks.

"I think so. I'm not sure."

"Well, let me know," she says. But there's something behind it.

"What?"

"It's just... there are things to manage here. There are bills. There's the apartment—"

"But it's subletted."

"And I'm managing it for you. The way that you left, well—"

She stops, and I can hear in her hesitation the ways she's been careful with me, the things she hasn't said. I hear her holding it back, until I say, "I needed to deal with this in my own way."

And then it spills out of her. "You just *left*. You left a mess, Hannah. Do you think it's easy to answer for you all the time? To act like I know what you're doing? To worry about you and check on you and not know if you'll even call or write?"

Her words try to pull me in, but they don't. I feel too distant now. "I'm sorry, Kate. I didn't ask you to cover for me."

"It's been months. I have my own kids to take care of. I mean, there's a limit. It's just like when you were sick. Nothing's any different. It's so... so..."

"What?" I prod.

"It's so selfish," she says, and then immediately, "I didn't mean that. I'm worried about you."

"It's okay," I say. "I'm okay. I'll sort everything. I will. I just need a little more time."

She sighs. "And, Hannah? Please don't get angry—but be careful. This Italian guy isn't going to fix everything."

I bristle. "This isn't about him, Kate. It's about me. This is about *me* fixing me."

I have a life here now, I want to say, *even if it's not quite like yours.* But she's right about one thing—I am selfish. And I was selfish before. I couldn't see anything beyond myself. And at the same time, I didn't care if I lived or died. That stopped mattering, too. And isn't it better for me to be here now, far from her, than a shadow of a person with her? I escaped it, I'm surviving it, I have more flesh on me now than so many months ago. I... I... I... It was selfish, is selfish, and yet I couldn't have gotten out of it in the way I've gotten out of it here. And as I sit on the balcony later that night watching the stars come out, I breathe a sigh of relief not to be leaving yet, selfish as it may be.

The next day is bright with sun and warmer, and I ask Lorenza if I can leave early and then hurry to the club in the late afternoon.

The men are already gone, but as I enter the locker room, anxious to change and get out onto the river before clouds move in, I find Francesca, bent before the mirror as always. She looks tired.

"The sun brings everyone out of hiding, I guess," she says. "Where've you been?"

"Working."

She looks surprised. "You work? Where?"

"At a library—the Biblioteca Serroni." I unpack my clothing quickly.

"Huh. Good for you. Guess you're staying for a while. Good." She begins coating her lashes with mascara, her eyes open wide. "A library. That would kill me, but good for you." And, when I don't respond, "I didn't even know that place existed."

"It's private. Mostly for students."

Francesca looks back at me, then returns her gaze to her own face before asking, as though as an afterthought, "You ever see Peter there?"

"No." I sit down and pull off my shoes.

"Nice kid," she continues, rustling through her bag on the sink ledge. "But a bit of a baby. That stunt out on the water?"

She pauses, waiting for acknowledgment, until I say, "I feel badly for him."

"Huh." She squeezes a bit of foundation onto a sponge and spreads it across her cheeks, under her eyes. "Who doesn't? But I already have a kid, you know? The last thing I need is another one."

I don't answer, but she continues with force.

"He acts like it's some big surprise that life isn't perfect. That it isn't fair. That *is* life. Not what you expect. And I have to explain that to him?"

I nod. I know very well what she means.

"Sure, you're old enough to know that," she continues. "You're an adult. Not him, though." She closes the little tube and rubs her hands together. "You can't blame me."

I sit up at that. "I'm not. I don't." Meaning it.

She meets my eyes in the mirror and nods.

I finish changing quickly. Pants off, shorts on, not quite looking at my body but no longer as afraid of it as before. Not perfect. But better. When I look back, Francesca is still in front of the sink, unmoving.

"He's a good kid, though," she says, catching my eye again. "You're his friend, right?"

"I guess so." Guilt tugs at me.

"Well, that's good. I'd say you guys should date, but I guess you got a man, huh?" She gives me her sly look. "I'm still waiting for details."

"Sure." I throw my clothes in my locker. "Another time, *va bene*?"

"Yeah," she says. "Who knows how long that sun will stay out."

I leave Francesca with her doubts. I enjoy my afternoon on the river. The water is freeing, the sun warm on my shoulders. But in spite of the lightness of the afternoon and the sense that I have room to breathe out on the water, I have my doubts as well. I don't think we can live in anticipation of disaster, and yet it often happens that we think tragedy has passed us by, or that we've survived the worst of it, when in fact we have witnessed only the initial blow.

Chapter Nineteen

"Hannah?"

The next evening, a regular Tuesday, I'm at the supermarket having the young woman at the deli counter measure out *due etti* of cheese when I hear my name followed by whispering, and then I turn to see her.

"Hannah!" she says brightly, approaching me around the vegetables. The same face, composed; her hair pulled back tight. The same voice from all those months ago—*Look at you*—but overly saccharine, as it was on the afternoon when I'd grown careless. No suit, but a sleek leather jacket that looks brand new, maybe purchased here in the market, and all I can manage is a soft "Claudia?"

"It is you! My god, I didn't recognize you for a minute. You look so good," she says, then quickly, "Not that you didn't look good before, but you look really great. Healthier." *Heavier* is what she doesn't say.

"*Basta così?*" the woman at the counter asks, glancing at Claudia. My face must give me away because she adds, "*Tutto a posto?*" Are *you okay?*

"*Sì, grazie,*" I say quickly, taking my little packet and holding her gaze a beat too long, wishing I could stay with her until Claudia disappeared, could forget I'd ever seen Claudia and get on with my life, but Claudia has turned around and is calling, "Matt, come over here!" to a tall man browsing the meats close by.

"Matt, this is Hannah. My friend from work." *My friend.* "You remember her, don't you? From the benefit? I told you it was her."

"Oh, sure," he says, the flesh gathering around his eyes as he smiles, and I know then that what he remembers is not speaking with me at the party, but whatever came afterward, maybe the conversation they had in the car on the way home, still tipsy, as they dissected the evening and he asked about the girl who was just a little too skinny and drank just a little too much—and Claudia would have assured him, her conscience clean, that she had already tried to intervene. *Look at you.*

And just like that, my old life comes flooding into this small supermarket in Florence.

My throat fills up. "What are you doing here?" I manage.

"Well, we got engaged," Claudia says.

"Oh my god. Congratulations," I say as she holds out her hand so I can see the ring glittering, large, on her finger.

"You didn't get my messages?" she asks. She sounds surprisingly hurt.

I shake my head. The e-mails. Shit.

"Anyway, I was dying to share the news with you. And then Matt found this great last-minute deal to Italy, and I thought, why not? I know it's the week before Thanksgiving, but I told Robert that I just *had* to take it. Everyone says this is the best time to be here, between the tourist seasons. And it's true—I don't think we've had to wait in a single line, have we, Matty?" Then they launch into a catalog of everything they've done so far, and I think about the last time I saw Claudia, when I swung open the door of that strange bathroom with a smile, as though she hadn't heard anything, couldn't see the red around my eyes or smell the bile coming off my breath.

Early June. We were in the home of one of the board members. His apartment was balanced at the top of a tall glass building, a great eye looking over the city. All windows, and nowhere to hide. Sparse everything, except for the drinks and the food, which kept coming—*Don't you want any? Aren't you hungry? You need to put some meat on those bones.*

They're envious, I'd thought. But I could feel their eyes—Claudia, the director, the trustees—and so I took everything they offered me. How much? I lost track. I couldn't hold on to anything anymore. Any time someone said something, I ate. Too much. Far too much. Too much to drink as well.

Our host joined our circle, began talking about something that seemed humorous, though his look told me I was wrong to laugh when I did, and so I excused myself, walked over to one of the many windows to look out. I tried to stay steady, but we were so high up, and it felt like the building was swaying, or I was swaying. Everything was swaying.

Slowly the haze began to lift, and then I could feel inside of me all the food, all the wine. A ticking bomb. And for what? I had to see myself. To empty myself. I couldn't wait.

I found the bathroom at the end of a hallway. Slate and marble with a broad mirror. I stripped off my blouse, my pants, watched my image swaying. Then I bent over the toilet—pressure in my head, cold tiles hard under my knees—I was clutching the bowl. There was no choice. I could see myself in the water. *If only you were...* Then I stopped thinking and let everything come up. I was crying. I always cried when I threw up.

I was not listening. I was careless. The door opened. I thought I'd locked it, but I must not have, because it opened. Though I didn't notice until I heard a quiet "Oh." A small person in the doorway. A girl. Seven? Eight? The daughter. The trustee's daughter. I stood up, mumbled something, tried to cover myself, but she fled. The room was spinning. I closed the door, locked it, dressed, turned on the faucet and let it run and run until there was knocking.

"Hannah?" a voice asked. Claudia.

It was done. I knew it was done.

"Hannah, some people have been saying..." In Robert's office again. He took off his glasses, rubbed his eyes. "Is there someone you can talk to?"

"I'm fine," I said, "I just need to take better care of myself."

He sighed. "I—we can't."

And then I knew that the eyes wouldn't leave me.

"We'll take care of you, of course—three months' severance."

I nodded. It was done.

He didn't look at me then, left his glasses on the desk. "I'm sorry" is all he said.

My sister in her well-ordered apartment: "You should sue."

"It's over. I made mistakes—other mistakes. It's in my contract."

"Still. You're not yourself. You're sick." She paused, then added softly, "Maybe you should get some help."

"I'm fine," I said.

"Hannah..."

"For god's sake, stop looking at me."

"It's so good to see you," Claudia says once they've caught me up to today, to this very moment in the supermarket. "You've been here for quite a while?"

Who told her that? I take a few steps away from the counter, giving a nod to my friend, as though walking Claudia and Matt away from her might keep this place mine.

"It's just a break," I say. But taking in their anticipatory expressions, I have the urge to defend it, and so I continue. "An extended break, to really get the experience of living here," and I tell them, then, that I belong to a rowing club, have a job, have some "Italian friends," which means, of course, that I'm learning to speak Italian pretty well—not fluent, but getting better. They're trying to look interested, but they overcompensate, grinning and nodding as you might to appease a small child, this couple, with their secure relationship and their excellent choices. Even if they find any of what I say valid, they won't admit it, I realize. My choices are the choices of someone who is flailing, and this is all I can think as I try to make my life here stick. *Look at you.* The more I say, the smaller I feel, and so I stop. I've already given them too much. She'll tell everyone again.

"That sounds so nice, doesn't it, Matt?" Claudia says. Then she checks her watch. "Honey, go pay for our stuff, would you? I'd love another minute with Hannah."

Dutifully he heads toward the cashiers.

"Girl talk," Claudia says to me, putting a hand on my arm just as she had that afternoon in the bathroom, her excitement camouflaged by concern. I look down at her arm in her new leather jacket.

"So are you seeing anyone here?" she asks.

"No," I say. "No." I won't let her have that, not him.

"Shoot. I was hoping for a little romance—you deserve it!" Her voice is higher pitched now. She waits for me to say more, but there is nothing left to say. "Well, you look great. *Much* healthier." *Heavier.* "You have to come to dinner with me and Matt. How about Saturday? Anyway, it has to be Saturday. After that, we leave for Cinque Terre." She says it with a soft *c* like an *s*, rather than the hard Italian *ch*. "Everyone talks about it. *Sinkwa Terra. Sinkwa Terra.* And then it's back home—it goes so fast. God, I envy you, just hanging out here." I wince, but she continues. "So, dinner Saturday? We've found this restaurant with the most amazing steak— and the waiters are delicious. Maybe we can set you up?"

I shake my head. "I have plans," and I do. Luca and I are driving to the coast. But my voice sounds hollow.

"That's really too bad." She pauses, gives me a moment to change my mind. "Well, how about this—we can grab a coffee tomorrow or the next day. There's *no way* I'm leaving this city without seeing you again. Just a quick coffee. I'll e-mail you tomorrow—sound good?"

She waits, keeping those same sharp eyes locked on me, no room for questions or doubts, no escape from the extended humiliation, and so I promise we'll meet and give her a hug that is too warm.

I wander the aisles, waiting for them to leave, my mind racing with the exuses I will fabricate. Then I leave myself without buying anything, abandoning the small satchel of cheese on a shelf. The city feels different when I get outside, like it might blow away with a strong wind.

Something has come loose. Just one small thing, but it's enough.

The next day I go to work in the morning and the club in the afternoon. I almost collide with Luca coming out of the locker room, and I must look terrified because his own surprise turns to laughter as he puts his arms around me.

"You thought I was a ghost?" he asks.

I have lunch with him and the men, and I smile and nod on cue, but I feel far from them. Walking back to the library, I glance around, as though I might find my old life at every corner. Claudia is still in the city, so I am not mad—this is a possibility, in fact. *There's no hiding here.* And like clockwork, her e-mail arrives—"Meeting up!"—outlining her itinerary and the many open windows in which me might connect. *We have so much to catch up on—all these months that you've been here. It's great to see you doing so well. You have to tell me your secret!* And though she doesn't say it, in the spaces between her words are the words *you will slip up. You will slip up again.* I do not respond.

The feeling stays with me all through the next day, and it is with me at Luca's house in the evening.

"*Stai bene?*" Luca asks, and I realize I've been staring out his kitchen window, unspeaking.

"*Sì,* sorry. I'm great," and I smile and smile, put my arms around him, feel the heat coming off him, and still I can't shake the chill. We talk, but I don't know what I'm saying. We make love, but I feel like there's someone else in my place. *You will slip up.* Because I'm faking it, all of it. I've been lying to him, I've been lying to everyone, sweeping my past away as though it didn't belong to me, as though it wasn't mine. What was I thinking coming here?

The next morning, I'm showered, dressed, and anxious to go, but when I come out of the bedroom, shivering with wet hair, it smells like coffee and I find Luca in the kitchen preparing breakfast, upbeat and humming.

"But you're late." I smile and try to look like the woman he's been with for weeks, try to remember what she might say, what she might do.

"First, breakfast. Then we go." He takes a tomato off the counter and tosses it to me. "*Dio spero,*" he says.

"A tomato?" I ask, letting it roll from one hand to the other.

"No, no." He produces a small knife and takes the red orb from me, slicing it evenly in two, index finger to thumb. "It is like a fruit. It is sweet."

He carefully hands me half. Its gelatinous insides are more orange than red and jiggle with the slightest vibration. My teeth cut the skin to find fruit like a plum. Juice spills out. Luca laughs and catches it in his palm.

"You like it?"

"Mmm..." I mumble, chewing slowly. "It's great."

We finish it between the two of us and it feels, for a minute, just as it always does when we are together.

"*Dio spero*," I repeat the name. "God hopes?"

"Divine fruit," Luca corrects, reaching for another one and pausing to inhale it deeply with a smile before putting an arm around me. "*Diospiro.*"

I try to hold on to the moment, to hold on to him as we rattle down the small roads into the city and he leaves me at the bridge near the library, reminding me that he'll see me the next morning for our trip to the coast. I try to believe that this is real, that this counts. But as I make my way through my usual tasks, it is hard to recall the sweetness of the morning, even as I keep mistranslating *God hopes* in the hope that there is someone somewhere, however distant, rooting for Luca, for me, for a safe end to this day, but I feel instead the weight of the past, the depth of my lies, and the desire to hide.

And so I'm not surprised that my hopes go unanswered when Luca calls that same evening.

"Ciao, Hannah, *mi dispiace*. I cannot meet tomorrow."

"It's fine." I'm more relieved than anything else. "It's no problem. Is everything okay?"

"I must go to Arezzo again. For the weekend and... for longer, I think." His voice is calm, but it falters when he adds, "My father, well, *ci vediamo.*" *We'll see.*

"I'm so sorry, Luca."

He sighs. "*Grazie.* It's possible I come over tonight? To say goodbye?"

I hear the need in his voice. But I can't bring myself to say yes. I have to think. I have to get back to myself. "I'm not feeling so well."

"*Davvero*? Then I can take care of you," he says, softer.

"I don't want to make you sick, too, Luca. I have to sleep. When you get back. We'll go to the coast. When you get back."

On Saturday morning, another message from Claudia—"Hello???" I think about responding with a slew of excuses about my busy life here. Instead I return to the supermarket and load up a cart, then spend the entire day at home preparing a meal, determined to make true the fact that I have plans, even if they are only cooking and sipping wine with the music from my small radio keeping me company.

I don't eat in the kitchen but instead set the table in the living room with the nicest silverware and dishware I can find. I've made braised chicken and vegetables, and a fennel salad with pine nuts and Parmesan. I light a candle and pour myself a glass of wine, turn out the kitchen lights, and carry the radio into the living room. But when I sit down to eat, I find that I'm not hungry. I take a few bites but then leave it. I go to bed early without having eaten.

In the days that follow, I try to get back to my rhythm, to be fully present as I sip my morning coffee on the balcony, chat with Lorenza about my reading, pull long strokes on the ergometer, eat lunch at the café, walk slowly home along the river, drink a glass of wine over dinner, turn up the radiator just a bit before I climb into bed. In these sensations—the steaming coffee always in the same cup, Lorenza's small smile each morning when I arrive, the *tap tap tap* of my fingers on the computer, the warm greetings of the men at the club, the rhythmic wheeze of the ergometer, the conversation buzzing around my table at lunch, the loud *clink* as I lock up the library, the chill that cools me on my walk home, the light snapping on in the stairwell, the smell of gas when I light the stove, the drip and hiss of the radiator when I drift to sleep—in each of these is the promise that this life can be sustained. As though by performing these actions in the same way each day, I might hold on to it.

You will slip up. As though the past with its ghosts doesn't exist if I don't look at it directly, like a child who closes her eyes tight and believes that, in her blindness, those things that she fears cease to be.

Thanksgiving arrives and I don't call home. When Luca phones the next evening, I am still not myself. So much weight in his voice—he's been gone almost a week, and it must be a nightmare, each day of his father's dying. I can hear, again, his need and then his disappointment when I say, after a few stilted minutes, that I have to go. My withholding feels like a dare, and I wonder if he will look for someone to fill the void left by my distance. Still, I remain detached. Because I'm not the woman he thinks I am. Something has changed in me. There is a heaviness growing that I can't get free of, and when I hang up the phone, my apartment hums with its own silence.

This is how it begins. Slowly at first. It creeps in. Without my having invited it, it comes, even as I am still going to the library each day, working out at the club in the afternoons, and cooking elaborate meals in the evenings that I eat. I do eat them. I stop eating in the morning, only the morning. It isn't so much a decision as it seems to just happen, and once it happens, it is so easy to stay with it. To sleep in a bit later, tell myself that I'm too busy, too busy even for a cup of coffee before I leave or an espresso on my way to work. *I'll save it for lunch,* I think, *something to look forward to.* Anyway, it's only for a few hours, and I have plenty of energy in the morning. For a couple of days, I leave it at that.

The elation arrives quickly—I'm surprised at how quickly it sets in—and the longer that I wait to eat and the less that I eat, the more it builds. Instead of going to the club or the café on my lunch break, I make my way up into the hills behind the library—strange it hadn't occurred to me to do this before. I spend the two hours walking, the cold and occasional drizzle refreshing, and Lorenza always comments on the color in my cheeks when I return. I feel awake and alive.

So I start to push it, a little more each day. I eat lunch a little later, and it seeps into the afternoons. It's so easy. It's so easy to push it a few more minutes, another half hour, another hour, and then another. And there's a promise in it—a prize waiting at the end of every minute that I hold out, and so I hold out longer. When I do eat, I'm barely hungry. I shrink lunch to a snack: yogurt, a piece of fruit. It fills me. I *do* eat in the evening, and so it is easy to say to myself, to anyone who might ask, that nothing is wrong, as I imagine throughout the day the meal that I will prepare, visualize it in detail.

The elation grows and, with it, a sense of clarity, anything non-essential dropping away. The city takes on a glow. It vibrates just slightly, as though I can see the life coming off the buildings, the crowds, the river.

It doesn't take long. Several days and I'm back to where I was months ago, but I am not afraid. It makes sense that I do these things, and I don't know now why I'd waited so long. I only eat one thing before dark: a piece of fruit, easily quantifiable. I drink an espresso, but with no sugar, just a boost for the late afternoon. And things are fine, they are always fine, for a while.

At work, I'm filled with energy, high on it. Lorenza asks me to reorganize whole sections of books or catalog members going back decades, and I perform these tasks like some sort of Olympic athlete. I continue walking up into the hills during lunch, feel the satisfying stretch in my muscles, proud of the emptiness that is able to sustain me for an hour or more up and then down, and Lorenza still comments on the color in my cheeks. In the evening, I go to the club and I'm unstoppable, an endless well of energy, burning, burning, burning, the excitement, the power of calories expended. I'm using more than I'm taking in, far more, and this is a triumph. I rarely run into the men I know, but when I do, I greet them warmly, unembarrassed, and confide, with appropriate solemnity, that, no, Luca's father is not well at all, and, no, I don't know when he'll be back.

I e-mail my sister every few days with long and detailed descriptions of the food I've eaten or would have eaten. I lie. It's so easy, and I wonder why I've been honest all these months, how I could have become so distracted. Luca calls, his voice sad, and maybe for this reason he doesn't notice a change in me. I'm glad that he's not here to interrupt this.

After a week, the fog sets in. But I am not foggy. I am clear. I am attuned, so attuned, my nerves pulled tight, waiting to be struck. And the city responds. It grows louder and brighter, the sounds sharper, the colors more vivid, the light sometimes blinding. Passing voices and distant bells echo long and loud. The statues in Piazza della Signoria twist and turn when I walk by them at night, the floodlights below carving deep shadows into the stone faces of Hercules, Perseus, and the Sabine woman with her sharply pointing finger. They each seem to have something to say, as everything in this city does, and the sensation is so strong that I have to look away. And when I hear, one evening, the man with the lone saxophone playing outside the Uffizi, just the touch of his song—one or two notes—brings tears to my eyes, as anything can now, though I don't feel sad. Only closer to something—something vital that everyone around me is oblivious to, something that only I can see as the trappings evaporate. *I stripped myself of everything.* The phrase drifts in, is wise, is true.

And when I'm alone, the fog, and the lights and sounds that penetrate it, feels safe and I feel lucid. But when I'm around others now—with Lorenza or the men at the club or on the phone with Luca—the clarity leaves me. That's not quite right—I still feel clear, but I know that they won't understand, and their very presence clouds my own understanding. And so I stay busy at the library but avoid Lorenza's eyes, my head bowed low. And when, two weeks after Luca's departure, I bump into Stefano leaving the club and he stops me with a "Hannah, *stai bene?*" and a look of concern, I stop going altogether, afraid of witnesses who might report something.

Not going to the club means that I need to do something else. Dinner cannot happen without it, and I'm smart enough to know that if I stop eating altogether, things will come apart. I need to sustain enough, just enough, to hold it together, to maintain this state of clarity without dropping over the edge. And so I walk more in the evenings, choose restaurants that are well beyond the gates of Florence, get lost on my way, arrive late, order a salad with grilled calamari, or a plate of vegetables, or a winter soup. My stomach hurts when I eat, so I eat less and drink more instead. Then the long walk home, with some regret, looking forward already to the clean slate of the next day when I will do better.

I don't feel lonely. Still, one evening after a few glasses of wine, I respond to the glances of my young waiter—a boy, really, maybe Peter's age—whose eyes suggest that I need him, must need someone, sad woman that I am. I let him give me a ride home on his moped, though I know I'll have to make up for the lost walk the next day, and I invite him upstairs. Once in my apartment, he is no longer a boy. He is aggressive, insistent, and when I feel the weight of him on top of me and tell him to stop, his face grows angry, older, and he hurls words at me in sharp Italian, tells me I'm a lonely old woman, a tease of a whore. But he leaves, and once he's gone and I lock the door tight, his words don't touch me. And when Luca calls that same night at the late hour that he said he would, I let the phone ring and ring, half guilty about the boy, though it is more than that. And when he calls again a few days later and leaves a message to tell me that he's back, would like to see me, would like to know that I'm okay, I don't respond.

Because the boy was wrong—I am not lonely. I don't need him or anyone else. Here's the thing: I am not alone. I have something more than myself. My old friend returned. We have a good grip on each other now. And it doesn't feel painful or cruel, this grip. It is not threatening, but intimate, immediate, necessary. It is an embrace.

Chapter Twenty

Friday afternoon. We are into December, but today is warmer, so I choose a different path into the hills, the smooth winding road and growing euphoria urging me on. I could walk all day, all night, and not grow tired. But when it is time to turn around, I am lost, surrounded by high walls with no way of knowing where the city is from where I stand. I remain calm—there is nothing threatening here. Being lost is inconsequential, is exciting even. I've eaten nothing today and I feel so light now that I could float away into whatever new place this road is taking me. But as I wander up one road and then down another, I curse myself. Because I'll be late getting back from lunch and my lateness will mean more conversation with Lorenza, when I no longer trust my voice with her, when all that I want is to have her eyes off me. Because I know that she knows something.

I take a wider road, hoping it will lead to a town, however small, or a vista, and when I come upon a shorter wall, I jump up to try to see over it, to see the city or suburbs or whatever lies in that direction, but each leap reveals only a flash of a large home and valleys beyond, all glowing, all trembling, as everything does these days. My head begins to ache and I try another road. After two more bends, I stop and lean back against the wall, ready to give up. Maybe I won't go back to the library at all. That will solve it.

It is cold but sunny, and I can feel some warmth coming off the stones as my bones press into them. I hear footsteps, a soft *pat pat pat* from somewhere below, growing louder until I see a figure jogging. I wonder if I'm dreaming. I never see anyone on these walks. As I watch his labored steps, the cadence of his body's movements become familiar—Sergio from the club. I want to hide then, but there is nowhere to go. There is just this single road surrounded by walls, and me and Sergio.

He glances once and then again before his brow releases and his face opens up, revealing his teeth, and it seems like it's been so long since I've seen anyone from that world that tears almost spring to my eyes. Then I remember my purpose and the feeling recedes.

"Ah! Hannah, ciao!" Two jarring kisses hello. "*Che ci fai qui?*"

"Just walking," I say, my head pounding. He looks at me quizzically. "Only I'm lost, I think."

Sergio nods but must not understand, because he says, "A beautiful day. *Ma va tutto bene?* We miss you at the *canottieri*. You are stranger."

A stranger, he means, though I must also seem strange now. I try to compose my face, to make my features less strange, but I know I still look not quite right. Why is it that the clarity abandons me so quickly, why now, when I most need it? Keep it together.

"*Davvero*, we are worrying," he says.

I nod. I'm seeing him through a fog and just following his words is exhausting. I cannot follow them and think at the same time. And I need to think. Because I'm not safe now. Things are coming loose, threatening to fall apart entirely.

"Luca says he also does not see you. He worries for you," Sergio says then.

Hearing his name startles me. How long ago was it that he called me? A few days? A week? I try to think back, to get a hold of it, but the details are vague, I can't quite grasp them. And I feel something settling hard in the pit of my stomach now, something like dread.

"His father?" I remember to ask.

"*Ah, sì.*" Sergio explains that he is okay—well, not okay, but alive—a small miracle, and so Luca is back for now.

As he speaks, I try to find an answer to this moment. I pull apart the pieces, examine them, but my head is a mess. Sergio falls silent, waits. I should say something. But I have no idea what he just said and so I nod and nod. There must be a way out.

Sergio smiles wide then, as if he's discovered the solution. "*Allora*, I see Luca today. I meet him in one hour. *Vuoi venire con me?*" Go with him? Such an easy idea, and the old me would have said yes right away, would have gone with him to assure everyone that I was fine; would have seen Luca, watched the lines grow like small bursts of light around his eyes; would have had a meal with them and then, perhaps, gone with Luca back to his house, where we might have been full with the idea of being close again, high on it, shy at first and then not as we remembered each other, and I would have tried to be the one who comforted. I can picture all of this and I'm about to say yes, that yes, in fact, I will go with Sergio, but he's looking at me oddly and I can read myself so clearly in his face, everything written across me.

I cannot go with him. I cannot go back to the club. It is impossible. That world is too distant, leagues from where I stand now, and I can see the chasm, wide between us—it will only grow wider when I am with Luca. I cannot face Luca, cannot face any of them. I've been there before and I know how I will look to them, to him. It is all there on Sergio's face.

"Today, it isn't possible," I say, and smile. I draw up all my energy, infuse my voice with it, my voice that sounds suddenly so loud, so unfamiliar. "But soon, *va bene*? Very soon. Say hello to everyone for me? Tell Luca I will call?"

Sergio looks skeptical.

"*Digli che lo chiamo io,*" I say, as though it's a problem of comprehension. Which it is. He doesn't understand this strange woman standing before him. How could he?

His face doesn't change, but he says, "*Ci vediamo presto, allora?*" He offers a hand, plants two more jarring kisses on my cheeks, and continues up the road, breathing hard. I'm breathing hard, too, and I lean back against the wall. Then I remember that I'm still lost.

"Sergio!" I call before he rounds the corner. "*Da che parte è Firenze?*"

I can hear his laugh, nervous, before he points to the road on my left and throws his arm down twice. "*A sinestra e poi dritto.*" Another wave and he's gone.

I walk slowly, my steps lead, the lightness of this bright day evaporated, the fog that has been so pleasant shifting. My heart is beating loud in my chest, pushing the blood fast through my body. I can feel the knot of fear expanding, the world changing, growing dark. The walls are heavy on either side, inching in as though they might swallow me, and by the time I'm back in the city, I am sweating and sick. I breathe slowly, in and out, push it all down—Sergio's expression, the shifting fog, Luca, the dread, the growing darkness—compress it until I can hold a stone face. But as I approach the library, a bitter taste wells up in the back of my throat. *You are stranger.* I can't go in there. I can't face Lorenza.

I turn around, walk quickly down a side street, moving fast as though the thoughts may stop if I speed up, but they keep on coming, my head filling, my skin flushing. If only I could keep it at bay a little while longer, just a few more days, a few more hours, a few more minutes. I'm not greedy. I'll take anything now. Anything.

It's too late, though. The world has changed and I can feel it. That familiar moan. The emptiness around me, the emptiness within me, not static but growing, a void with no center, feeding on itself, a void of my creation. *Welcome,* I keep saying, again and again. *Welcome. Take this body. It is yours. Take this pain.* I walk with heavy steps through one of the city's gates and dig my nails into my hands instead of screaming. A bike races past, bell ringing loud; a voice shouts and I jump onto the curb. The sidewalk ahead comes sharply into focus before it drops away, a camera shutter closing to a point, and the moment, the day, the last few months, begin to dissolve. I am here, then I'm underwater, the pressure in my head beating, nausea setting in. Tears pool into my eyes, threaten to spill over, and my insides pitch one way and then the other. *Don't,* I think, *don't,* but I can't keep it down. I duck into a bar, keep my eyes averted. *Don't look.* I walk to the back, into the bathroom, into the stall where everything comes up fast and hard. There's nothing in me and still it comes, with a loud retching that must shake the whole bar, followed by tears that I let run and run until there are no more. I sit on the dirty floor, exhausted, thinking about all the bathroom stalls that I've disappeared in, all the floors, toilets, walls that I've knelt on, bent over, leaned into.

And then I feel, again, that moan, distant but deep.

Look at me.

I close my eyes tight, but something breaks. Something has broken.

Look.

I am at the bottom. Just like all those months ago when I arrived as deep and as low as I would go.

Look at me.

I can feel it on top of me, ahead of me, the weight of it. I keep my eyes shut, waiting for it to disappear, but it remains, large and looming.

Look.

It is too late. It will not be ignored.

Look at me.

My heart picks up, my mind moves. I snap my eyes open, go to the faucet, wash my face. Back through the bar—"*Prego, signora*"—but I keep going, out into the street. I walk toward the center, weaving through side streets, keeping my head down. I walk until my legs are shaking and my skin feels slick under my clothes. I walk until a thunderous roar engulfs me. I look up. I'm in the piazza in front of San Frediano in Cestello. The church's doors are closed, the gate locked, but it sounds like there is a great force inside, a waterfall rushing or a supernatural being breathing loud. I stand there and stare, listening to this roar. It is as though the church is filling with the sea, the doors about to burst and wash me away. After everything, this is how it will end. I back up, away from the roar, and the sound changes. It is coming from behind me now. It is the river, pouring across the spillover, the pounding echoing off the church's facade. There are no demons here. And no answers, either. I'll go home.

But then I see that the tall gates of the convent—always locked tight—are open, and so I enter, cross a gravel lot and walk through a dark open lobby into a cloistered garden thick with plants, four trees anchoring its corners. One wall of the cloister is a small chapel, windows glowing, and I can hear voices chanting in an unfamiliar language.

I take a few steps before I see her: a stone woman at the garden's center, the evening fog rising around her. It is her. It must be. She looks like she might stride right off the pedestal. Her halo is bent back, flying from her head as though it is being torn away by an invisible hand. I walk around the cloister until I'm standing in front of her and can read her name cut into stone before me: SANTA MARIA MADDALENA DE' PAZZI. Mary Magdalene of the Crazies. Of course. This is where she lived. Where she died. I look up. Her eyes are globes. I step to one side, then the other, and they follow me. I sit down on a bench in front of her. On the other side of the courtyard, there are two signs: HOSTEL DE' PAZZI and, in blue block letters that tumble down the edge of a doorframe, BAR DE' PAZZI. A few chairs. A game table. All empty and quiet. And so this is how she is remembered, in this overgrown garden with her back to this bar. Bar of the Pazzis. Bar of Crazies.

When the service ends, there is an avalanche of voices as people file out, shades walking away, leaving me in the growing dark. I wait until it is silent and I am alone, and I feel, finally, calm. Far from the afternoon. Far from Luca, from Sergio, from Lorenza, who must be closing up the library now, wondering what's become of me.

A light blinks on across the courtyard, buzzing over the falling letters. I freeze. There's the sound of clinking inside the little bar and then, a few seconds later, loud English, and two men step out holding beers. They walk over to the game table, begin playing, the clicks and spins echoing. A third man, tall with a grizzled beard, appears and leans against the wall next to those falling letters looking out. It is dark here, I remind myself. It is dark. The table clicks and spins, and one of the players curses. Then I see the tall man's look change, grow focused, and he lowers his beer.

"Hey," he says. "Hey! There's someone out there."

I stop breathing. The clicking and spinning stops.

"Hey, who's there?" He takes a step forward, his voice gruff.

"It's a statue, idiot."

"No, behind it, right there."

"What the fuck?" says a third voice. "Who's there?"

The tall man begins making his way around the garden, under the arcade.

"Are you staying here? What are you doing here?"

"Nothing," I say loudly, and this stops him for a minute. "Just sitting."

But he keeps coming, the others behind him, and so I jump up, walk fast out of the garden and back through the convent. I start running. I can hear them following, and a voice shouts, "Hey!" as I run into the lot. There is light, revealing me. I run for the gates. They are closed. I panic, then see a button to one side. I push it hard and the gates begin to creak open. As I slip through the widening crack, I hear, "It's just some woman. What's her problem? It's just some woman."

I keep running, filled with rage now. How dare they? Chasing me off like vermin. And now there's nowhere for me to go. I slow to a walk and then stop, sweating, and lean against the wall. I won't scurry for them. The bells of San Frediano in Cestello begin to ring, long and loud. *Love itself is not loved. Love itself is not loved.*

The night guard at the library's entrance nods sleepily as I pass her. I mumble about having forgotten something. *There's something I've forgotten to do.* I walk up the dark steps and down the hall, push my key into the lock and open the door, half expecting to see Lorenza there waiting. But the library is silent. I turn on one of the lights, find my bag, then make my way back to the shelves, to all those books I'd returned weeks ago. I run my hands along the spines. They chased me out, those men. That place might be theirs, but these are mine. *The Life and Miracles of St. Margaret of Cortona. The Dark Night of the Soul. The Order of the Poor Clares.*

I begin to pull out books, one by one, and put them into my bag. I take one and then another and another, the corners catching on the shelf with a loud *thunk.* One cover tears—*The Blessed Angela.* Of course. But it doesn't matter. I can never come back here. I resist the temptation to open them, to read the first few lines. Later. Later. It is amazing—there is so much here and it feels as though I have my arms deep down in mud, digging with cupped hands. It's so obvious now. So obvious that there must be an answer hidden amid the muck. Something I missed. Something they didn't tell me about. Something that could free me. I squeeze the last book into my bag, then turn out all the lights in the library except for the one in the hallway where Signora Arcelli's portrait stares at me accusingly. I find my way down the stairs, past the night guard. I imagine she will stop me, search me, ask me about all these books, but she only nods.

As soon as the night air hits, I'm frantic to get home, as though something might happen to these books or to me between now and then. I cross the street, hugging the wall along the river. I look down at the club as I pass and it seems like a memory from long ago.

I don't stop for food, but I do stop at the all-night *vineria*, squeezing in between the group of men huddled around the small, fluorescent window gripping plastic cups. I smile but I cannot look the elderly vendor in the eye as I pay for four bottles of wine. *Look normal*, I think, but what could be normal about buying so much wine at this time of the night with this odd grin? Say something.

"*Grazie.*"

Then I walk fast, almost running the final few blocks, loping and off-balance, the bag heavy at my side. Everything looks misaligned and the sidewalk feels unsteady, as though the ground is not solid, as though the earth is not earth but something gelatinous. Chills scale my legs and I'm light-headed. I've felt this before, the ground giving way. Felt it for months back home. Just like old times.

"*Ciao, bella*," I hear as I approach my door. I don't stop. I just need to get home.

The light in the stairwell is out, and I'm forced to walk up slowly, my shoulder screaming from the weight, feeling along the wall until I reach my floor, where I use all my energy to push open my door. From far below, I hear that haggard voice—"*Signorina*"—and I slam my door, triple-locking it. Too bad.

The apartment is dark and I turn on only the small kitchen light. I take off my sweater, lay it over the back of the chair, walk down to the bathroom, empty myself, wash my face, dry it, and return to the kitchen. I open the doors to the balcony and the cold air feels good. I am calm now that I have a direction, a task. I need to think clearly. Puzzle it out. There is an answer. There must be.

I open the wine, pour myself a tall glass, take out the books, and begin, one by one, unearthing the words.

Do not ask me to give in to this body.

The words that stare up at me are different, though, transformed as though the texts have changed. Though perhaps it is only I who have changed. This is true. I am not the same woman who read these words before. That woman is gone. And what of all the women before her? If I could go back to the time before I was carrying this emptiness, before I was carving away. If I could find that moment when everything shifted—*when did this start?*—that kernel, however small.

Do not ask me to give in to this body.

Because there was a time when I was safe in my body. A long time. The years when Kate and I shared a room. I was grounded, practical, somewhat oblivious. Even after our father left. I didn't act out, didn't adopt extreme behavior. I didn't start wearing makeup early, wasn't the last girl in the grade to get my period or the first to get a bra. I was average, normal. I was safe.

Between me and my body there must be a struggle.

A gymnasium. Three girls lined up, standing at attention. He went down the line with his finger, labeling our breasts. We did not look at one another. We did not speak of it.

Between me and my body there must be a struggle until death.

But that's not right. That was a story people told me. *This is where it begins*, they said.

Priests cannot preach it.

In health class they talked about eating disorders; we read dramatic testimonials in a text that tried to be contemporary but wasn't, that tried to shock us into identification but didn't. None of the girls in the book sounded like me. I knew girls in real life who didn't eat. They looked like ghosts, but the boys still liked them.

They do not understand what they preach.

I wasn't jealous—my boyfriend didn't like them. He took off my shoes one cold winter evening, warmed my feet with his hands. And I knew things were coming and I only had to wait.

They babble.

I wasn't like the ghost girls and I didn't want to be like them. Anorexia was something for other people. Not eating was something other girls did.

My delights have heretofore been bodily and vile...

Even in college when I gained weight, I didn't care. I had sex for the first time when I was at my heaviest. Did I think about the additional flesh? Did I want to live any other way? There must have been women in school who were sick, but I wasn't like those women.

...because I am a body.

I graduated, got one job and then the job at the museum. I had friends. I dated and had relationships. Nothing that lasted, but what does in your twenties? I was safe in my body. I was fine.

She did not seem to be the same.

And then I wasn't fine. At some point, I found myself in that fog. It sat thick around me. Impenetrable. How long did it last? Years. For years I fell in and out of that state.

She did not seem to be the same person.

And then Julian arrived.

I saw a brightness.

I felt hopeful. I close my eyes and everything returns vividly, months compressed. A break in the fog. Finally. Someone good. Someone kind. The beginning, the warmth and elation, as though a great light were shining on me. I see myself then, satisfied in the glow.

Let the tongue of the flesh be silent.

And I see, too, when things began to change, the sadness creeping in, expanding between us. He peppered me with questions as I pulled away, asked me to describe that thing I had no words for. *Leave me alone.* Those were the words I had.

Let the tongue of the flesh be silent when I seek to express my love for you.

Why won't you talk to me? he'd asked, the room coming apart in ribbons around us. I remember his hand sliding up and down my arm, along the scabbed line where I had cut myself—not on purpose, though it felt like it had happened because of some error on my part. There was something in the pain that felt good.

Let the tongue of the flesh be silent...

I kept going, carving deeper into my flesh, watching it disappear around me. *How do you cut so close to the bone?* they asked. The truth I did not tell: *I have found a shortcut.*

...when I seek to express my love for you.

It was not his voice that I heard. He never said, *Starve yourself, shed yourself, change form, disappear.* He cared about me.

Strip yourself of everything.

Leave me alone, I said.

Of everything.

Leave me alone. Until he did. And I kept going, digging deeper and deeper, sculpting and scratching, then bending over so many toilets.

Of all attachments.

Because it wasn't his embrace I wanted. It was that other voice I clung to. *If only you were.* It wasn't the voice of anyone I knew. It didn't belong to my sister, my mother, my friends. It came from somewhere else, from somewhere within me. A need. A hope.

Even your very self.

And when that voice appeared—*if only you were*—I grabbed hold of it tight. *This is mine,* I said. I gave it words, I gave it language. I wrapped it around me, slipped down into it. And once I was down into it, it had nothing to do with anyone else.

Do not ask me to give in to this body of mine.

I knew what that voice was saying with its grip. *If only you were.* I heard it. I embraced it. And I replied. Digging ditches around the bone, I replied, *If only I were.*

Between me and my body there must be a struggle.

And still I didn't recall the ghosts in the hallways of my high school. Those girls remained in the domain of after-school specials, and I was different. At work, at the gym, over dinner, women—specific women, *my* colleagues, *my* friends—talked endlessly about appearance and dieting, and I was different from them, too. *How do you cut so close to the bone?* It was a secret. It was mine but not mine to tell.

I have reached the summit of perfection.

They were talking about taking away—bellies, thighs, age. I wasn't taking away.

The eyes of my soul were opened.

I was constructing. I was revealing. With every bite I didn't eat, I was creating.

I comprehend the whole world.

I am disappearing. Like a hiccup, this phrase emerged before vanishing just as quickly, eclipsed by other thoughts—the food, the exercise, a safe place to throw up.

It seems I am no longer of this earth.

I existed in two worlds then. Like a mini-nap for the sleep-deprived, I would nod into that second world—the one where I lived most of the time—even as I was speaking with my sister, the doctor, a friend.

I saw a fullness, a brightness...

Walking down the street, I would have five or six flashes of that tower of food.

...with which I felt myself so filled that words failed me.

Winding through a party, I would smile instinctively at a familiar face, while thinking about my clothing, which felt tighter. I didn't need a scale—the tools were on my body. Lifting my shirt in the bathroom, I measured the distance between the waist of my skirt and my belly button.

I am continually in this state.

At some point, I could no longer tell when I was present and when I was drifting into visions; when I was asleep and when I was awake. *If only you were.*

It is like a stone flung in the forge to melt into lime...

Did I dream about that voice?

...it crackles when it is licked by the flames...

Did I dream about food?

...but after it is baked . . .

I'm not sure.

...makes not a sound.

My days became:

    Chills.

    Sunlight too bright.

    Sounds attacking me.

    Counting.

We must fast every day.

What I ate, when I ate, counting and categorizing, tearing apart a plate. I built my day around these rituals.

I stripped myself of everything.

I no longer accepted invitations to meals. I could not hold my wine.

Even my very self.

Could not defend myself against questions and suggestions. Sleep more, eat more.

I forgot to eat.

Hannah, you can't forget, she'd say, looking at my journal, now filled with gaps. *Do you understand what will happen to you?*

Priests cannot preach it.

I was filled with rage. Rage at the impossible things she asked of me. Rage at her inability to understand. All she did was disrupt my rituals.

I have reached the summit of perfection.

Because it wasn't denial, a rebellious refusal to consume. I was consuming something. The promise of something.

I comprehend the whole world.

St. Catherine knew.

I am continually in this state.

Counting and categorizing, dividing my days into consumption and expulsion, dividing my body into parts I could look at.

And when I am in this state...

My image in a mirror, naked and growing.

...it seems I am no longer of this earth.

These were the things they didn't understand.

Wholly true. Wholly certain.

These were the things I believed in.

Wholly celestial.

This was where I put my faith.

Even if the whole world were to tell me otherwise...

I gathered people around me as witnesses to something—my isolation? My demise?

...I would laugh it to scorn.

But I was not sad. I was proud.

She did not seem to be the same person.

Look at you. This isn't you. When did this start? They were wrong. All of them. They could not see that I was not only taking away. They could not understand.

Priests cannot preach it.

My rituals.

They do not understand what they preach.

My body in a mirror.

They babble.

But then I saw. One afternoon in a shop window, I saw. Everything written across me.

She was filled with love and inestimable satiety,

And still I clung to it.

which, although it satiated,

I clung to it.

generated at the same time inestimable hunger.

Here is the truth.

In touching her it seemed to take the form of a sickle.

I loved it.

Love took the form of a sickle.

It hurt me, but I loved it.

I could not imagine a death vile enough...

It was mine and I loved it.

...to match my desire.

There was something in the pain that felt good.

I could not imagine a death vile enough.

I was a repository for pain. I was a sponge.

For when love is pure you see yourself as dead.

I invited it back in.

I have fled the world.

I gave it words. I gave it language.

I have changed my life.

Take this body, I said. *Take this pain.*

Is it not enough?

My eyes well up. I slam my palms down on the table. The apartment rings with it and the pain stops the tears.

There is in my soul a chamber...

Why?

...in which no joy, sadness, or enjoyment enters.

They erased themselves, every single one.

Let the tongue of the flesh be silent.

They were erasing, but they were creating.

I saw a fullness, a brightness...

A persona, a voice, a belief in something more.

...with which I felt myself so filled that words failed me.

The body disappears, language disappears, the self disappears, but something remains. Something beyond language.

Wholly true.

They had God, but what did I have?

Wholly certain.

Why was *this* where I found my meaning?

Wholly celestial.

Why was *this* my anchor?

For you will have understood...

Why was *this* my answer?

...that you cannot understand.

I was born in the wrong time, I think.

This is my last thought.

Chapter Twenty-One

My phone is ringing. My head is pounding and each shriek punctuates the pain. I listen until the wailing stops. It is probably the library. By now Lorenza will have discovered my late-night activities, the empty shelves. I'm in my bed—I must have found my way here during the night. I watch the shadow of the shutter move across the wall, listen to the city humming outside. It is light, but I'm not sure what time it is, what day it is. I concentrate on the details in the room: the faux-gilded mirror frame curled in a smile, the dark armoire in the corner, the wool blankets piled heavy on top. If I stay here a few more weeks, I may need those blankets. The radiator turns on and off without warning and this apartment could grow cold. I think about the books still in the kitchen. There is more to read but not with this pain in my head. I feel light, like I might disappear. I drift off again.

I wake sometime later to the sound of music across the way—a piano. Scales and scales and scales. The pain in my head is gone but there is an ache in my stomach. I can't remember when I last ate. Time is bending. I try to fall back asleep, but the pain persists. I throw off the blanket and walk to the kitchen, take the pitcher of water out of the fridge, and pour myself a tall glass. There are ways of tricking your body. This is one of them. I drink the entire glass and look at the clock. It is just before three thirty. It will be dark again soon. I pour another glass and stand out on the balcony.

I'm dizzy as though I've been playing in the sun too long, holding hands with someone and spinning in place. In my backyard. In my backyard. And now the courtyard is off-balance, moving just slightly. Focus on a single point. I remember my legs tucked into the wooden shell, remember gripping those wooden handles. Focus on a single point. And slowly the vertigo passes.

But the pain will not be ignored. I go back inside. My options are limited. I take out a box of crackers. Stale, but I eat one, then another. Still, the pain lingers. I open the refrigerator. Mozzarella floating in a jar. I take out the jar and lift the cheese from the water, let it drip over the sink. I cut off one thin slice and then another. The third I place on a cracker. Then one more of the same. I drop the cheese back into the jar and return it to the fridge, snap the cracker box shut. I feel awake, better, and I sit down to continue reading, but the old feelings return immediately.

Doubt. Regret. Guilt.

I begin with the crackers, stack them one on top of the other. I can't remember how many, not exactly.

The cheese there's no way to account for. I can feel it moving inside of me.

And the wine—I cannot think about the wine. I know better than to convince myself that it doesn't count. Everything counts. And now there's nowhere to put it all. Why had I eaten?

I feel the pull from the end of the hall. I squeeze my eyes shut and then open them. It is probably broken anyway. I stand up, walk down the hallway, my bare feet sticking with each step, and into the bathroom. I slide the scale away from the wall, drop my pants to the floor, pull my shirt up over my head. I step on. It is freezing and I can feel my flesh rise into goose bumps as I wait, the scale shuddering beneath me. The wheel spins. It is not broken. It was never broken.

It stops.

The numbers stare up at me.

Heavy.

How could I have let this happen? It is too much. Too much weight, too much wine, too much guilt. I've added instead of subtracting.

I feel it all expanding in my stomach. I will never recover from this. Tomorrow I'll be even heavier. I lean down over the toilet and throw up. But not all of it, I don't think, not everything.

I get dressed, walk back to the kitchen, and look at the books fanned out across the table and floor. There are no answers here. There are no answers. The problem is mine and only mine, and now I've made it worse instead of better. *It's not real,* Pam had said, sitting on the curb in Cortona. *It is real,* I'd wanted to say then, but maybe she was right. Maybe it's only because it's not real that I have survived here for so long.

And still it had returned. So much talk about this disease, so many doctors, so many studies, so many voices. And still it has been here for centuries, and still it exists, continues to exist. Like a rat or a cockroach, a pest capable of outliving us all.

The pain at the center of me is howling now. I pour a glass of water. This is what you get. This is it. I'm pouring another glass when the sound of the buzzer crashes through the silence. My hand shakes and water spills across the counter, and my first thought is not *Who is it?* but *How do they know?* The empty bottles, the strewn books, my bloated body come momentarily into focus. I hold my breath. A minute passes. I set down the glass, begin to sop up the spill. But the buzzer sounds again and then again, the shock reverberating off the wall. Then the phone is ringing. It is a full-scale attack. When the ringing stops, the buzzer kicks back in, a long moan. I cover my ears until it cuts silent. I wait for a full minute. Then I walk to the living room window on tiptoe. I can see a figure on the street below. The head raises and I duck back but then remember that my apartment is dark, hiding me. I peer down again. The person is no longer looking up but down at his wrist. I recognize the jacket, the hair, the stoop of his shoulders.

Luca rubs his hands together. He looks up and down the street. I remember. He buzzes again. I remember my panic that first evening at his house. *There is in my soul a chamber.* His hands framing my body. I remember his kindness. But what would he do with this? He could not sustain this. It would not hold. It is too heavy for him. It is too heavy for me, too, but I can bear it more easily alone.

And then I see the door open and Luca disappears inside. Someone's let him in. Sounds in the stairwell. Voices, confused. Then steps and more voices, rising and rising. I walk down the hallway, not breathing, steady myself against the wall. Luca's voice and then the rasp of that witch, close now. What are they doing? They can't, they can't.

A knock on the door, loud.

"*Signorina?*" Signora Rosa.

"Hannah?" Luca.

Don't breathe. Don't breathe. They'll have to leave.

But he's trying to convince her to open the door, calmly and then not as he argues with sharp words I've never heard from him, his voice interrupted by the stubborn rasp, that rasp that I am suddenly grateful for. She will not. She will not. There are laws, after all. And she is all hard edges. She will not. Then the voices descend and I go back to my window. Luca steps into the street. He glances up at my apartment, and I want to cry out with the tenderness that finds its way to the surface, and then I think I will call out to him, ask him to come back, fill this apartment with life. But it is impossible. My time with him is so long ago—it seems like years ago that I woke up beside him. There is no way to reconcile it with this moment. I stay silent. Luca turns and walks to his car. His head is bent. He looks broken. But what can I do for him? Nothing. This is not the woman he knows but it is the woman I am. I have nothing to give him.

And now this place isn't safe. Not anymore. He may come back. It is time to go.

The sun attacks me. It doesn't seem like winter with all this light— an orange hue growing deeper by the minute. The color is nauseating and I'm sweating in spite of the cold. I can feel the food in my stomach, can feel the wine, can feel all of it heavy within me, thick and slopping side to side, absorbing into my form. I squint as I walk, but I cannot make out details. I pass the silhouette of a woman, shoes clicking—Claudia? But she's gone. She's been gone.

I put my head down. I must seem mad. I turn around when I reach the corner to look back at my street, a river of light and bodies, my apartment tucked silent and dark above it.

I keep going. I almost collide with two silhouettes of men rounding the corner—we dance right and then left, right and then left, until they laugh and split around me. I wipe my face on my arm. What do they care? A bell cries out somewhere far off. I need to get to the water, follow it east, find my way up to the grove. I turn onto a busy street and am hit with sound, evening noises stampeding with vibrancy and volume: the bars packed for the *aperitivi*, jammed with bodies and laughter; the cars rattling in an endless line down all the streets and funneling toward the bridges; the shopkeepers closing metal gates with a definitive crash; the bells of churches all over the city crying, *Evening, evening, go home, come out, to the hills, to the city, to the family, come, come, go, go.* I arrive at the Arno where the mopeds congregate at the river's edge. They dart around me like so many shining silver fish, and their buzz, that searing buzz, envelopes everything, inescapable. I cover my ears and walk away from the center, turning only once to look back at the Arno's curving body and then down to the patch of green that is the club, where figures are gathered for sunset. I turn away. They would not recognize me. That has nothing to offer me anymore.

I take the easternmost gate, the Porta alla Croce, into a residential area where the streets grow wider and the buildings larger. I look for a way north across the railroad tracks that cut a divide between here and the hills. Along the tracks are thick glass walls stenciled with the silhouettes of birds, as though they've crashed there and remained, a grotesque smattering of corpses. I keep looking for the place where I have crossed, only from the other direction, on my way home from the grove on so many Sundays. But somehow it doesn't work, everything looks strange, and I see only busy overpasses for cars.

I pass a small food stall where men are buying bowls of tripe, hot and dripping. I feel ill and stop with my hands on my knees, but I don't throw up. I keep going, each dip in the sidewalk an effort, each step shaking me, until I spot a small sign for a footpath. It is growing dark, but I take the path under the train tracks to the other side, where I find another busy road. It looks nothing like the road I'd taken on those Sunday afternoons, but I follow it and look for a way up into the hills. I will know the turnoff when I see it. Three boys fly by on bikes, shouting phrases at me that I don't understand. Trembling, I hurry on until I see a smaller road, an offshoot. That could be it, might be it. I take it, the stone walls embracing me, the road beginning to climb as I walk up and up toward the light. The road splits and I follow a still smaller road up to the next divide. One of these must be the road, my road. I trace a long arc, and the city appears and disappears, growing brighter before it grows dark, and then I can no longer see it at all and no longer know where it is. I know only that I am going up and not down.

It is cold here, but the sun is still warm on my eyelids, the hills clutching at its rays. And it is quiet, finally, except for short beeps announcing cars or mopeds around blind corners. Otherwise there is no sound, only my feet on the stones. Images drift in and out and then fall away. The numbers that stared up at me; the thousands of words on the hundreds of pages; Luca, bent, waiting by my door. He must be home in his small town now, where the church bells will be ringing, and the silverware clanging, and the voices rising. If I were with him, I would be going south instead of north. South to dinner, to the baths, to another town. These memories pierce, but they are nothing compared with everything that came before and everything that has happened since—it circles and consumes them.

The road ends at a commune of vertical homes—this is unfamiliar. It is a small town, but not Luca's, not one I've ever seen. I don't want to backtrack, so I walk into this town, nothing more than a street with quiet homes and a single bar. A group of construction workers is packing up for the day. "*Ciao, bella,*" one says languidly, out of interest or habit, I cannot tell. I say nothing. I place my hand on the rough surface of a building for balance, pushing off with each step, drawing energy from its warm walls. And then I am alone again, the town disappeared behind me.

The road splits and I choose the path to the right. This will take me to the grove or it won't. Either way. The sun begins to drop, glinting off the bits of glass that are dug into the tops of the walls like broken teeth. I'm tired. So tired. And something else. Deflated. The subtle descent. When this feeling comes, it always enters this way, small wings beating against the heart. Soft. Unpredicted. Then consistent.

I could vanish. If I lay down on the other side of these walls, I might never be found. I stop and lean back against the stone with my eyes closed, slide down until I am out of the light, sitting on the ground, the cold seeping in through my coat and then my pants and up my back, the chill making its way to the front of my body. I'm becoming part of the road, part of the wall, welded to it by the cold. If only things were this simple: to be an object on some-one's path, to be a wall anchored to a road. I begin counting, try to remember the crackers, the cheese. I stack them, set them apart. I look in the faces of the empty wine bottles. How many glasses in a bottle, how much liquid in a glass? I separate out each bottle, measure it. Even so, it must be gone. I imagine the path up, which looks long in my mind. I must be empty by now.

The walls and the road grow hazy and my vision swims. I feel ready for anything, close to something, and light, as though I might float off this road, up above these walls, out over the city. Who would believe it? Who would believe any of it? And yet, it is true. *I am continually in this state.* If I stayed here long enough, I know that I would feel myself separate from this place and float right up to that vanishing point where everything disappears and comes together.

My soul languished and desired to fly away
languished and desired
and desired to fly
desired to fly away
in this state
away

I open my eyes with a start. I'm cold, damp, and there is a sharp pain in my chest. I'm still in the same spot on the same road, but the sun is lower, everything around me flattened by long shadows.

I draw my legs in tight. I can smell smoke somewhere far off, I can smell night descending, and I want to close my eyes, but something stops me—when the sun drops fully, there will be nothing to light my way except the slivered moon. And I have no idea where I am. All I know is that I have gone up and not down and that the walls have grown higher and the houses farther apart. The grove is nowhere. It has disappeared. I am lost, again, but there will be no Sergio this time. There is no one up here now to point the way. There is no one. No one here and no one who knows that I'm here. Even the city, hidden somewhere below, doesn't notice my absence. I do not exist. I am not missing because I am not missed. I am a woman alone on the empty, caged roads outside Florence. I am a woman alone. I am alone. And all the life in the city below, everything I've done in the past months, everything I've done in all the years leading up to this year, is separate, is gone. *I stripped myself of everything.* It does not matter who I was before or who I had become.

I lean back against the stone, cold again, and I hear that familiar voice. Because the truth is that I am not alone. I haven't been alone for weeks. I've had my companion, that companion that has been with me, always with me, since I first invited it in. I've been denying it. I've sought solace elsewhere, turning my back on my old friend, and still it was there in the shadows, hushed. Even as I rowed and kissed and ate, it kept its nails in me.

I will never leave you, it is saying now with its grip. I imagine it silenced, frozen by the cold, but it persists. I do not breathe. I do not make a sound. I cannot silence it.

I will never leave you. Though what it means is *I will never let you go.*

No.

No.

Dark. It is almost dark. I stand up, my legs shaking, my coat catching on the wall's surface. I begin to walk downhill—slowly, evenly, and then quickly. The town. I will walk back to the town and decide what to do from there. Decide there. The road becomes steep, the stones sliding easily under my boots, but by the time the sun is almost gone, and with it any warmth, I'm still not back at the little piazza. I stay to the right, take a turn at a narrow fork. Over a rise, I glimpse the hills in the distance, blue and gray, climbing and falling. The town must be this way.

And then I know it isn't right, cannot be right. If I were walking in the right direction, the roads would not be growing narrower. They would be widening, spreading. But the roads *are* growing narrower. I could just as easily be descending into an empty valley as the lit bowl of Florence. There is a monstrous pain in my chest and my head and I'm getting dizzy. I come to another fork and go left this time, trailing my hand along the wall until my fingers jump at the cold bars of a gate, the house behind it crouched silent in the dark. There is no one home. There is no one here but me and that other figuring traveling these channels alongside me. It is only me and it. I keep moving, faster now.

I will never leave you.

I begin to sweat, tear off my coat as I speed up. I try to hold on to the belief that the next turn will be the right one, but around the bend is more unfamiliar road. I start to run, around more strange curves, more strange road, filled with the truth that I might not find my way out. I might never be found.

I will never leave you.

I run faster and faster, until it is fully dark, the night stretched out before me, waiting to engulf me with every turn.

I will never let you go.

I cannot. I cannot. I cannot. This repeats and repeats as I run with no care of direction. My heart is pounding. I just have to keep running, keep moving. The road curves sharply up and then down, now blue with the moon, now black without, now narrow, walls squeezing from either side. I trip and splay out, my teeth clattering, my body skating, the stone tearing into my pants, my knees. I leap up and keep running, my purse beating against my side, my shoes slapping, the slaps echoing, the echoes following me down and down and down. I see myself from above then, a small shape darting up and down this game board, ready to meet that figure at every dark corner.

I will never leave you.

Sound grows thunderous—my footsteps or the coursing of my blood, I cannot tell.

I will never let you go.

I'm almost sliding, arms out, stone scraping at my hands as I round corners. If the roads are growing narrower or wider, I cannot tell. I let myself be pulled by gravity, pushed by momentum. I run and run and it is as though I have never not been running.

Until a soft glow appears above the walls, then bright flashes in my periphery. Homes. I don't stop at the first or the second or the third. I fall again and get back up, my limbs awkward and loose. I don't stop when I reach, finally, the little piazza, the nameless bar, now dark. I keep running, aware of how loud I must sound to whoever lives up here, and find the road that I hope will take me to the center and take it down and down and down. I run until I hear sounds of life—first sporadic voices escaping the windows of low buildings, then collective laughter, low music, utensils striking dishes. The road widens and spits me out onto a busy street by the train tracks. I wait for a break in traffic, then keep running, under the tracks and back into streets with buildings and people. Civilization rushes in, lights and noise wash over me, crushing after the panicked quiet. I keep going, running even though people are staring. Still I run until I'm back at the Arno. I run straight up to the river's wall and let it catch me hard in the stomach before I stop, breathing loudly.

Gradually my eyes adjust, my breathing slows, and the pressure in my ears dulls as the sounds of the city separate into distinguishable parts: the bass from a club beating low, shouted greetings close by, the orange night bus wheezing, splashes in the river below, and somewhere a band playing music, music, music. Here Florence sits, filled with life but somehow empty, oblivious to the expansive darkness just beyond its lit perimeters, creaking and moaning.

My body aches, my muscles scream, and I'm covered in scratches. I look up and down the river. The Ponte alle Grazie is visible in the distance. I'm only a few blocks from home. I stare at the river, my arms shaking as I press them into the wall's ledge. I push up my sleeves to feel the rough surface on my flesh, and still I cannot anchor myself. The city that had held me with such care feels different, gone suddenly like the folded parcels of the street vendors when the *carabinieri* arrive.

Where is the woman who had been held by this place and found joy in it?

And then a new question drops, heavy. I hear it. Hear it clearly. The only question that matters.

Why did you come here? Did you come here to—

I don't finish the thought. I don't have an answer. Maybe if I knew what had caused this. But I hadn't found an answer to that, either. Instead, I ended up drinking, whittling down, throwing up, disappearing. And now here I am, alone again and facing this impossible question with no answers and no way of moving forward. Because what would be the point? What would be the point of finding new places and new people and new lives, or returning to the old, when either way this friend might be waiting, might return as much as I will it not to? What is the point of living as a question mark if the answer is always the same? In the hills, I felt like I could break free, float clear away, join those saints who knew more, saw more, felt more. Could disappear along with them. But instead, I woke to the dark, to the fear, and I am still here, cold and tired and afraid, and I wonder if the saints had felt this frustration, if their searches felt as futile.

I hear the question again and I try to take all the moments of the past year, line them up in my mind, weigh them against what the future might hold. I think about my mother's hardness, my sister's pain, my loneliness, my confidence, the bathroom floor. About my first day at the club, the stares of the men, Luca's broad smile, the uneven pull of water. About Dario sweating in his bar, Francesca bent over a sink, my body curled over an oar, and the brilliant afternoons in the grove. About the dust in Orvieto and the birds in Cortona, and all the saints whose corpses litter these cities. About Luca's hands, about waking up in his bed, about waking up without him. And finally about that day months ago, when it all came apart, and I could feel the weight of this thing that I could not look in the eyes. Here it is again, staring me down.

Did you come here to—

I feel something then. It is a physical sensation, a movement from deep within me. The question repeats but it is irrelevant. It doesn't matter anymore why I came here. There is only one answer. It was there when I left Boston. And it was there tonight. My friend was still with me, yes. But there was something else with me, too— something stronger than the impulse to disappear. It had chased me out of those hills, back to this city. It didn't feel stronger than my old friend, but it was, must be, because here I am. Here I am.

I am still here. That is the only answer. For the time being, there is no other answer.

As soon as I think it, the weight lifts and the city comes back into focus: the beat of the bass from the club, the bridge glowing in the distance, the band playing. I stand and listen until the song hums to a close and I feel a shot of hot breath in my ear, a presence at my back.

"Dove va?"

I don't turn to look but begin to walk quickly, listening for steps that do not follow, past the club, past the bridge, and, finally, home.

Chapter Twenty-Two

I sleep late. Then I shower, wash the dirt from my hands, arms, and knees. I clean the cuts and cover them. I go out to the store. The world is still foggy, but I am determined. Once I begin to weigh out vegetables, I'm ravenous. I force a smile for the cashier as she rings up my groceries, and then walk quickly home with my provisions. I make a plate of mostly produce, but add several thin slices of cheese at the last minute. I will take small steps, just like before. I cut a slice of bread, toast it, and drizzle it with oil. I eat it all without regret.

I pick up my phone and begin to dial the library, then put it down. It is Sunday. There is no one there. I send Lorenza an e-mail, tell her that I will be back tomorrow. I call Kate and am relieved to get her voice mail. I leave a brief but friendly message. I think about calling Luca but don't. I'm not sure what I want to say.

I collect the books that are scattered in the kitchen and stack them on a shelf, wipe the wine stains from the counter. I fill the bottom of the aluminum coffeemaker with water, level espresso into the little nesting basket, replace the top, light the stove, and wait for the sound and the smell. Then I sit out on the balcony for a long time. There is no sign of the old woman today, her shutters closed against the chill.

The buzzer rings just after dark. I look out the window. Luca. He is looking up and I raise my hand slowly, unsure of whether he can see me. He shakes his shoulders, rubs his hands, then rings again. I don't wait for the landlady to appear. I step back from the window and buzz him in. I check my face in the mirror—I don't look well, I know. I don't look well at all. There's nothing to be done. For the moment, this is who I am.

"*Ma cos'è successo?*" Luca asks in a rush as soon as I open the door. "Are you sick? Your arms. You are hurt? How?" He puts his hands on my arms, scabbed from the falls, and I step back. His figure in my doorway is overwhelming. I want to hug him, want to wipe the concern from his face. But I don't know what to say. I don't have the words for it. It has been days since I uttered a sound to anyone—it feels like years.

"I'm okay."

"What happened? I was afraid. I call. Nothing. I come here. Nothing. Sergio tells me he sees you, but I cannot find you. I go to your work—"

"You went to the library? When?"

"Friday. The woman—she doesn't know. I thought maybe you left Firenze. That you went home—*non lo so*. Without telling me. But then I thought you wouldn't, *no*?"

"No." I take his hand and lead him down the hall to the living room. Outside, the lights of the city are twinkling on. We sit down.

"What happened?" he asks again.

"Your father?" I finally say, surprised by how clear my voice sounds.

"It's okay," he says quickly, the last syllable lilting up.

"He's all right?"

"Now, yes." He shrugs. "Tomorrow, after tomorrow, we don't know, but now he's okay. I will tell you—later, later. What happened?" He squeezes my hand. "You were sick? You look sick—*no, mi dispiace*. You look nice, *come sempre*, but also I think you were not well." He puts his hand to my cheek. "Are you hungry? Did you eat?"

"I ate. I'm tired. I don't know—I don't know where to start." I can't look at him, so I turn into his shoulder. Everything about him is warm. The crevice of his neck. His arms around me. I feel raw beside him, cold and stiff. And then determined not to be, I lean into him and kiss him, tasting my tears in the kiss. He responds without questioning it, though it must seem strange to him, all of it.

I'm here. I'm still here. But I have to do more. *Why won't you talk to me?* If things are going to be different, I have to do more. I take a breath and speak into his neck. "I've had some troubles for a while."

"*Sì,*" he says quietly. "*Lo sapevo.*"

"You knew?" I pull away.

"I knew there was something. Some..." He gestures with his hands, looking for the words. "Troubles, like you say."

"Then why did you go out with me?"

Luca smiles. "You think I would not see you because you have some troubles? We all have some troubles, *no*? *Tutti.* You, my father—*sì*—and also me. And so what can we do? Speak to no one? Be with no one?"

I shake my head.

"Maybe you have greater troubles. I don't know. You are a puzzle. I knew there were some things..." He pauses. "Sad. But I thought if you don't want to talk about it, *va bene.*"

I nod. We sit in silence for a moment.

"You want to talk about it now?" he asks.

I realize I'm holding his hand tight—I don't even remember reaching for it. "Maybe."

"You want wine?" he asks.

I shake my head.

"Water?"

I nod, and he disappears and returns with two glasses of water. Then he sits down next to me, puts a hand on mine, and smiles. I take a sip, look at him, take in that broad smile, the crinkles around his eyes. I can see some pain in his face, but something else, too. Hope. Resignation. Warmth.

"For a while," I say, "I didn't eat." It feels strange to say it directly like that. It is so simple. It is just the starting point, or the ending point—I'm not sure which. But right now, here with Luca, it is a beginning.

"*Niente?*"

"Not enough."

"*Ah, sì.* I understand. In Boston?"

"And also here."

"Here? Not so easy in Firenze—the best food in the world, *no?*"

I laugh. "True."

He looks concerned. "*Scusami.* I don't mean to joke. It is serious. *Allora*, you did not eat. Why not? Not to be so skinny—it is not necessary."

"I don't know." I sigh. "It wasn't a decision. It started as one thing and then it became something else."

Luca nods.

"It crept up. Like an illness."

"For how long?"

And so I tell him. Slowly. I don't tell him everything, not all of it, but I tell him enough. More than I've told anyone else. Luca doesn't interrupt, even when I pause, self-conscious. He keeps his hand on mine, waits for me to continue. And so I continue. Luca will understand or he will not. Will bear it or not. Will leave or not. But I have to speak. The words take on a life of their own, filling the room. It is such a relief not to be hiding, for the first time in months and months, not to be lying.

"And now?" Luca asks.

"Now? I don't know. I mean, I feel better right *now*, sitting here with you." He gives my hand a squeeze. "But I've also felt better before. And so I worry. That it will all happen again."

Luca looks confused. "*Ma perché?*"

"Because I don't understand it. Because I can't control it. Because you can't—" I sigh and my voice shakes, but I am adamant. "How can I prevent something if I don't know why it happened in the first place? I went to a doctor. It didn't help."

"*Allora*, you think there is nothing that can help."

"I don't know. What if this is just who I am?" My voice catches and I feel I might begin crying again. I want to live. *Someone who wants to live.* That is a part of who I am now. But there is also that other part—the part of me that might end up back in that place, back at the edge. I don't know how to make Luca understand. I don't have the language. Or maybe it's just that this illness has its own language reserved for those inside of it. "It's like it won't let go of me," I finally say.

"It?"

"The illness, the disorder—whatever it is."

Luca takes a sip of water, considering. "*Forse. Forse* it will not let go. But—*non lo so.*"

"What?"

"You have to let it go, too, *no?*"

I nod. "I'm trying. But I can't stop thinking about the past. And worrying about the future."

"*Sì,*" he says, "it is good. We must think of the past—and care for the future. But there are things to do now, yes?" He looks at me with his eyebrows slightly raised. He isn't making light of this. He is asking a serious question.

There are things to do now. And he's right. I'm tired of fearing the other, tired of living in anticipation of it. *There are things to do now.* It's enough. For now, it's enough.

"Things," I say, "like what?"

He puts his arm around me. "*Come,* we can have a walk or take some dinner. *Se vuoi,* we can go to Spain or Francia. We can visit Argo, who now is lonely and also missing you."

I put my arms around him, smiling. "And..."

"Or perhaps we stay here and I can kiss you for a while, which I was missing."

I lean back into him. We kiss for a long time and then I lay against him without speaking, trying to hold on to the now.

I'm nervous about returning to the library, but as soon as I open the door on Monday morning, I hear "*Eccola!*" and Lorenza has me in a hug. It is so uncharacteristic, so strange having her small arms around me. She steps back and I hoist my bag off my shoulder; it is heavy with books.

"I was worried," she says. "Extremely worried. Especially when your friend came by."

I'm here. But I have to do more. "I'm sorry. I'm so sorry. I wasn't myself." This is true. "It won't happen again. But I understand if you can't keep me on. I know—"

"You can't possibly leave," Lorenza says. "It's the end of the term—we're flooded with students. I think it's the only work they've done all semester. You have to stay on."

"Of course. Thank you."

She smiles and eyes my bag of books. "Now that that's settled, let's get those back where they belong, *sì*? Did you find what you were looking for?"

Later that week, I see Peter at the club. He's walking down the hall of boats.

"Hey!" I say.

"Oh, sorry." He tries a smile. "Ciao, Hannah."

"How have you been? I've missed seeing you."

"That's strange. I've been here."

"I bumped into Pam, and she said—" I stop when I realize he isn't listening as his eyes dart around. I know how it feels to hide. "Anyway, maybe we'll see each other back in the States?" I ask.

"Sure." He nods, looking at the door. "Sure."

The next day, I'm greeted with another surprise. Blood. My period for the first time in more months than I can remember. I'm confused, not sure of what to do, and for a moment I am an adolescent again, awkwardly wadding up toilet paper. The blood is light, pale, little more than a few drops over the course of a day, but it is still there, recognizable. It is a relief. Because even though I've been eating well again, my hair is thinner, my breasts smaller, and it is difficult to put on flesh, as though my body can't regain its footing. It is like waking up to find someone else has lived my life, warred with my body, and left me with these remnants of battle. The blood is a small victory. I begin eating more.

The final days of work are a mad dash—for Lorenza, for me, for the students frantically researching, typing, printing—and then my duties are officially done. Lorenza asks if I want to return in

January for the new term, and I tell her what I haven't yet told Luca—that I've decided to go home. I've promised Kate I'll be there for Christmas, and I will. She won't have to cover for me, explain why I'm not there, because I'll be there. I'll sort things—the bills, the apartment, the questions. And then? I don't know. I only know that if I'm going to move forward, I have to account for what I left behind.

When I tell Luca that I'll be leaving, he immediately says, "*Allora*, then you return for Capodanno!" New Year's. I smile, but tell him that I don't know how long I'll be gone.

"*Va bene*," Luca says. "You don't know when—*va bene*. But you come back. *Certo*. You always return to Firenze." And then we drop the subject altogether and continue, as Luca had suggested, with the now, the finality of my departure making each day more urgent.

It seems as though everyone will be leaving for the holidays, and the wives and children who have been so invisible emerge at the center of the conversations at the club now. Gianni is going to Florida with his family. When I ask him, "Why Florida?" he shrugs and says, "Why not? It's nice there, *no*? Miami," he croons. *Meeeee-aaaa-meeee*. Stefano and his family will be in the Lake District, and Sergio and his wife are visiting her relatives in Rome. Even Carlo will be taking his children skiing.

"Carlo has children?" I ask Luca, remembering this revelation when we are at his house reading later that evening, my feet propped up in his lap.

"*Sì, sì. Due*. One boy, one girl," Luca says without looking up.

"I'm surprised."

"Why?"

"I only thought of him as Carlo the Wolf."

Luca laughs. "*Sì*. But any person can have children." Luca returns to his reading, then adds a few seconds later, "*E davvero*, he is a good father."

The next day, Francesca waltzes into the club during lunch with her daughter and a small bag of gifts in hand, to wish everyone a good holiday. Each person receives an embrace and a chocolate.

"*Buon Natale*, Hannah," Francesca says. "I'll see you in January?"

"I'm not sure. I'm going home for a while."

"You can't leave!" Francesca exclaims, and she looks legitimately concerned, but then she tempers it. "I mean, you'll come back, right? You got your man here. We have a lot to talk about, *no*?" and with two kisses, she's on to the next. Marco arrives a few minutes later. He shakes hands with everyone and kisses his wife for all to see. Francesca accepts his affection without hesitation. There is no eye rolling or sly commentary from the crowd, even after the family departs. I wonder if Francesca and Marco do this every year, if life simply resets for them and everyone else.

"It is always the same," Luca says later. "People talk but then she is married. And also it is Christmas."

It is Christmas and the city glows with it, the lights around Florence transforming every street, painting every piazza gold. It is odd to witness the holiday preparations I'd dreaded when I didn't know where I would be or where I was going. I still don't know where I'm going, but it is good to be where I am. It is a gift to walk around Florence with Luca, stopping for roasted chestnuts or slipping into one of the oldest bakeries for *ricciarelli*, a holiday treat. It is a gift waking up with him, the day stretching ahead of us.

One evening I take him to the olive grove. He's surprised, impressed even, that I had found it.

"My town," he says, pointing across the valley.

I nod.

"And from here you watched me?" he asks slyly.

"No," I say, laughing. "Sometimes I thought of you, though."

As it turns out, Luca will be leaving the day before me to be with his family. He invites me to join him, and I remember when I thought he would never invite me into that circle. "Next time," I say. The evening before his departure, we exchange gifts. For him, a warm scarf from the market. For me, a book on the saints. "In Italian," Luca says. "You practice." It brings tears to my eyes.

"I'll go with you," I say that night as we lie next to each other. "To the station, I mean, to see you off."

He is already sleeping. I grasp for his hand to ensure that he's still there.

"Say something."

"*Cosa?*" His response is delayed.

"*Dimmi qualcosa.*"

"Say what?"

"Anything," I say. "It's too quiet."

There is a moment in which the silence is full of his thinking. "*Ci sono troppo poche lune per la gente.*"

"What does that mean?"

"*Non lo so.* I made it up." I can hear his smile in the dark. Then, "It means I'm happy you're here."

I move into him and he shifts to gather me.

"You could stay," he whispers again a few minutes later. He means this, I think. It comes from a place that is sincere, that believes the future could be as easy as the now.

I squeeze his hand. "I'll see you off tomorrow."

"Mmm," he mumbles, already gone.

The next morning we drive to the station in the rain. In the daylight, it feels a bit overly dramatic to be going with Luca. But people do these things, after all—in real life they do. They see off their lover who has not hurt them and whom they have not hurt, but who may soon be gone from their life forever.

We make our way up Via Camillo Cavour and Luca pulls to a sudden stop.

"*Aspetta,*" he says, heading out into the rain with his jacket tented over his head, and I remember that first evening when he drove me home, stopping the car to get water and bread, the small pieces he passed to me slowly. And still he did not run away.

"*Panettone,*" he says upon returning, wiping the rain from his face. "For the evening." I open the bag and find a small Italian Christmas cake wrapped in brown-and-gold paper.

The train station is packed, the people harried. Everyone is going somewhere—to family or holiday homes, or to Rome or Bologna for flights elsewhere. As always, many of the trains are delayed, and Luca and I have more time than we'd imagined on the platform. We kiss and then sigh, leaning into each other.

When his train finally pulls in, Luca says, "You are sure you will not come?"

I nod.

"*Va bene. A presto. A prestissimo.* Until *very* soon. *Hai capito?*" He raises his eyebrows.

"*Sì.* I understand. *A prestissimo.*"

Luca climbs onto the train and I look for him through the amber windows among the many bodies searching for seats. I cannot find him and feel panicked, but then I hear a small tap and see him a few windows down, his head against the glass. I walk down the track and align myself with him. We smile, but there is nothing to say now. I shrug my shoulders and look away but do not leave. Next to me, a tall woman blows a kiss to the train and then shifts her hip to one side with a large smile. Beyond her, an older man grips his son tight, then watches him board. We stay, committed to our stations. There is a promise in the waiting. *I will remain here, just as I am, until you return.* Finally, the doors close; the train exhales, leans back into the bumper, and crawls forward. I wave to Luca a final time and try to hold in my mind his broad smile as I watch the train curl out of the station and feel the loss setting in.

But when the last car passes under the station's overhang and out of sight, I find that it is not unbearable, not yet. Beside me, the father looks at his watch and walks away with small, brisk steps. The tall woman sidles down the track, her head thrown back. Then they are gone and the face of the station is already changing as a new set of travelers arrives. I stay for a moment and watch the crowds, before the reality of my own departure propels me out into the city and toward the things that remain ahead of me. There are things to be done, after all—cleaning and packing, a final meal. The panettone in the little bag at my side helps, as perhaps Luca knew it would.

I'd planned to row today, but the weather isn't cooperating, and I walk back to the center in the rain, feeling Luca's absence, feeling my own time slipping away with each step. It is still early enough that I witness the complex choreography of Florence in the morning, when it is owned by the Italians, and I take in the sights and smells and sounds as though I might carry them all back in my person. The urgent, lyrical voices of two men who hurry by me, gesticulating wildly; the young mother weaving her children through the tight streets with a repeated *"Andiamo, ragazzi, andiamo!"*; the crowded coffee bars, humming with conversations; the *ding* of so many small spoons dropped onto saucers, and the smell of sweet pastries slid onto plates, and I remember the cookies I had with Luca on All Saints' Day.

I keep going, past the Duomo, where the *thump thump thump* of suitcases sound on cobblestones as tourists follow this well-worn route. I walk through Piazza della Signoria, the arms of the Uffizi, and across the Ponte Vecchio to the Oltrarno. Here the streets are quieter and I have a strange sense of déjà vu as I recognize a shopkeeper on the adjacent corner. I've never been in his shop, but I've seen him always outside. Even on this rainy day he stands under the awning, smiling and giving a small "Ciao" to a passing friend. As I round the corner, a man passes a woman with a young child.

"Dove vai?" the man exclaims, putting a hand on the boy's head. *"A tua nonna?"* and the boy squeals and runs into a café.

Francesca was right—this is a small village. This morning is every morning, and every morning, this morning. It is reassuring to think that even when I'm gone, these movements will continue, will repeat each day, and that when I return they might all still be here waiting. *It is always the same,* Luca said, and I hold on to the phrase. It cuts the feeling of loss. It promises a future here.

I stop for breakfast at my favorite bar. After I eat, there is a break in the rain, and I race home to grab my rowing clothes. It is already drizzling on my way back, but I remain hopeful. I pause at the green door of the *canottieri* and take a deep breath before I push it open and make my way into the cool foyer and then down and down until I reach the small coffee bar where Manuele is behind the counter reading a paper.

"Ciao, Hannah of Boston," he says, offering a hand and a cheek.

By the time I've changed, it is raining heavily again. There will be no rowing today. Still, I walk down the quiet hall of boats and stop by my scull, *Persefone*. Seeing it, I realize how badly I want to be out on the river one last time, to feel the oars drawing against weight, to pause under one bridge and then another, to look up at the bodies lining the walls, to look down at the silent water, to feel the soft clanging against the dock when I pull back in and the weight of the wood, dripping, on my shoulder. The prospect of it not happening seems unbearable.

I hear a faint shuffle and turn to find Correggio walking toward me.

"*Posso?*" I ask when he reaches me, the plea leaping out involuntary. *May I?* As though he might not notice the weather, might, in this moment, act against the core of his character, which is utterly consistent, made of the very *it is always the same* that is the fabric of this city. But a crack of thunder shakes the club, making my request ridiculous, and I'm embarrassed. Correggio looks at me, looks at the boats, looks at me. He doesn't say no or laugh. He pats me softly on the shoulder with a smile.

"*Alla prossima,*" he says, *until next time,* and then continues his shuffle down the hall.

I work out in the empty room of ergometers, feel the stretch in my arms, listen to the slow exhale of the wheel. I take a long shower, and when I emerge, I find that Stefano has already left for lunch. Manuele gives me a piece of paper, and I take my time composing a note of thanks that he promises to deliver.

I don't go home immediately, but walk up two bridges and cross to the library. I want to say good-bye to Lorenza, as I had promised I would. I step quickly—my final trip to the club has made me late, and I fear the library will already be closed for lunch. And it is. The door is dark. I'm deflated. No final afternoon on the river, no good-bye to Stefano or Lorenza. How can I leave without these things?

As I reach the Ponte Vecchio, it begins to rain harder, and by the time I step into Piazza della Signoria, it is coming down so intensely and with such wind that I'm forced to duck into an open vestibule. I stand there and watch as the storm empties the piazza and paints the buildings, adding to their facades a new sheen. Thunder smothers all the street sounds, and an old man flies by silently on a bicycle, grinning as though fleeing the scene of a crime. My vision is blocked then by a couple, drenched and kissing as they pass my doorway. I remember walking across this piazza at night with Luca, the lit tops flying high into the air, and the memory softens the day's disappointments. I look across the square to the loggia of statues where the Sabine woman is safe from the rain but still not safe from her attacker, her body twisted and her jagged finger pointing upward to where she might go if she could only escape. She is unwilling to recognize the futility of her efforts. And maybe they aren't futile; maybe she's already beyond the hands that hold her—and what then?

You have to let it go, too, no? Luca had said. I had known it before he said it. I had known it that evening in the hills. And I had known it months earlier. *You have to let it go, too.* But here is the truth: I didn't want to die, but I didn't want to let it go. It gave me a center. That void became my center. It had the capacity to kill me, but it was exciting. On the brink, always. Of death, of life. I could do anything because I was outside of everything. With all else stripped away, things came into focus, sharp and clear. Long after Julian left, after I lost my job, after I lost friends and alienated family, it remained the constant. I had disappeared from my life, but I was not alone. I had that other being with me and I loved it. It had hurt me, but I still loved it. It was mine. I loved the body that had been wrecked by that stranger. I loved the body and the stranger. I loved that other self even as I was horrified by it. How could I wish it away? How could I wish myself away?

Control, beauty, insecurity, failure in love, perfectionism—these were the explanations I had been given. But having known it, the allure is something different. It is the promise of something closer, something separate, something the mystics knew. An existence. "I, Catherine." "I, Angela." "I, Clare." *There is nothing of mine*, St. Angela wrote, and yet in the "I," a being is created, a self of one's imagining. And wasn't that worth something? I remember the description of Angela in rapture: *rays of astonishing beauty, some thick, others slender, radiated from her breast, unfolded or coiled as they as-cended upward toward heaven.* The body disappears but the outline remains, a burning profile lit from behind, created out of the dis-solved figure.

My own insistent disappearance. It isn't a way to live. And still, as I lean against the doorway of the vestibule and watch the sky grow lighter and the stones grow darker, there is a part of me—not a small part—that longs for it, desires it. Even in this moment when I have just, again, escaped it. I know there will be evenings, my eyes between bottles in a bar mirror, when I will see it, taste it. I can tell myself that I will keep it at bay, hold a steady course. But the truth is that I don't know. Because it is not the reminders that I'm afraid of. It is this missing. It is in the missing that I will need to remember who I am now and will need to see that past without envy, so that I mourn it instead of inviting it back in. Because I *will* miss it. In those glimpses, I will miss my old love. More than I will miss Luca's arms, or the perfect afternoons in the grove. More, even, than the feeling of the oars pulling water smoothly, finally balanced.

The wind finds its way into the lobby, swaying the old glass lantern above me, and slowly the rain lets up. On the hour there are bells from many directions ringing at different times. A small chime close by. Then one far off—in the hills, maybe. They are out of synch. The bells of the Duomo sound the loudest, layered, com-pleting the chorus and singing the longest until there is only a sin-gle bell striking the time. *You are here,* it rings solid. *You. Are. Here.* The square is empty now, the crowds chased indoors, the final drops of rain chased into the drains, leaving only puddles and re-flections. As I step out into the piazza, my existence becomes vivid and hovers before me and around me, quivering with possibility. Each nerve stands at attention, ready to receive a breeze, a chill, a caress. The beauty of this moment is too blinding for any fear to exist. This moment has its own force. I can breathe easy, without knowing.

This, too, could be life.

Author's Note

While researching the lives of the saints and the history of eating disorders, I was fortunate to have at hand the books of people who have done this work for decades. I used a variety of translations when quoting the saints, making occasional adjustments for clarity and consistency. The following texts informed the book: *Holy Anorexia* by Rudolph M. Bell (University of Chicago Press, 1985); *Fasting Girls: The History of Anorexia Nervosa* by Joan Jacobs Brumberg (Vintage Books, 2000); *Holy Feast and Holy Fast: The Religious Significance of Food to Medieval Women* by Caroline Walker Bynum (University of California Press, 1987); *Butler's Lives of Saints: New Concise Edition*, edited by Michael Walsh (Burns and Oates, 1985); *The Book of the Divine Consolation of the Blessed Angela of Foligno*, translated by Mary G. Steegmann (Chatto and Windus, 1909); *Angela of Foligno: Complete Works*, translated by Paul Lachance, O.F.M. (Paulist Press, 1993); *The Life and Doctrine of Saint Catherine of Genoa* (Christian Press Association Publishing Co., 1907); *Catherine of Siena: The Dialogue*, translated by Suzanne Noffke, O.P. (Paulist Press, 1980); *Saint Catherine of Siena as Seen in Her Letters*, translated by Vida Dutton Scudder (Kessinger Publishing, 2010); *St. Catherine of Siena* by Johannes Jørgensen, translated by Ingeborg Lund (Wipf and Stock Publishers, 2012); *The Life and Revelations of Saint Margaret of Cortona* by Fra Giunta Revegnati, translated by F. McDonogh Mahony (Burns and Oates, 1883); *The Life and Miracles of Saint Margaret of Cortona* by Fra Giunta Bevegnati, translated by Thomas Renna, edited by Shannon Larson (Franciscan Institute Publications, 2012); *Maria Maddalena de' Pazzi: Selected Revelations*, translated by Armando Maggi (Paulist Press, 2000).

Acknowledgments

While writing is often solitary, it does not happen without the generous communities of people who make it possible. I was fortunate to have many people who were a part of the life of *Florence in Ecstasy*.

Thank you to my brilliant agent (my saint!), Sarah Burnes, for believing in this book and its author, for your wisdom and counsel over many drafts, and for finding *Florence in Ecstasy* a wonderful home. Thank you to Logan Garrison Savits, Rebecca Gardner, and Will Roberts at The Gernert Company for all of your support and for inspiring enthusiasm for the novel, both here and abroad. Thank you to the unparalleled team at The Unnamed Press for ferrying this book out into the world with such care: Chris Heiser, for your sharp editorial eye and mind, which made this a better novel; Olivia Taylor Smith, for your passion, creativity, and savvy in getting others excited about the book; Jennifer Tanji, for helping to publicize it; Jaya Nicely, for the stunning cover; Nancy Tan, for the excellent copy edits; and J. Ryan Stradal, for your matchmaking in bringing the novel to Unnamed. Thank you to Kimberly Burns, publicist extraordinaire, for championing this book and for your vital support and advice throughout the process.

Thank you to my first writing mentors and dear friends Christina Moustakis, John Byrne, and Jennifer Fell Hayes for instilling in me a love of literature and writing, and for giving me the courage to pursue it as a vocation. Thank you to my Hopkins mentors—Richard

Macksey, Stephen Dixon, Alice McDermott, and Tristan Davies—remarkable and passionate writers and thinkers who inspired and guided me both on the page and in life. Thank you to my literary mothers at City College: Linsey Abrams, who—with profound wisdom, care, and soul—nurtured this novel, and me, from the book's inception all the way to publication; and Felicia Bonaparte, whose brilliant mind and generous guidance enriched the novel and my own understanding of it. Thank you to my CCNY family: David Groff, Frederic Tuten, Fred Reynolds, Harold Aram Veeser, and Rebecca Chace, who supported and mentored me in the classroom and beyond. Thank you to my CCNY peers for helping me to shape the novel, and to Robin Blair, Linsey Abrams, and Michelle Valladares for publishing an excerpt in *Global City Review*. Thank you to the Lippman and Himmelfarb family for believing in this novel early on and honoring it with the Doris Lippman Prize.

Thank you to the institutions and residencies that gave me the space, time, and wonderful communities of people among whom to work: the Ox-Bow Artists' Residency, the Virginia Center for the Creative Arts, the Lower Manhattan Cultural Council, and the New York Public Library's Wertheim Study. Thank you to the Institute for International Education and to the Italian Fulbright Commission, and especially to Paola Sartorio, for the gift of a year in which to search for saints and complete the novel amongst an incredible group of peers. Thank you to Florence University of the Arts for hosting me, and to Gabriella Ganugi, Grace Joh, Federico Cagnucci, Isabella Martini, and Nicoletta Salomon for supporting my project, for your friendship, and for making a home in Florence for me and Brendan. And thank you, Nicoletta, for being my Italian reader and editor! Thank you to Mark Roberts at the British Institute Library in Florence and to Piera Cusani and Cristina Mondadori at the Mondadori Foundation/WE–Women for EXPO for your invaluable partnership and support. Thank you to the Società Canottieri Firenze, a true oasis in Florence, for your generosity and friendship. Thank you to Scuola Lorenzo de' Medici. And thank you to all of my friends in Florence for your kindness and for sharing your experiences and expertise.

Thank you to early readers Claire Messud, Katherine Howe, Krys Lee, Katie Freeman, and Jessica Anya Blau—to have the support of such talented writers and remarkable people is deeply meaningful to me. Thank you to dear, longtime friends Georgia Elrod, Anne Thell, and Beth Macri—my fellow Florentine adventurers whose input and friendship I treasure. Thank you to cherished friends Abby Santamaria and Vadim Shick for all of the help and encouragement. Thank you to Judi Culbertson and Tom Randall for being early readers and loving supporters of my writing. Thank you to my Words Without Borders family and my Cathedral family, and especially to Edith Thurber, my mentor in teaching and in life, for her guidance, wisdom, and friendship.

Thank you to the Chaffee and Lange families for all of the love, laughter, and support. And thank you to my grandparents, Charlotte and Hubert Chaffee, and Sophie and Paul Lange, who were storytellers, adventurers, and my heroes growing up. Thank you to the loving and spirited Kiely and Shannon clans for welcoming me into the fold with open arms. Thank you to Tom and Maryanne, Niall and Trish, little Bridget and Leo, and Grandma Jane for loving me, encouraging me, inspiring me, and for all of the wisdom and kindness you instilled in Brendan. I love you!

Thank you to my extraordinary parents, John Chaffee and Heide Lange, my first teachers and first readers. Mom and Dad—thank you for decades of boundless love and sage advice, and for teaching me the most important lessons of all: to build a life of meaning and purpose, to courageously pursue passions, and to love deeply. And thank you for showing me every day how it's done. Thank you to my brother, Joshua Chaffee. My world grew exponentially when you arrived, Joshua. Thank you for being my confidant, my partner in crime, and my champion over many years, and for everything that you have taught me about strength, authenticity, and love. And thank you, Garima Prasai, for opening your heart to our family. Your warmth, intelligence, and beautiful spirit have been such a gift to us.

Thank you to my soul mate, my life partner, my husband Brendan Kiely. Almost a decade ago I walked into a writing workshop with a novel in mind—I had no idea that I was also walking into my future. Thank you for saying yes to that future, Brendan, for leaping with me then—and then again and again. Thank you for showing me how deep and how full life and love can be, and for being my muse, my rock, my home. Here's to you, my love, and here's to all of the writing, leaps, and loving to come.

@unnamedpress

facebook.com/theunnamedpress

unnamedpress.tumblr.com

www.unnamedpress.com

@unnamedpress